CHRISTMAS WISHES AT THE CHOCOLATE SHOP

JESSICA REDLAND

Boldwood

First published in Great Britain in 2021 by Boldwood Books Ltd.

Copyright © Jessica Redland, 2021

Cover Design by Debbie Clement Design

Cover Photography: Shutterstock

A CIP catalogue record for this book is available from the British Library.

Paperback ISBN 978-1-80048-452-8

Large Print ISBN 978-1-80048-453-5

Hardback ISBN 978-1-80280-204-7

Ebook ISBN 978-1-80048-455-9

Kindle ISBN 978-1-80048-454-2

Audio CD ISBN 978-1-80048-447-4

MP3 CD ISBN 978-1-80048-448-1

Digital audio download ISBN 978-1-80048-450-4

Boldwood Books Ltd
23 Bowerdean Street
London SW6 3TN
www.boldwoodbooks.com

For my grandparents, Louisa Jane and Ted Williams,
Jack and Polly Wiseman. No longer here in person,
but forever here in spirit xx

1

'Goodbye, Nanna,' I whispered, turning in a circle and scattering her ashes across the sand dunes. 'You're with your wildlife now. And Grandpa.'

Spurn Point Nature Reserve – a three-mile-long peninsula curving between the North Sea and Humber Estuary – had been my grandparents' favourite place and it wasn't hard to see why. On a sunny August day like today, when the bluey-green sea was calm, I felt like I was on an island in the middle of nowhere rather than twenty-five miles east of Hull.

I watched the dust settle among the sand and grasses, exactly as Nanna had wanted. A tear slipped down my cheek and I quickly swiped at it because that's exactly what Nanna *hadn't* wanted. I could imagine her whispering in my ear, 'Come on now, Charlee, lovey, turn the tap off. Crying won't bring me back.' I couldn't help it, though. I missed them both so much. After my mother, Stacey, abandoned me the day I was born, my grandparents had brought me up so losing Grandpa five years ago and Nanna in May had felt like a double impact each time: grandparent and parent rolled into one.

Sitting down on a nearby sand dune, I closed my eyes and let the mid-afternoon sun kiss my face. Such a beautiful day. Nanna would have loved it. If cancer hadn't taken her, she'd have been sitting beside me enthusiastically identifying the birds and wildflowers. But she wasn't here and never would be again.

At the start of April, the doctors had given her a week, two at the most. I knew that she was desperate to celebrate my thirtieth birthday on 1st May. I also knew that she was tired, in pain, and ready to be reunited with Grandpa. Holding her frail hand in the hospice as she drifted in and out of consciousness, I whispered that it was okay to leave but, somehow, she hung in there and made it through my milestone birthday – just – dying at 1.08 a.m. on 2nd May with me by her side.

I don't think I've ever known another couple quite as devoted as my grandparents. All my memories of them together were happy: giggling as they prepared a meal, holding hands everywhere they went, slow dancing in the lounge when they thought I'd gone to bed. Nanna had quite literally fallen for the boy next door. Grandpa had moved in when he was ten and had invited her to help him build a den in the woods. They'd been inseparable for the next seventy-two years until a fatal heart attack stole him from us. A true gent to the core, he'd been adored by everyone who met him, but he only had eyes for Nanna. It was my forever wish to be fortunate enough to find a love like theirs. Perhaps I'd already found it with Ricky. After nearly six months together, I knew I was smitten and couldn't imagine my life without him, but I was aware it was still early days. A terminally ill grandparent hadn't exactly provided the backdrop for a happy, carefree start to our relationship although him not ditching me in favour of someone with less emotional baggage suggested he might feel the same way about me.

'Charlee!'

I snapped open my eyes and looked in the direction of the shout, shielding my eyes against the bright sun. 'Ricky?'

He ran across the sand, waving.

'I thought you couldn't make it.' Heart racing, I picked up my bag and the urn and ran down the sand dune into his embrace.

'Biffo's finishing up. It's about time he pulled his weight, lazy git. I didn't want you to have to do this on your own. I'm not too late, am I?'

I pulled away and held up the empty urn.

He grimaced. 'Sorry. How was it?'

'A bit emotional, but...' My voice cracked and tears welled in my eyes.

Ricky put his arms round me again and pulled me close as I sobbed against his chest. At six feet tall with strong muscles from his work as a joiner and labourer, his hugs were powerful and comforting. I always felt like I could face anything after a Ricky hug.

'Sorry,' I said when I'd calmed down. 'Since we met, all I seem to have done is cry on you.'

I'd met Ricky in late February while out celebrating my best friend Jodie's thirtieth birthday. He'd been on a stag do pub crawl in Hull city centre, but the pubs hadn't been welcoming of a large all-male group, so the men offered our small group a couple of free rounds if we accompanied them and made the group mixed. I was attracted to Ricky instantly. With his dark blond hair in a buzz cut style, twinkly blue eyes and high cheekbones, he reminded me of Brad Pitt in his younger days. When Ricky took my number at the end of the evening, I genuinely hadn't expected to hear from him, but he rang a couple of days later and took me out for a meal the following night.

The first five weeks together were fantastic. Ricky was interesting, fun and attentive and I could easily see myself falling for him but suddenly I had something different to focus on. Nanna was admitted to hospital then moved to the hospice after her devastating prognosis.

'What sort of boyfriend would I be if I ran off when things got tricky? Come here, you.' He wiped my tears then cupped my face in his hands, his eyes fixed on mine for a moment before tenderly kissing me. His hands moved into my hair as the kiss deepened, making my heart race again. I moaned softly as his hands shifted to down my back and then up inside my T-shirt, gently grazing the sides of my breasts. A momentary fizz of excitement gave way to annoyance and I stepped away, frowning. Had he just tried to feel me up, today of all days?

'Come on, Charlee,' he said, his voice husky and full of longing. 'There's nobody around. You know I can't resist you.' He moved in for another kiss, but I took a further step away.

'I know and I'm really flattered, but it's not really the time or place, is it?' I held up Nanna's urn to illustrate my point, but it was hard to keep my tone light and not add: 'Show some respect.'

He nodded. 'Sorry. I should have thought. Forgive me?'

I relaxed my shoulders, unable to resist those puppy-dog eyes. 'It's okay. I'm just a bit emotional today.' I rolled my eyes. 'A bit more emotional than usual, that is.' I took his hand in mine. 'Thanks for being so patient with me. I know I've not exactly been the dream girlfriend, crying all the time and squirming at the thought of having sex in my grandparents' house, but I'll make it up to you.'

I had a serious amount of making up to do. We had slept together, but it hadn't been a regular thing. To save money to pay off his credit card debts, Ricky had been sleeping rent-free on his workmate Biffo's sofa so staying over at his wasn't an option. Before Nanna took a turn for the worse, he'd slept over at ours a couple of times. She'd insisted on him sleeping in my room

saying she wasn't completely naïve about modern-day relationships but I'd far rather she'd banished him to the third bedroom.
The thought of having sex while Nanna slept – or tried to sleep –
in the room next door made me shudder. After Nanna died, I
assumed the discomfort would go but it hadn't so far. My strategy
was either avoiding intimacy altogether or lying back, crossing
my fingers, and faking it. I wasn't proud of myself.

'Tonight?' Ricky asked, sounding hopeful.

'We'll see.' I put the urn in my bag, thankful I could turn away
in case my expression gave away how I really felt about the
prospect.

Hand in hand, we ambled towards Spurn Point, the tip of the
sand spit.

'Biffo asked when you want to do the big refurb. He's been
asked to plaster his brother's house and he doesn't want to book
that in if you need us to gut your place first.'

I sighed. Making the decision to refurbish my grandparents'
home had caused me several sleepless nights. It desperately
needed bringing into the 21st century, but I felt guilty about
changing all the things that Nanna and Grandpa had chosen.
They'd loved that house and it was so them. It wasn't me, though.

'I'm still not sure what to do. Mr Winters called round again
last night. He's desperate to buy it for his daughter. I'm wondering
whether I should sell it to him and buy somewhere that's
more me.'

'Sell it? Since when? When I suggested it, you were adamant
you weren't going to move.' He sounded a little put-out, and I
could understand that. I *had* been adamant at the time but my
neighbour, Mr Winters, had made a good point: if I was planning
to refurbish it, it wouldn't look like my grandparents' home
anymore so was selling up and moving to a new home that much
different?

'I know and I was determined to stay at the time but I'm having doubts. The house needs a lot of work and I don't know if I can bring myself to have it gutted. It might be easier and less painful to cut the ties completely, sell up, and buy somewhere new with the proceeds.'

We continued in silence for several minutes before Ricky spoke. 'I think you *should* sell and my logic for that is that you're not comfortable there. Even when your Nanna was alive, you always acted as though you were a lodger. I thought you'd be different after she died, but nothing's changed. You're still tense.' He looked at me pointedly. Did he know that I'd been faking? 'I think you need a fresh start.'

Reaching the Point, we sat down on the beach facing each other. I scooped up some warm sand and let it trickle through my fingers as I took in the stunning view. To my left was the sea, twinkling deep blue and turquoise in the sunshine. To my right I could see back along the peninsula to the low lighthouse on the beach and the high black and white striped lighthouse in the grassy dunes. I could hear birds and insects and smell salt in the air.

'Have I upset you by saying that?' Ricky asked, raking his hands back and forth through the sand.

I shook my head. 'No. It's just a lot to think about. You're right, though. It doesn't feel like my home anymore.'

Growing up it had felt every bit my home, but I'd moved out when I was twenty to share a flat with Jodie. I'd always known that living with my best friend wouldn't be a forever arrangement. Sure enough, after four amazing years together, it was time for her to move in with her long-term boyfriend, Karl. Unable to find another affordable flat within a short commute to work, I moved back in with my grandparents. It was only meant to be temporary but, within a year, Grandpa died, and Nanna seemed to age a decade overnight. She kept telling me that there was no rush to move out and I knew her well enough to realise that was her way of asking me to stay. So I did, but I felt like the lodger. It wasn't anything she said or did. It was all completely in my head, but I knew I wasn't settled.

'So, what are you going to do?' Ricky asked.

'Sell to Mr Winters. I think. Should I?'

He picked up a pebble and tossed it into the sea then turned to face me.

'Yes, because it would be quick and easy, but only if he gives you a good price. I'd get a few estate agents in to value it first because houses like that are in demand, even when they need work. But only if selling is what you *really* want. It's your decision.' He brushed the sand off his hands then took my hand in his and fixed his eyes on mine. 'Sell or stay, I'll still love you.'

My eyes widened. He loved me? He'd never said that before. I studied his earnest expression and kicked myself. I was being silly. It was just a turn of phrase. It didn't mean he actually loved me, did it?

Ricky ran his thumb over my hand. 'Did you hear what I just said, Charlee?' His voice was gentle, and he looked a little uncertain of himself which was adorable.

My heart raced. 'Yes, I did, but I wasn't sure if...'

He smiled as I tailed off. 'I *did* mean it. I love you, Charlee. I'm sorry I haven't said it sooner but there never seemed a right moment. I'm not sure this is it, either, but it kind of slipped out.'

I knew I adored him but, at that moment, I realised it was more than that. I'd fallen in love for the very first time. He'd been my rock for the past six months and I wanted him in my life forever. 'I love you too, Ricky.'

He leaned forward and tenderly kissed me and, this time, he didn't push for more. We lay back on the sand, hands clasped, staring up at the sky. The wispiest of clouds – like tiny sections of aeroplane trails – were the only break in the bright cornflower blue. I thought about what Ricky and I had just said to each other and the patience and understanding he'd shown me, and an idea took hold. I wasn't an impulsive person but occasionally an idea presented itself out of the blue that felt so right that I had to act on it immediately. It was a big step and one I'd never come close to taking before.

Butterflies fluttered in my stomach as I tried to find the best way to say it. I drew strength from Ricky's hand squeezing mine and rolled onto my side. 'I have something to ask you.'

Ricky adjusted his position to face me. 'Ask away.'

'It may only be for a short while given the conversation we've just had about me selling up, but I was wondering...' I paused, trying to get control of my nerves so that my voice wouldn't wobble. 'I was wondering if you'd like to move in with me?'

His eyes lit up. 'You mean that?'

'It's got to be better than sleeping on Biffo's sofa, surrounded by empty lager cans and his dirty undies. It'll still be rent-free, of course.'

Ricky laughed. 'If I say yes, you know that it won't be for those reasons, don't you? It'll be because I want to be with you.'

I nodded.

'In that case, it's a yes. When?'

'Now?'

He grinned then hugged me tightly. 'Thank you so much. Should we go and get my stuff right away and then go somewhere to celebrate?'

The butterflies fluttered in my stomach for a different reason now and my cheeks coloured as I said, 'How about we go home to celebrate first, then we get your stuff?'

Ricky stood up and reached out a hand to help me to my feet. 'Well, when you put it like that...'

* * *

As our naked bodies entwined on the lounge rug an hour later, I had to keep telling myself to relax and enjoy the moment. I knew I was sexually compatible with Ricky because we'd been away for his birthday and it had been fantastic, but I simply couldn't relax in my grandparents' home. I wasn't sure whether it was because it felt disrespectful or whether I half-expected one of them to walk in on us. Ricky's fingers and his tongue worked with expert precision, yet I had to fake it again.

We lay on our sides, facing each other. He gently ran his hand down the curve of my body. 'Am I doing something wrong?'

I gulped. 'No! Of course not! Why do you ask?'

'Charlee! You know you're like an open book.'

Busted! He *did* know. 'It's not you. It's just ...'

'It's just this place, isn't it? As I said earlier, you're not comfortable here, and I don't think that's going to change.'

I wrinkled my nose. 'Sorry. I know. I can't live like this, can I? I'll call some estate agents in the morning.'

'I think you should, but only if you're sure.'

'I'm sure. I need to be in my own home, not my grandparents'. Or rather, *we* need to be in *our* own home...'

2

'Hi, gorgeous, I'm back.' Ricky poked his head round the lounge door a couple of evenings later and his smile slipped. 'I didn't know we were expecting visitors.'

'It's okay. I was leaving.' Mr Winters took the last glug of tea, put his mug down on a crocheted doily on the occasional table beside him, and stood up. 'I'll be in touch again as soon as I've briefed my solicitor. Pleasure doing business with you.' He shook my hand, smiling.

'And you, Mr Winters.'

'Stop it, Charlee!' He pretended to look stern then broke into a grin. 'It's Neil. Mr Winters makes me sound like a teacher.'

I laughed as I realised how ridiculous it was calling him by his title considering he was only about five years older than me. 'Sorry, Neil. Nanna referred to all the neighbours as Mr or Mrs – even her best friends – and it's a habit now. I'll see you out.'

I glanced at Ricky loitering in the doorway. He stepped aside, and the two men nodded at each other, but didn't speak. I remembered my manners. 'Neil, this is my boyfriend, Ricky. Ricky, this is Neil. We've just agreed a deal on the house sale.'

'So I gather.' He folded his arms and raised his eyebrows at Neil. 'I hope you haven't tried to pull a swift one.'

I flinched at his hard tone and the rudeness of the comment. 'Ricky!'

They stared at each other for a moment, like stags sizing up the competition before locking antlers. Then Neil turned and headed for the door while Ricky pushed past me into the lounge.

'I'm sorry about that,' I muttered as Neil stepped outside.

He shrugged. 'Don't worry about it. It's good that you've got someone looking out for you.'

'I thought you said he was buying the house for his daughter,' Ricky snapped when I returned to the lounge.

'He is.'

'An investment for when she's older?'

'No. It's for now. She's eighteen and getting married this summer.'

His body seemed to relax, and his tone softened. 'He's got an eighteen-year-old daughter? Really? He doesn't look much older than us.'

I leaned against the doorframe, smiling. I'd intended to have words with him about his rudeness towards Neil but, instead, found myself amused by what I could now clearly see as insecurity and jealousy.

'He isn't. Nanna said he became a dad when he was eighteen, so he'll be about thirty-six now. You're not jealous, are you?'

Ricky stiffened. 'No! Should I be?'

'Not at all but you are! You're so jealous. You assumed Neil would be in his fifties or sixties instead of young and hot, didn't you?'

He narrowed his eyes. 'You think he's hot?'

'Of course not! And, even if I did – which I don't – he's very, very happily married, and you know my views on infidelity.' It wasn't something I'd personally experienced, but I'd been there to support Jodie a couple of years ago after she discovered that, before she'd moved in with Karl, he'd been with several other women. What a dickhead. They'd been together since they were fourteen so that was a fourteen-year relationship flushed down the toilet because he felt there was something he needed to get out of his system before settling down in a monogamous relationship. Like Jodie, I'd never, ever forgive anyone who did that to me.

I knelt on the carpet in front of Ricky. 'Do you know who I think's hot?' I asked in a teasing voice.

'No idea.'

It was so hard not to laugh at his gruff voice and petulant expression. I unfastened the belt on his jeans. 'Do you know who I think is *really* hot?'

The corners of his mouth twitched slightly. Ha! I knew he couldn't keep sulking for long. It was cute, though, and reassuring to see that he had a flaw after he'd been pretty much perfect over the past six months.

'No,' he said, his tone lighter.

Trying not to keel over with embarrassment because being forward so wasn't me, I undid his zipper and pulled his jeans open. 'Do you know who I think is really, *really* hot?'

'No. Who?'

I seductively licked my tongue across my lips. 'That bloke who presents the weather on the local news.'

Ricky laughed. 'Sorry for being grumpy.'

'Crap day?'

'Yes. But I'll tell you about it in a minute.'

I arched my eyebrows. 'A minute? Is that all it's going to take?'

'Two, then,' he said, lunging for me as I squealed.

* * *

'So why did you have a crap day?' I asked, serving up a dish of pasta an hour or so later and sitting down at the dining table opposite Ricky. Nanna had always insisted on proper sit-down meals in the dining room; another habit I hadn't yet broken.

Ricky stabbed at a couple of pieces of fusilli with his fork and sighed. 'Big announcement at work today. House sales are slower than predicted. They've put phase three on hold.'

'No! How long for?'

He sighed again and shoved the pasta into his mouth. 'Indefinitely.'

My heart sank for him. I'd always thought that Tenley Meadows was a ridiculously ambitious project: 1,650 new homes, a school, doctor's surgery, shops, pub, and other amenities situated north-east of Hull. It wasn't the best location for commuting into the city centre, there weren't enough jobs in that immediate area to justify so many houses, and the area was prone to flooding. Of course, I'd never voiced my concerns when Ricky secured a contract as one of the joiners on site shortly after we met, focusing instead on the great news at getting a long-term contract. Only it now looked like it wasn't going to be long-term after all.

'Do you know how long you have left?'

'They're not even going to finish phase two, so they reckon maybe a month, six weeks at a push.' He stabbed at his fusilli again.

'Oh, Ricky. That's crap.'

He nodded.

'What are you going to do?'

'I'll have to find another contract. One of my mates reckons they need more joiners on the housing estate where he's working.'

He didn't sound too enthusiastic, presumably still reeling

from the bad news so I injected as much enthusiasm into my voice as I could. 'That's brilliant news! Is he going to put in a good word for you?'

'He will if I ask him to. He reckons I could start immediately too.'

'Even better, in case they mess you around at Tenley Meadows. Which development is it?'

'It's called Lower Glendale.'

I pondered for a moment. It didn't sound familiar. 'Is that the one near North Ferriby?'

Ricky put his fork down and sighed. 'No. It's in Whitsborough Bay.'

I stopped, forkful of pasta midway to my mouth, and stared at him, my stomach churning. The North Yorkshire seaside town of Whitsborough Bay was where Ricky had been brought up and where his best mate Smurf still lived. It was only the next county, but it was a ninety-minute drive north from where I lived in Brockington near Hull and that was on a good day. With single-track roads all the way, the travel time could easily increase.

'Smurf was the mate who told me about it,' he continued, his tone flat, his expression apologetic. 'Say something.'

'Sorry, I...' I put my fork down and pushed my bowl aside, appetite gone. 'You're going to take it, aren't you?' I asked in a small voice, knowing that he didn't have much choice as he couldn't not work.

'I'm going to have to. I made some calls this afternoon and there's nothing round here at the moment. I moved to Hull because there were no jobs in Whitsborough Bay but the work's dried up here and, typically, there's plenty of work back home.'

'Then you should ring Smurf and tell him you're interested, before someone else secures it.' I tried to sound cheerful, but it wasn't easy.

'Don't look so sad,' Ricky said. 'It doesn't mean things have to change between us, you know. I still want to be with you. I know it's not ideal, but it's not the other side of the country. It's only the next county. We can make the distance thing work. Assuming you want to, that is.'

'Of course I do!'

Ricky came to my side of the table and put his arms round me. I snuggled against his stomach, my arms round his waist. 'You could always move to Whitsborough Bay with me,' he said, stroking my hair.

'I can't do that.'

'Why not? You're selling this place and you don't have any family here now. I'm sure that you and Jodie will still see each other wherever you live, especially if you live in Whitsborough Bay. She loves it there, doesn't she?'

'It's her favourite place. She'd be a constant visitor. But I still can't move there, Ricky. My job's here.'

'So find a new job in Whitsborough Bay. Or take some time out. It's not like you'll be strapped for cash after this place sells.'

I wasn't strapped for cash now as my grandparents hadn't lived an extravagant lifestyle, leaving me a sizeable inheritance. But move to Whitsborough Bay? I didn't know anyone there. Not that I knew many people in Hull either. Jodie was the only friend I regularly saw out of work. I occasionally went out for a meal with my boss Pierre and his wife Lillian but that was it. It wasn't like I'd be leaving behind a big circle of friends and a busy social life.

'I don't know,' I said, pulling away from him.

Ricky crouched on the floor beside me. 'It's not a definite "no" then?'

I couldn't help but smile at his eager expression. 'It's an, "I'll think about it," but please don't get your hopes up. I love my job and I have an amazing boss.'

'Who has an evil daughter who likes to make your life hell.'

'Yes, but I only have to work with Gabby twice a week.'

'You wouldn't have to work with her ever again if you moved to Whitsborough Bay with me.'

A world without Gabby? A delicious thought. 'It's tempting, but Grandpa set up that business. I know he sold it to Pierre when he retired but I still think of it as Grandpa's chocolaterie. I couldn't imagine selling his home *and* leaving his business.'

'You could always set up your own chocolate shop in Whitsborough Bay in his memory. I bet you'd do really well.'

I leaned forward and gently kissed him. 'You've thought all this through, haven't you?'

'I don't want to lose you.'

'I don't want to lose you either.' I kissed him again. 'But I don't think I can leave Hull. Not yet. It's too much change all at once.'

Ricky nodded. 'I understand. But here's a thought. How old is Pierre?'

'Sixty-five.'

'Do you think he's going to keep working forever? What if he decides to retire? You think it's hell working with Gabby twice a week? Imagine if she was your boss.'

I shuddered and my stomach lurched at the thought. Pierre was so passionate about his craft that it was easy to assume he'd never step away, but he had to at some point. There was no way Lillian would accept him working forever. The baton would pass to Gabby when he retired and there was no way I could work for that woman, although I suspected her first decision as the new owner would be to take great delight in giving me my marching orders.

I took in Ricky's eager expression and ruffled his hair. 'Go on.

Phone Smurf and get that job secured. We'll work out the distance thing somehow and I'll think about what you've said about moving but I'm not promising anything.'

As I listened to him talking animatedly in the hallway, I felt excited for him but apprehensive for us. Even though he'd said he loved me, was our fledgling relationship strong enough to survive that distance? Would he still want to come back to Hull to see me when he was finally back where he'd always wanted to be, among his family and friends? It would be so much easier for us if I did live in Whitsborough Bay but that was an enormous decision and one I wasn't ready to make yet. I'd never lived anywhere else. I'd never even considered it. Moving out of my childhood home was scary enough. Could I really leave my home, my job, and the people I knew to settle in a town I'd only visited a couple of times as a child?

3

I stood in the middle of the lounge the following morning, feeling quite overwhelmed at the speed of change. Ricky had left for his final day at work at Tenley Meadows a short while earlier. Final day? It all seemed so quick. Smurf had wasted no time following their conversation and had got straight onto his boss who'd phoned Ricky half an hour later and, after a quick chat, offered him a job on the Lower Glendale development starting on Monday. Ricky had then called his boss who'd agreed that he could leave with only a day's notice. I suppose it made sense when they were planning to lay them all off, but it all seemed very real very quickly. In the space of four days, he'd moved in, lost his job, found a new one, and was going to be moving out again. I'd scattered Nanna's ashes and agreed to sell her house. I could scarcely catch my breath!

Turning in a slow circle, I took in the furniture and possessions that epitomised Nanna and Grandpa. The mahogany sideboard displayed Nanna's posh Royal Doulton dinner service and her cut crystal glasses. The matching tall bookcase was stuffed full of the historical romance novels she'd loved to read. I wandered over to it and ran my fingertips along the spines. She'd spent many an evening in the armchair, paperback in hand, her changing facial expressions telling the tale of what she was reading. I'd read most of them myself too, enraptured by smouldering heroes in frilly shirts and riding breeches.

I closed my eyes and took a deep breath. It was going to be hard to leave, but I'd made the right decision. Definitely. And if I was moving out, I was going to need to bite the bullet and clear the house, preferably starting today while I was still off work, but I had no idea where to start.

Wandering into the kitchen, I made a cup of tea instead. I wasn't thirsty but any opportunity to delay the sorting was most welcome.

Returning to the lounge, mug in hand, I looked at the bookshelves again. I'd start there, clearing out all the books I'd read. Easy. I reached for the first book, but I hadn't read it so left it where it was. The second didn't seem familiar either and the third was one of Nanna's favourites.

By the time I made it to the end of the shelf of roughly forty books, I'd only removed one: a ten-year-old edition of B&Bs in Cornwall. There was no point continuing. I needed to be ruthless, and I wasn't sure I could be. Jodie wasn't one for sentimentality so I texted her to see if she could help later.

Upstairs in Nanna's bedroom, I opened her wardrobe door and lightly ran my fingers across the dresses, predominantly in delicate floral prints, and the rainbow of silk blouses. Her perfume wafted at me as the clothes swayed on their hangers and I could almost feel her presence. A lump formed in my throat as I pictured Nanna dressed in her favourite clothes and outfits she'd worn for special occasions. I shook my head and closed the door. Too hard. I definitely needed Jodie by my side for sorting through clothes. There had to be something I could organise that wouldn't be difficult or upsetting.

Twenty minutes later, I'd stuffed the entire contents of the airing cupboard – Nanna's linens and towels as well as my own – into several binbags. I'd had the same towels and bedding since I moved out and it was time for a proper fresh start.

Feeling a sense of achievement, I decided to tackle the attic next. The Christmas decorations seemed as good a place as any to start. Nanna had loved Christmas. She'd insisted on a real tree each year in the bay window of the lounge with a colour theme – usually silver or gold and one or two other colours – although it was a case of anything goes for the small artificial tree in the dining room for Grandpa who'd believed that trees should be decorated with an explosion of colour.

The decorations were packed into crates, each clearly labelled by colour. I lifted the lid off the first of two 'red and cream' crates and smiled. Full of material and felt animals and shapes as well as more traditional baubles, it was my favourite set and looked stunning accompanied with gold decorations. She'd done that last year. Back then, I'd had no idea it would be our last Christmas together. I pictured her unwrapping her gifts from me, spraying herself with Opium Eau de Toilette – a fragrance I'd always associate with Nanna – and snuggling into her new soft grey cardigan. She'd smiled and thanked me, told me I'd spent far too much as usual, then had glanced at Grandpa's photo on the mantelpiece, eyes sparkling. Had she known back then that she'd soon be joining him?

The lump in my throat had returned and I blinked back my tears as I replaced the lid and pushed the crate aside to start a 'keep' pile.

The next crate was simply labelled 'blue', filled with baubles, snowflakes and wooden decorations in navy, royal, and pale blue.

I loved that colour scheme too. In fact, I loved them all, and I knew for a fact that none of the boxes contained old, tatty decorations, because Nanna always took such pride in her tree, so they really didn't need sorting out.

There were ten colour-themed crates in total, a box containing the artificial tree for the dining room, a couple of bags for life containing tree lights, plus a further crate with miscellaneous items like the hooks for hanging up wreaths, card holders, spare Christmas cards, and tree hooks. That was a lot of Christmas decorations, but there was no way I could let any of them go considering how much Nanna and Grandpa had loved Christmas. Plus, they'd get used. I'd never need to buy another decoration in my life.

A couple of cardboard boxes stood behind where the crates had been. There was nothing written on the lid of either of them. Crouching down, I opened the flaps on the first one. Inside were another two smaller cardboard boxes. I lifted the first one out and smiled at the words in marker pen on the lid: *Charlee's Creations.* Surely she hadn't kept everything I'd made at school. Peering into the box, it seemed she had. From a cotton wool covered toilet roll tube, which I'm assuming was meant to be a snowman, to an impressive-looking angel made from what looked to be a folded Reader's Digest sprayed silver, she'd kept the lot.

I reached for the other box. Marked on the lid was one word: *Stacey.* My birth mother. I sat back on my heels, my heart thumping. Did I want to open it?

Over the years, I'd often pondered on how I should feel about the woman who'd abandoned me on the day I was born. I'd settled on indifference. Perhaps if I'd had a miserable childhood, I'd have hated her, but Nanna and Grandpa had been amazing. I definitely hadn't missed out.

Biting my lip, I opened the lid of the box, then smiled. It

wasn't photos or letters. It was full of childhood decorations too and, funnily enough, that included a cotton wool covered toilet roll tube.

After studying the various items, I put my decorations and Stacey's back in the larger cardboard box and pushed it to one side: the first box in my pile for the tip.

I lifted the lid on the second cardboard box and took out a large red photo album with my name written across the front in marker pen. Sitting cross-legged, I placed the album in my lap and opened the first page. The caption in Nanna's flowing script read: *Charlee's 1st Christmas*. She'd clearly made it a Christmas tradition as there was a double page spread for the next two decades, stopping when I moved in with Jodie. Each year was represented by five photos all following roughly the same format: my unopened gifts, obviously taken after 'Santa' had visited on Christmas Eve, me in my Christmas outfit, me playing with my presents, me with Nanna, and me with Grandpa.

Returning to the start, I looked through the album again, smiling at the memories of my favourite gifts and shaking my head at presents I'd completely forgotten about. I remembered her taking lots of photos at Christmas, but I'd had no idea the album existed. What an amazing keepsake of all our Christmases together.

'Thank you, Nanna,' I whispered, closing the album and stroking my fingers across the cover. 'I'll definitely keep this.'

Standing up, I placed it on top of one of the crates of decorations and peered back into the cardboard box. There were old Christmas cards sent to Nanna and Grandpa from people I didn't know, odd crackers which had obviously been spare and forgotten about, a box of well-used red candles, recycled gift bows, and another photo album. I lifted out the cream album and blew some dust from the cover. There was no name written on this one, but somehow I knew. It was *her* album.

My mouth felt dry and my hands shook as I opened the first page and read those words: *Stacey's 1ˢᵗ Christmas.* The photos were faded, but the format was the same as mine. I stared at the grainy images, trying to spot similarities between my birth mother and me. Twisting round, I grabbed the red album and opened that on the first page too, comparing the images. Did I look like her? I'd never seen a photo of her. Nanna said she'd been angry with Stacey for leaving and had destroyed the photos she had of her. All she'd tell me was that she had dark hair like me and that she'd worn it long throughout childhood. Nanna and Grandpa had both had dark hair so discovering Stacey was a brunette hadn't been a surprise revelation. I had no idea whether my hazel eyes, easy-tan skin and freckles were inherited from – her or my father.

Nanna never talked about Stacey and, although I'd initially been curious, I learned not to ask because it seemed to upset Nanna too much. She'd been their only child and she hadn't just cut herself out of my life; she'd severed ties with them completely too.

Studying the albums now, Stacey's early photos were too grainy but, as the years passed and the image quality improved, I could see similarities, but I definitely wasn't the spitting image of her. I'd never know if I looked like my father instead because, according to the spare snippets I'd had from Nanna, Stacey hadn't known who he was.

I wondered whether Stacey and I were similar in personality at all. We certainly weren't in one respect: I would *never* abandon a child at birth and disconnect myself completely from my family from that moment. In some ways, I understood why she'd stayed out of my life, but why had she cut off her parents too? It didn't make sense.

Sighing, I closed the albums. As Ricky had pointed out last night, I didn't have a family anymore and I wished I did. It felt strange being completely alone. I had Jodie, Ricky and Pierre, but it wasn't the same as having Nanna and Grandpa. I had no interest in finding Stacey. She'd had thirty years to find me – not difficult when my grandparents had never moved house – but she hadn't bothered so why would I want to meet her? To me, she was simply the woman who'd given birth to me; she wasn't my mum.

I placed my precious keepsake album back on top of the crates of Christmas decorations and dumped Stacey's on the box of childhood decorations to be thrown out. Then I hesitated, picked it up, and placed it on top of mine. I had no idea where Stacey was, I had no way of contacting her, and I didn't want to contact her, but that was a special photo album and had to have been important to Nanna, given that she'd created the same thing for my childhood. I had no intention of looking through it again, but it somehow didn't feel right to throw it away.

* * *

Jodie stopped by after summer school finished for the day. She was a teaching assistant at Brockington School but earned extra money during the summer helping run a summer school for foreign exchange students.

'The cavalry's here!' she announced, hugging me. She removed a bobble from the pocket of her jeans and scraped her long wavy hair back into a high ponytail. I loved Jodie's hair. It was naturally dark blonde with lighter blonde and honey highlights giving it a glorious sun kissed look. My hair was too dark to experiment like that. I'd tried but blonde streaks didn't suit me, and red tones only lasted a couple of weeks.

'And I definitely need the cavalry. It's not going well.' I led her into the dining room.

'This is all to go to the tip?' she asked, pointing to a pile of crates, boxes and bags at one end.

I grimaced and pointed to the opposite end. 'No. That's the pile to go.'

Jodie looked towards the two cardboard boxes – one containing the childhood Christmas decorations and another with a few broken items and dodgy lampshades that I'd found gathering dust in the attic – and laughed.

'You weren't kidding when you said you needed my help. What's in the crates you're keeping?'

'Christmas decorations.'

'In *all* of them?'

I shrugged 'Pretty much.'

Jodie sighed and shook her head. 'What am I going to do with you?'

The tears I'd managed to hold back for most of the day found their escape and spilled down my cheeks. 'I miss them so much, Jodie.'

'Aw, I know you do.' She put her arms round me and hugged me. 'But keeping everything they've ever owned is *not* going to bring them back.'

She made me a mug of tea then led me upstairs and into Nanna's bedroom, clutching a roll of binbags. She fixed her blue eyes on mine. 'I know it's hard, but it has to be done,' she said gently. 'And we have to be brutal. Is there anything of your Nanna's that you could imagine wearing? And if you say any of her flowery nylon dresses, I'll throw this roll of binbags at you.'

I thought for a moment. 'There are a couple of snuggly cardigans which I bought her for Christmas last year and the year before. I love them, but that's about it. Does that sound awful?'

'Of course not. You're thirty and she was eighty-six. I'd be slightly concerned if you did have the same taste in clothes.'

Jodie ripped two binbags from the roll while I took the two cardigans out of Nanna's drawers. She billowed out one and handed it to me.

'We'll bag everything else up. *Everything.* You take the wardrobe and I'll take the drawers. The easiest way to do this is to just systematically fill the bags, as quickly as possible. Don't pause to look and remember because that will just break your heart.'

She was right; doing it quickly was better like ripping off a plaster. But my heart still broke into a thousand pieces.

4

'Charlee! Welcome back, *ma petite chocolatière!*' Pierre greeted me with a kiss on each cheek and a hug then stepped back, smiling at me.

'Thank you. Good to be back!'

At sixty-five, Pierre was one of those men who'd become even more handsome with age with a full head of grey hair, a neatly trimmed beard and warm dark eyes. He was well over six feet tall – maybe six foot three – and had broad shoulders and a flat stomach thanks to a passion for cycling. I knew for a fact that some of the regulars – male and female – came for more than the chocolate. A flash of his dazzling smile and his dulcet French tones had them floating out of the shop on a happy cloud. To me, he was a wonderful boss, friend, mentor and the closest thing I had to a father figure since Grandpa died.

'You have had a good week?' he asked, following me into the large room at the back of the shop, which we used for chocolate-making parties.

I shrugged off my jacket and pulled on my apron. 'Not really.

It's been a tough week. I finally did it. I scattered Nanna's ashes on Tuesday.'

'Oh no. I am sorry. You did this at Spurn Point as she wished?'

I nodded. 'She's with Grandpa now.'

'They were a lovely couple. Ted and Louisa-Jane were very lucky to love so deeply. It is a rare and beautiful thing. If only—' His face fell.

'What is it?' I asked. 'Has something happened to Lillian?' His wife had been seriously ill over the winter with bronchitis. She hadn't been right since, suffering from a series of chest infections and a couple of asthma attacks.

'Please sit down.'

I perched on one of the wooden stools surrounding the preparation table, feeling anxious at the formality. What was he about to tell me?

'I have news. Lillian. She is not well, but she is not worse so do not fear. She will, however, not improve while we live in this cold place. We have made a difficult decision. We will return to *La France*.'

My heart thumped as my mind raced with what this meant. It was a relief that Lillian hadn't taken a turn for the worse and, for them, it was absolutely the right thing to do for her health and wellbeing. But for me, did it mean that I was out of a job?

'I think that's the right decision for you both,' I said. 'I really do. Please pass on my love to Lillian.'

'I will. I do not wish to leave England but Lillian, she needs to. I have little choice, *n'est pas*?'

'When do you go?'

'Lillian will leave tomorrow and stay with her sister. I will follow in three, four... maybe five weeks.'

I gulped. First Ricky, now Pierre. Why was everyone leaving me? And why so quickly?

'I expect you are wondering about the chocolaterie?' he asked. 'I am not selling so your job is safe.'

My stomach lurched. If my job was 'safe', that meant…

'Gabby will be the new manager here.' Pierre's wide beam told me what a proud father moment this was for him. He had absolutely no idea that his daughter was conniving, vindictive, and absolutely hated me. She always put on a good act in front of her parents, pretending we were friends, and I'd never had the heart to suggest to Pierre that everything was not as it seemed.

'Really?' I tried to keep my voice even. 'Gabby's going to be in charge?'

He nodded. 'I asked her to keep all staff and she says of course.'

Hmm. And I bet she had her fingers crossed behind her back when she said that. There was no way she'd keep me on. At least it was her day off today so I'd have an evening to psyche myself up to facing her smugness.

'She will be in later,' Pierre said. 'I will make the chocolate now and, after that, the chocolaterie will be my Gabby's and I will step back with my hours.'

She was in today? She was going to be in more frequently and Pierre less? That was going to be hideous. But Pierre was looking at me, evidently waiting for a response so I nodded vigorously, not trusting myself to speak for fear a sob would escape instead.

He patted my hand. 'Do not look so sad. This is not goodbye, *ma petite chocolatière*. I will stay in touch.'

'You'd better.' Tears clouded my eyes and I was grateful to melt into his hug so that he couldn't see how upset I was. The news that Gabby was taking over was bad, but I was more concerned about Pierre's departure. I'd miss him so much.

'I promise I will. You are welcome to visit France. Our door will always be open to you, Charlee.'

'Thank you. And thank you for being the best boss, ever. Well, second best boss after Grandpa, that is, but very close.'

Pierre laughed. 'I cannot be offended. This is high praise indeed.'

* * *

I paused for a mug of tea mid-morning and took the opportunity to text Ricky:

✉ To Ricky
Unexpected news this morning. Pierre and
Lillian are moving back to France and Gabby's
taking over. Glad you've found a new job
because I think I might be about to lose mine
Hope your 1st day is going well. Missing you
already xx

✉ From Ricky
That's crap. It could be great, though. You
know you can't work for that woman, so this is
your last tie to Hull gone. Time to move to the
coast? Charlee and the Chocolate Shop. Sounds
good! xx

Ricky certainly deserved ten out of ten for persistence. Was he right? Should I take this as a clear sign that the chapter of my life in Hull was over and I needed to start a new chapter in Whitsborough Bay?

* * *

I felt her eyes on me a little after 2 p.m. and gulped as I resealed the bag of chocolate drops then turned round with a fixed smile on my face; the one that I reserved especially for her.

'Gabby! I hear congratulations are in order.'

She scowled. 'Papa told you? I wanted to have that pleasure.'

I ignored the cruel tone to her voice. 'It's a good move for them. I think it will make such a difference to your mum.'

'Did I ask for your opinion?' She planted her hands on her hips and glowered at me. She was only an inch taller but had perfected the art of looking down on me – usually with a sneer on her face like right now – making me feel significantly smaller than her. Her short dark hair was dyed bright red with a long fringe swept across her eyes and she wore her signature style of large, hooped earrings and crimson lipstick. She was effortlessly stylish and would be considered beautiful... if only she would smile instead of snarl all the time.

'We've got a children's party at four,' I said, picking up the booking diary. 'Do you want to run it, or would you like me to?'

'How old are the kids?'

'The birthday girl's turning seven, so I'm guessing mainly six or seven. We're expecting twelve of them.'

Gabby shuddered. 'Urgh! Little brats pawing at me with their chocolatey fingers. I can't think of a more revolting way to spend my afternoon. They're all yours.'

No surprise there. I'd never been sure whether Gabby genuinely hated children or whether she simply hated the chocolate-making parties because they'd been my idea. It was probably both. I loved them, though, so I had no problem running this afternoon's.

Assuming that the conversation was over, I turned to put the bag of chocolate drops away.

'Did I say I was finished with you?'

I closed my eyes for a moment and sighed inwardly. This was how it was going to be from now on, wasn't it? Every single day. Fake smile. *Yes, Gabby. No, Gabby. Three bags full, Gabby.*

I turned to face her. 'Sorry, Gabby. Is there something else you want me to do?'

She smirked. 'There certainly is. I want you to clean the workshop.'

I frowned. 'It's already clean.'

'Are you arguing with me?'

'No. It's just that I clean it every day and it's only going to get messy during the party.'

She narrowed her eyes at me. I knew that she was loving this. 'I want a deep clean. Now.'

A deep clean? Was she mad? A proper deep clean meant removing all the furniture and equipment. 'That doesn't make sense, Gabby. The kids will be here in in less than two hours, and I need thirty minutes to prepare for that. There isn't anywhere near enough time for a deep clean.'

She ran her perfectly manicured scarlet fingernails through her silky hair. 'Who's the boss here, Charlotte?'

I hated it when she did that. 'My name's Charlee,' I said through gritted teeth. I wasn't being pedantic. Charlee genuinely was the name on my birth certificate. Stacey had chosen it before I was born and, despite her walking out, my grandparents had honoured her wishes. She'd always called Grandpa's shop his 'chocolate factory' so had decided on Charlie for a boy or Charlee for a girl. Very droll.

'And *my* name's on your payslips, Charlotte,' Gabby quipped, tapping her finger against her crimson lips. 'If you get any more of them, that is.'

My stomach dropped to the floor. It was starting already. 'What's that supposed to mean?'

'I've asked you to do a deep clean and you've refused to do it. If you're not willing or able to carry out basic instructions, you know where the door is.'

I stared at her for a moment. The physical resemblance to her parents was unmistakable, but there was nothing of Pierre or Lillian in her personality. It wasn't just me who saw the real Gabby. Her interactions with customers were blunt and several regulars had made a point of telling me they deliberately avoided the chocolaterie on the days Gabby was working. God help the business when she took over Pierre's hours. She'd destroy it.

As to why she hated me so much, I wasn't sure. I could only assume that it was professional jealousy because, no matter how hard she tried, or how much additional training Pierre gave her, she wasn't a naturally gifted chocolatier. Everything I designed or made always sold so much better than any of her creations.

'Are you going to do the deep clean or not?' She narrowed her eyes at me. 'I suggest you think carefully before you answer that.'

I bit my lip as I considered my options. I could either put up and shut up – which would be both difficult and miserable – or I could bite the bullet and start afresh in Whitsborough Bay. I'd spent the day there yesterday with Ricky before he settled in at Smurf's flat and it had been lovely. We'd ambled along the seafront eating chips, wandered hand in hand by the shore and had a ride on the big wheel before heading into the town centre. Ricky kept pointing out empty premises and asking, 'Would that make a good chocolate shop?' and I had got swept up in the excitement of it all. I'd particularly liked Castle Street, a cobbled street off the main pedestrianised area, full of independent shops and cafés and, yes, the perfect place for a chocolate shop. Could I do that? Could I really set up my own business? I wasn't sure, but as I stared into her cold eyes, there was one thing that I *was* sure about: I could not and would not work for Gabby. It had only been bearable before because it wasn't every day and working with Pierre the rest of the time more than made up for the grim days working alongside his daughter. Without him in the picture, what reason was there to stick around? I could still honour Grandpa's memory by establishing my own chocolaterie in Whitsborough Bay. It may be different premises, but the business would be built on everything he'd taught me.

Reaching behind my back, I unfastened my apron and lifted it over my head. 'No, Gabby, I'm *not* going to do the deep clean. I'm *not* going to do the party. And I'm *not* going to work for you.' I'm not sure how I managed to keep my voice so strong and confident when I was quivering inside. I'd never stood up to her before.

Her mouth dropped open. 'You can't just walk out.'

'I think you'll find that I can.' I headed to the back of the workshop to collect my belongings.

Gabby followed me. 'What am I supposed to do about the party?' she snapped.

I pulled my jacket on. 'You can either phone the mum and explain that the party is cancelled because your member of staff walked out after you placed ridiculous, unreasonable demands on her simply because it made you feel strong and powerful. Or you can keep your customer happy and have a revolting afternoon being pawed at by chocolatey fingers.' I lifted my bag over my shoulders. 'It's not my problem.'

'You can't do this.' For a moment, Gabby looked panic-stricken and almost human, but I wasn't going to let it fool me.

Driven by the hurt and anxiety caused from years of hostility and pettiness, I felt like I was the strong and powerful one at last. I straightened up, raised myself onto my tiptoes, lifted my chin and gazed down at her. Two could play at that game. *Keep going. You've got this!*

'I've already said that I can and I am. It didn't have to be like this, but I cannot and will not work for a bully. I love this place and I love your dad, but I have no loyalty to you. I don't know why you're looking so worried. You've always made it clear that you can't stand me so I'd have thought that me walking out would make your day.'

'I promised Papa you'd keep your job.' There was a hint of desperation in her tone, as though she wanted me to back down. No way.

'Messed that one up, didn't you?' I rolled my eyes as I passed her and stepped into the shop. 'Goodbye, Gabby.'

'You won't tell Papa, will you?'

'Good luck with the business, by the way. You're going to need it.'

She flashed her eyes at me, and the old Gabby was back. 'Meaning?'

'You know exactly what it means. You may have finally grasped how to make semi-decent chocolate but that alone isn't going to keep this place alive. You've got sod all business sense, you're rubbish with customers, and you've no idea how to treat your staff. Hardly a recipe for success, is it?'

I marched towards the door and left before she could say anything else. Somehow, I managed to hold it together but, when I knew I was out of view, I sank onto the nearest bench, shaking. My heart was racing, my palms were sweating, and my stomach was churning. I hated confrontations but there was one more difficult conversation I needed to have, and I needed to do it right now before I chickened out or she got in first with a vicious lie.

'Charlee! How is *ma petite chocolatière*? Missing me already?'

'Very much. But I'm not a chocolatier anymore,' I said.

'What do you mean?'

Much as I'd have loved to spill the beans, I couldn't hurt him by doing so. 'I'm so sorry to let you down, Pierre, but with everything that's happened lately, I need some time out. Ricky lost his job and he's had to move back to Whitsborough Bay to find work and I've agreed to sell the house to a neighbour. It makes sense for me to start afresh where Ricky is.'

There was a pause. 'I feared this may happen,' he said. 'Gabby pushed you out *n'est pas*?'

'No! It was my decision. I was thinking about it last week.' I crossed my fingers against my little white lie.

'You are not a good liar. I know how Gabby is. I'd hoped being manager would change her but perhaps not. I am sorry that she has not been a friend to you over the years. I should have done more but you never said a word, so I thought you were not hurt.'

My shoulders slumped. He knew? 'I didn't want to say anything because I didn't want to upset you.'

'I thank you for that but, deep down, I always know how she is. What will you do now?'

'Ricky thinks I should open a chocolaterie in Whitsborough Bay.'

'Oh, Charlee! I agree with him. It would be *fantastique*.'

'You really think I have what it takes to run my own business?'

'Who do you think has run La Chocolaterie for the past eight years? It was not me. It was certainly not Gabby. The ideas like the parties? All yours. The best-selling designs? All yours. You have a gift. You should use it.'

After we'd said our goodbyes, I sat on the bench for several more minutes, feeling quite tearful. I'd always known Pierre rated me highly but to suggest that I was the one who'd made La Chocolaterie a success was quite overwhelming. It also filled me with excitement and hope that I could start over with my own business.

I didn't want to get Ricky into trouble on his first day by phoning him, so I sent him another text:

✉ To Ricky

You were right. I can't work for Gabby. Have just walked out. Looks like a chocolaterie in Whitsborough Bay could really happen! xx

✉ From Ricky

Best news ever! We'd better start house-hunting and shop-hunting! xx

5

After walking out on Gabby, the life changes seemed to happen at lightning speed and sometimes I had to pause to catch my breath and remind myself that it would all be fine and I was doing the right thing, particularly about moving to Whitsborough Bay. I'd had several months to ponder on what to do with my grandparents' house. In the end, agreeing to sell to Neil Winters felt comfortable but relocating to Whitsborough Bay had suddenly been thrust on me by a series of circumstances out of my control. Not having time to fully weigh up the decision unnerved me.

With no chain on either side and Neil Winters eager to start on the renovations, we completed on the house sale just over a month after agreeing the price. Jodie spent many evenings in the run-up to completion helping me sort through the furniture and contents. I'd really appreciated her help but also her company with Ricky not being around. She suggested enlisting a house clearance expert in case any of Nanna's ornaments or furniture were worth something. It turned out she had quite a few valuable pieces, including a hideous floral milk jug that I'd have added to the pile for the tip. The sale of that and various other items provided valuable additional funds to invest in my new business.

I only saw Ricky on Sundays as there'd been some overtime available at the construction site, so he was working a six-day week. We could have met up mid-week but it was a long drive for a short time together so we agreed to Sundays only knowing it would only be short-term.

Before the house sale went through, Ricky convinced me to view some houses in areas he rated. It had been a useful exercise in understanding what I could get for my money in Whitsborough Bay, but buying was definitely a step too far. I didn't know the town like Ricky, and I needed to be much more settled and familiar before I'd make such a big commitment. The priority had to be the business rather than the house because, if I didn't find suitable premises – and I'd seen nothing suitable so far – I might have to look outside the area.

Ricky claimed to understand and support my logic and he agreed to my suggestion that we rent together initially, but his comments about renting being 'a waste of money paying someone else's mortgage' conveyed his disapproval. It was my money, though, and I wasn't going to be guilt-tripped into making the wrong decision. I also had a growing concern which repeatedly woke me up in a panic. I had the financial means to buy a decent property straight out, but Ricky's mounting debts meant he could contribute nothing. Would he accept me buying a house in my name only or would he be offended and think it meant I didn't love or trust him? If he was fine with it, would he pay rent and half the bills or would he expect to live rent-free because I'd be mortgage-free? What if I *did* buy in joint names but things didn't work out? Would he fight me for half the value when none of the investment had been his? We loved each other and I had no reason to think that our relationship wouldn't last, but we hadn't been together that long and who knew what the future held. It was too risky. The situation between Jodie and Karl had made me wary and cautious. Their split had been difficult enough but selling their flat and detangling their finances had been horrendous.

Renting had to be the way forward for now. There was no need to rent anywhere big. We didn't have enough belongings between us to justify the space and I had no income coming in so couldn't justify the expense either. We secured a small fully furnished one-bedroom flat on the second floor of a modern apartment block ten minutes' walk from the town centre. Number twenty-four Coral Court was bland and soulless, but it was clean and functional; ideal as a base while I set up the shop.

It was now a week into October, and we'd been living in the flat for almost three weeks. I'd put down the deposit and had offered to initially pay the lion's share of the rent plus all the bills so that Ricky could chip away at his debts. I didn't mind doing that for a short time knowing that he'd be able to contribute more when his debts were cleared.

I'd fallen in love with Whitsborough Bay and, for the first fortnight, I'd felt like I was on holiday. While Ricky was at work during the day, I explored the town, the park, the castle and the seafront at North and South Bay, loving how different the two bays were. On an evening, Ricky and I went to the cinema, the arcades, ten pin bowling, or the pub although the latter was typically with his friends. We also ate out on numerous occasions. Ricky was worried about money so I insisted on paying for everything. It seemed the fairest thing to do when I had the funds, and I was the one initiating the nights out in order to familiarise myself with my new surroundings.

This past week, that holiday feeling had faded and reality had set in. I'd been unusually frivolous and I needed to reign it in while I had no income and no idea when I might start earning again. I stopped suggesting nights out and had assumed we'd go for a few romantic walks or enjoy cosy evenings in front of the TV together. Instead, I'd barely seen Ricky. He'd been round to Smurf's once, worked late twice, then last night was a night down the pub with Smurf and a bunch of their mates. 'You're welcome to join us,' he'd said, but I politely declined. I'd already had my fill of evenings with his former schoolmates. They were typical 'lads' for whom a night out meant copious amounts of beer and talk of football, cars, and women. I'd tried my best to strike up conversations but we had nothing in common and we didn't have the shared history and banter that they had with Ricky so I very much felt like an outsider.

I didn't begrudge Ricky going to the pub. I didn't begrudge him time with his friends. It was obvious how happy he was being back in Whitsborough Bay with them, which made me happy, but it also made me feel lonely. I missed Nanna – although I'd have felt the same if I was still in Brockington – and I missed Jodie and Pierre. Would I be able to establish new friendships here? I hoped so.

* * *

Despite arriving home in the early hours reeking of a brewery, Ricky was up and out early on Saturday morning picking up a few hours of overtime. He promised he'd be finished by 12.30 p.m. and we could spend the afternoon together.

I tried to keep myself busy but there wasn't much I could do in a small space on my own. By 11 a.m. I was going stir crazy so decided to walk into town. It was a gorgeous October morning with a blue sky that could fool you into believing it was summer if it wasn't for the nip in the air. I was glad I'd made a last-minute grab for my scarf as I definitely needed it.

The chain stores on the main precinct didn't interest me. Instead, I headed straight for my favourite place: Castle Street. As I'd done on numerous other occasions, I walked up one side of the cobbled street and down the other, gazing into each shop window and imagining what it might look like with a tantalizing display of chocolates. I felt like Goldilocks as I made my assessment of the different premises: this one's too big, this one's too small, this one's just right.

The thing I loved about Castle Street was that every single shop was an independent one and they all seemed to offer something different. There were shops selling flowers, teddy bears, clothes, cakes, furniture, books, wedding dresses, craft supplies and guitars to name just a few. Each time I'd visited, the street was busy which emphasised to me that this was the right place to open my own chocolaterie.

I smiled at the early signs of Christmas in several of the window displays; just hints rather than full Christmas displays. A fur-lined cape was draped round one of the mannequins in The Wedding Emporium, a small selection of children's Christmas books was nestled among the non-festive offerings in the window of Bay Books and Carly's Cupcakes had an amazing Santa's Grotto Christmas cake on display with a sign stating 'Christmas Orders now being taken' beside it. I wondered whether I'd find anywhere this side of Christmas and, if I did, would I have time to get it ready? It wasn't looking good which saddened me as I suspected Christmas on Castle Street would be quite magical.

I'd already picked out my dream premises: a double-fronted shop called Oak Bespoke that sold hand-crafted oak furniture. I'd stupidly tortured myself by going inside and imagining where I'd put everything. I'd mentioned it to Smurf on one of the nights down the pub, but he said it had only opened in the spring and was apparently doing really well which wasn't what I'd hoped to hear. If that was true, there was no way it was going to become available any time soon. Even so, I was drawn to it now and peered through the window, my imagination wandering away with me once more.

I'd set a deadline of the end of the year after which time I'd need to re-think and maybe look outside Whitsborough Bay. The one thing I wasn't going to re-think was opening a chocolaterie. That was definitely happening. I'd already decided on the shop name – Charlee's Chocolates – and the branding. I'd worked out a stock list, found suppliers for the equipment I needed, drawn up a marketing plan and pricing strategy. All I needed was premises.

Reluctantly, I stepped away from Oak Bespoke and headed towards home but I paused by the florist's, Seaside Blooms. I couldn't have the business premises I wanted but I could cheer myself up with some flowers, especially when today was a special anniversary.

* * *

'You have great taste in what goes well together.' The florist – a pretty brunette who I suspected was a similar age to me – smiled at me as she began arranging the autumnal flowers I'd selected into a bouquet. 'Are these for a particular occasion?'

'It would have been my Nanna's birthday today, so I wanted to mark the occasion.'

'Aw, I'm sorry about your loss. Was this recent?'

'May so it's the first birthday without her.'

She gave me a sympathetic look. 'The firsts of every occasion are always the toughest.'

She was so kind and gentle and, watching her work on the flowers, I wondered whether she might be able to help with my problem. Shop owners were probably the first to hear about premises becoming available.

'It's a lovely shop,' I said. 'Is it yours?'

'It is. My auntie set it up, but she passed it onto me when she retired three years ago. I'm Sarah.'

'Charlee,' I said. 'Do you know many of the other business owners on this street?'

'Nearly all of them. Why?'

'You don't know anyone who's thinking of selling up, do you?'

She stopped arranging the flowers for a moment. 'You're thinking of setting up a shop on Castle Street?' she asked, her tone curious.

'If I can find suitable premises.'

'What sort of shop?' Because if it's a florist's, you realise that I'll have to beat you to death with my thorniest roses.' She narrowed her eyes at me then winked and smiled, confirming she was joking.

'Definitely not a florist's. I may have a good eye for what goes together, but I wouldn't be able to arrange them if my life depended on it.' I hesitated. Sarah seemed friendly and I wanted to tell her, but I feared word getting round and someone beating me to it. 'This is going to sound awful, but I'd rather not say. I can confirm that I definitely wouldn't be in competition with you or anyone else on this street.'

Sarah resumed her arranging. 'In that case, you are safe from death by roses. There are a couple of empty shops further down but I'm assuming you've already looked at those and they're no good.'

'Not big enough, unfortunately.' If I'd only wanted to make and sell chocolates, they'd have been ideal, but chocolate-making parties were a valuable income stream all year round and it would be crazy not to secure premises big enough to hold them. I wanted to promote more than children's parties, too. I suspected there'd be a market among adults, perhaps for hen parties, team building activities, or simply individuals wanting to have a go at a new craft.

'Are you looking to buy or let?' Sarah asked.

'Preferably buy but I'd consider letting if it was the right premises and the right price.'

Sarah handed me a pad and pen. 'Scribble your contact details down while I wrap these. I'll ask around over the next week or so and let you know if I hear anything.'

'Thank you so much.'

'You're welcome. I know I'm slightly biased but it's a great street to be on. Best in town, I'd say.'

'From what I've seen, I agree. If I'm going to do this in Whitsborough Bay, it has to be Castle Street.'

* * *

I'd only been out an hour so Ricky wouldn't be back at Coral Court yet but, by the time I'd arranged my flowers, unpacked my shopping and made some lunch, he would be.

At half twelve, I prepared a sandwich for each of us on a fresh baguette I'd bought in town. Ignoring my stomach growling in protest, I covered the food and waited for Ricky. And waited. And waited.

One o'clock arrived. Then quarter past. With each minute ticking past, I battled with feelings of disappointment and frustration. Would it have killed him to text me to say he was going to be late? And why was he late when we were meant to be spending the afternoon together?

At half one, I gave up and grabbed my sandwich. I was halfway through it when Ricky's key turned in the lock.

'I thought I was going to have to send out a search party,' I called. I tried to keep my voice jovial, but I could hear the edge to it.

'Sorry,' Ricky called from the hall. 'They kept us longer than expected. I won't come through. I'm covered in sawdust. I'll jump straight in the shower.'

I heard the bathroom door open and close before I could respond. Sighing, I finished my sandwich while flicking through the latest copy of *Chocolatier Magazine.* Images of melting chocolate and delectable creations would help me calm down. I loved reading the real-life success stories and became engrossed in one about a master chocolatier who'd set up her own business after being made redundant. She'd now moved into bigger premises and her story filled me with hope that I could do the same. I'd suggest to Ricky that we drive up the coast to see whether any of the other towns or villages would be suitable locations for Charlee's Chocolates just in case I had to rule out Whitsborough Bay.

When Ricky appeared with a towel fastened loosely round his waist, my stomach did a little backflip at the sight of him, damp and half-naked. He leaned forward to give me a kiss on the cheek.

'I missed you,' he said, still leaning over me.

'How much?'

'Loads.'

I glanced at his towel. A quick flick and it would be free, but I had no confidence when it came to things like that.

'Fancy showing me how much?' I asked, cringing that I sounded desperate rather than seductive.

He hesitated. It was only for the briefest of moments, but it was long enough for the colour to rush to my cheeks and for me to curse myself for trying to play the role of temptress when it was so not me.

'Joking,' I said. 'You must be starving. I've made you a sandwich. I'll just fetch it.'

I ducked under his outstretched arm and pretty much sprinted into the tiny kitchen. Yanking open the fridge, I grabbed a can of lager and held it against one cheek, then the other.

'Maybe tonight?' he called.

'I thought you were going out for Smurf's birthday.' I put the can back in the fridge, took out his sandwich and removed the cling film.

'I am,' he called. 'Are you sure you don't want to come?'

I took a deep breath and exited the kitchen, hoping that the lager had done its job and my cheeks didn't look radioactive. 'I'm sure.' I didn't fancy another night in alone, but it was still more appealing than a night out with the lads.

Handing him his sandwich, I curled up on the sofa beside him. He took a huge bite and made appreciative groaning noises as he chewed.

'Where did the flowers come from?' he asked, stopping mid-chew.

I recognised that same flicker of jealousy from when he'd met Neil Winters. 'I bought them in town earlier. It would have been Nanna's birthday today.'

'Shit! Really?' He swallowed his mouthful and put his plate down in his lap. 'I didn't realise. Are you okay?'

His concern was touching. I nodded, blinking back tears. 'I'm fine. Nanna loved flowers and I felt like I wanted to acknowledge the day.'

He picked up his sandwich and took another bite. Thinking about his jealous reaction just now, it struck me that I wasn't jealous of him spending time with his friends, but I was jealous of how much time they had with him when I had so little. This was the perfect opportunity to suggest some ground rules before it came between us.

'You know I don't mind you going out with your friends,' I said. 'You can't be expected to stay home just because I don't know anyone yet.' It genuinely hadn't bothered me that I didn't know anyone in the area because I'd hardly had a busy social life in Hull, but saying it aloud suddenly made me feel very alone and my voice cracked at the end of the sentence. I took a deep breath. 'But between you working late and seeing your friends, we've barely seen each other this week. Can you make sure there's still time left for us, otherwise I might as well have stayed in Hull?'

Ricky put his half-demolished sandwich down on the floor and took my hand. 'Do you regret moving here?'

'No! It's just that...' I swiped at a rogue tear. 'I'm just frustrated at not finding suitable premises. I think it's getting to me.'

'Are you sure that's all?'

'Definitely. I really like Whitsborough Bay. I'll be fine when I've got the shop to focus on.'

'Good.' He picked up his sandwich again. 'I just want you to be happy. You know that, don't you?'

I nodded. He'd done everything he could to help me feel settled. He'd shown me round, he'd introduced me to his friends, he'd invited me out with them. It was *my* issue that I didn't like spending time with them and I wasn't going to become one of those women who demanded he didn't have a life of his own so I encouraged him to go out, despite my niggles about money. As long as it wasn't to the detriment of our relationship.

When he'd finished his sandwich, he wiped his hands down his towel. 'That was the best sandwich ever. Thank you.'

'You're welcome.'

'Why don't you ring Jodie and see if she's free tonight?'

I shrugged. 'I could do.'

Ricky stared at me for a moment, frowning.

'I'm fine,' I reassured him. 'Honestly. I'm glad I sold the house and I'm glad I moved here. I love this town and I love you. I'm just having a moment, so you can stop looking at me like that. No regrets.'

His frown remained and he sighed. 'I've got a regret.'

His voice was dripping with it and my heart thumped. Was he going to say that he regretted telling me he loved me? 'Oh yes...?'

'My regret is that I put a shower and food ahead of you. That was my bad.'

I smiled, relieved that it was nothing more serious than that.

'You should always be the top priority,' he continued. 'I'm sorry if I haven't made you feel like that recently. I got carried away being back with the lads. I promise there'll *always* be time for us.'

'Good. That's all I want.'

He cupped my face and ran his thumb over my cheekbone, sending a flutter of passion through me. 'You're so beautiful when you're angry.'

'I'm not angry.'

'You are and you're right to be. This afternoon I'm going to make it up to you.'

'How?'

He winked at me. 'I'm not wearing very much but you, Charlee Chambers, are wearing far too many clothes and that's something we're going to have to rectify.'

He leaned forward and gently tugged my T-shirt over my head. He cocked his head to one side. 'It's an improvement but still not quite right.'

I giggled as he unzipped my jeans, then pulled them off in

one speedy manoeuvre, causing me to slip down onto my back on the sofa.

'Looking a lot better, but you've still got two items of clothing on and I only have one...'

I swiftly released his towel, my pulse racing at how ready for me he clearly was.

'...and now I have none. You don't play fair.'

Instead of whipping off my bra and knickers and getting on with it like I expected him to, he straddled me and stared into my eyes. 'Was there anything you had planned for this afternoon?'

I shook my head. Exploring other locations for my chocolaterie suddenly didn't feel like my top priority.

'Then let's take this really slowly. I've been neglecting you and I need to make it up to you.'

And, oh my God, did he make it up to me? Wow! He kissed, caressed and teased until I was begging for him to take me. Straddled across his body on the sofa, I screamed as I finally let go and multiple orgasms shook my body for the first time ever. That would *never* have happened at my grandparents' house. Moving to Whitsborough Bay had definitely been the right decision. I just needed to be patient about the shop as it would happen eventually. I'd make friends of my own here eventually too and Ricky was going to make more time for us. If I stopped stressing and relaxed more, look at the amazing things that could happen!

6

'Have I told you lately how jealous I am of you living in Whitsborough Bay?' Jodie asked as we walked round The Headland later that evening, heading for a few drinks in Blue Savannah in North Bay. At Ricky's suggestion, I'd given her a call and she'd been more than willing to drive straight up.

'Only *every* time I speak to you,' I said.

'I mean it. I absolutely love this place.' She stopped and leaned on the stone sea wall, looking out towards the North Sea and to the curve of the bay in the distance where we could just make out the white domes of the Sea Rescue Sanctuary thanks to a bright moon. 'Look at it. It's stunning, even at night-time.'

I couldn't argue with that. There was something so calming about being by the sea. I'd always felt it at Spurn Point and I felt it here too. 'I wasn't sure if you'd be free at such short notice.'

She shrugged. 'I'd love to say that I ditched a hot date or a big night out but, let's face it, my ninety-six-year-old great grandma has a better social life than me.' Jodie had severed most of her friendships when she dumped Karl because they were mutual friends. She didn't want to hear them telling her how sorry he was or how much he missed her, so it was easier to make a clean break. 'And now my best mate in the whole wide world, the only person who I care about spending time with, has bogged off to live at the seaside, leaving Billy No Mates here with nothing to do except gorge on Spam sandwiches and watch the soaps every evening.'

Although her tone was humorous, I could tell there was truth in her words and I felt terrible. She was right. We'd been inseparable for the past two decades. Even when she'd moved in with Karl, we'd spent loads of time together, but now I'd gone and abandoned her with very little warning. 'I'm sorry,' I said. 'You do understand why I moved, don't you? I couldn't work for *that* woman.'

'I know. Gabby was an absolute cow. I'm amazed you stuck it out for as long as you did. It was the right time for you to move on and coming here was definitely a good move for you, or at least it will be when you find a shop.' Jodie straightened up. 'I'm not annoyed with you. Well, maybe a little bit, but only because I miss you so much.'

'And I miss you too.'

She smiled. 'Come on. Let's get a drink before we both start crying.'

'Why don't you move here?' I suggested when we set off walking again.

'I'd move here in a heartbeat. But playing gooseberry to you and Ricky...?'

'Believe me, you wouldn't be. He goes out loads with his friends so we'd have plenty of time together and, even if he didn't, I'd still have time for you.'

'Does that bother you?' she asked. 'Ricky going out so much, I mean.'

'Not at first but it has bugged me this week as he's been out with the lads three times. To be fair to him, he has invited me, but I don't like them. That sounds awful, doesn't it? They're just so loud and laddish together. His best mate, Smurf, is okay but the rest of them are a nightmare.'

'Smurf? Is he blue and white?'

I laughed. 'I don't know his real first name but his surname's Smurthwaite so everyone calls him Smurf, even his mum, apparently. When they're all together they act like they're sixteen instead of in their early thirties. It's as though they've just discovered alcohol but the world's supply is about to run out so they need to consume a lifetime's quantity in one evening. A couple of them can't string a sentence together without the f-word and their idea of a good night out is to fall over, throw up, or get into a fight. And don't get me started on how they talk about women.' I shuddered as I thought about the lecherous comments and behaviour I'd been witness to.

'They sound like absolute charmers. Have any of them got girlfriends?'

'Why? Do you want to audition for the part?'

Jodie laughed. 'Can't imagine anything worse. I was just thinking that they sound like blokes who've either gone through life with no meaningful relationships or ones who have some stupid ditzy lass hanging on every word who thinks they're hilarious instead of offensive.'

'It's actually a mix, although I don't think any of the ones with girlfriends are particularly long-term except for Smurf who's been with his for six years. She's often out with them and, I hate to say it, but I can't stand her either. She's like a real-life Barbie doll with long blonde hair, huge boobs, tiny waist, and trowelled-on make-up. I know I shouldn't judge her for her appearance, but her personality is as fake as her nails. She pretends to be friendly to me when Ricky's in earshot then walks off when he's not around.' My fists clenched just thinking about her unbelievable rudeness. 'Bloody BJ. She's so two-faced.'

'BJ? What sort of name's that?' Jodie giggled. 'Does it stand for blow job?'

I giggled too. 'I suggested the same thing to Ricky and he got a bit shirty with me, although what it really stands for isn't much better. It's Big Jugs apparently. She was an early developer so it became her school nickname and, bizarrely, she loves it. All the boys adore her. She can drink nearly as much as them, she's into football, and she was a gymnast when she was younger so her party trick is doing the splits or the crab in the pub, flashing her knickers and bra to everyone.'

'She sounds like a delight too. I'm not surprised you don't want to socialise with them.'

'BJ and her girlfriends have made it clear that I'm not welcome and I don't have anything in common with any of the lads.'

We walked along in silence for a few minutes and I felt quite tearful now that I'd put it in words. Was it me? Was I the unreasonable one not giving his friends a chance? No. I'd gone out with them twice with every intention of making new friends but it hadn't worked. They were a clique with years of history and I couldn't infiltrate.

'I really wouldn't be cramping your style if I moved here?' Jodie asked, interrupting my thoughts.

I stopped walking and grabbed her arm, a squeal of excitement building in me. 'Are you seriously thinking about it?'

She shrugged. 'With my parents back in Bradford and you being here, there's nothing to keep me in Hull except my job. It's not like they don't have teaching assistants in Whitsborough Bay, although I'm wondering if it's time for a career change anyway. I've always fancied living here and taking up sailing or surfing.

Karl and I talked about moving here but he decided it was too quiet for him. Probably not quite enough women for him to work round in his shagging season.'

'I still can't believe he did that to you. Such a waste. You were so perfect together.'

'Yeah. I thought so too, but apparently not.' She looked out to the sea. 'Living here would be a dream fulfilled, but are you sure I wouldn't be in the way?'

'Yes! Having you here would be the best thing ever.'

'I'd better hand in my notice, then, hadn't I?'

'Oh my God! You're really going to move here?'

She grinned. 'I'd love to move here.'

I flung my arms round her and we bounced up and down together, squealing.

'That's the best piece of news I've had all year,' I said, when we'd stopped our happy jig. 'This calls for cocktails. Do you have to drive back? Can't you stay over? I know it's not ideal but the sofa's really comfy.' I blushed as I thought about what Ricky and I had done on the sofa earlier.

'Go on then. I'll have to be home by lunchtime, though. I've got stuff to do. Will Ricky mind?'

'I'll text him.'

✉ To Ricky

Hi you, I've convinced Jodie to have a few
drinks. Would you mind if she sleeps on the
sofa? xx

He responded a few minutes later:

✉ From Ricky

Why don't you both have our bed? I can have my
old bed at Smurf's. Have fun xx

'Aw, he's such a sweetheart,' Jodie said when I shared his response. 'You should hang onto him.'

'I'm certainly going to try.'

'But maybe detach him from those Neanderthal mates.'

I sighed. 'That may be slightly harder.'

* * *

My mobile rang when I was half way down my second cocktail. I didn't recognise the number.

'Hello, Charlee speaking.'

'Charlee. Hi. It's Sarah from Seaside Blooms. We spoke earlier about business premises.'

My heart thumped. Did she have news? 'Hi Sarah. I wasn't expecting to hear back from you so soon.'

'I always think that there's no time like the present. I've done some digging and one of the bigger premises is about to become available.'

I nearly squealed with excitement. 'Which one?'

'The one next to the teddy bear shop, almost opposite me.'

I frowned. That couldn't be right. 'Next to the bear shop? But that's Oak Bespoke.'

'That's the one.'

'Someone told me that it had only just opened and was doing well.'

'It is, but there's been a change of circumstances. It's a sad story, actually. The guy who set it up, Ronnie, makes all the furniture and opened after he got the all-clear from cancer but now his wife's been diagnosed with the early stages of Alzheimer's.

They've decided that life's too short and they want to see the world while she's still able to.'

'That's awful,' I said.

'I know. They're apparently both really positive about it but they're keen to sell the shop quickly so they can fund their travels. It's a successful business but he can't sell it because he's the furniture maker so they're looking to sell just the premises. I know you haven't looked round but do you know the shop? Would it be a good size for your plans?'

Hadn't looked round? Quite the opposite. I'd been in there a handful of times in reality and a million times in my dreams. 'It's perfect, Sarah. It's my dream premises but I didn't think I had a chance of securing it.'

'It's obviously meant to be yours.'

'I feel bad about swooping in when they've had such bad luck, though.'

'You'd be doing them a massive favour if you bought it. Would you like me to see if I can set up a meeting with Ronnie so you can have a good look round and talk finances?'

I couldn't stop grinning. 'Would you? That would be amazing.'

'Leave it with me.'

'I gather that was good news,' Jodie said after I'd ended the call.

'Brilliant news! That premises I love is going to be available and I'm first in the queue. And my best friend's moving to the area. It's finally coming together.'

7

Sarah set up an appointment for me to meet with Ronnie at 11.00 a.m. the following day. Jodie returned to Hull first thing so I phoned Ricky to see if he'd join me. Although it was my business, Charlee's Chocolates would hopefully provide for our future so I wanted Ricky to be with me every step of the way, especially when it had been his idea. His phone went straight to voicemail which I'd half-expected. They'd probably been up drinking until the early hours so were likely still asleep.

I tried phoning again just before I left the flat but there was still no answer so I texted him to let him know where I was going and set off into town, nervous butterflies in my stomach.

Ronnie showed me round the ground floor which went back further than I'd expected, making the premises even more perfect for what I wanted, then he showed me round the large two-bedroom flat upstairs which had a separate entrance next-door.

'The flat probably needs a bit of updating,' he said. 'I was going to do it up and let it out but I never got round to it.'

We discussed the price. It was a bit more than I'd hoped to pay but, if Ricky and I moved into the flat, we could save on rent and we'd actually be better off. Ronnie said that time was of the essence for him and he'd be willing to reduce the price if I completed quickly. I had the money in place and was good to go so we agreed that a fortnight would give him time to hold a sale, clear everything out, and for our solicitors to complete the relevant paperwork.

'You've just bought yourself a place to start your business,' he said, shaking my hand.

I nearly squealed with excitement.

* * *

I was buzzing when I returned to Coral Court, desperate to share the good news with Ricky. His bag and shoes were dumped in the middle of the entrance hall indicating he was back.

'Hello?' I called.

Silence.

I pushed open the lounge door. He was lying on the sofa, a muted football match on the TV, snoring lightly. The room smelled of alcohol so I'd been right in my assumption about it being a big night.

Fighting the urge to rush round and open all the windows, I crouched down beside him and gave him a gentle shake.

He opened his eyes and squinted at me. 'You're back.'

'Did you have a good night?'

'It was messy. I might still be a bit drunk.' He adjusted position so I could sit beside him. 'Did you buy a shop?'

I grinned at him. 'I did. Oak Bespoke.' I gushed about my meeting with Ronnie and how I excited I was that it would be mine in a fortnight. 'I was thinking we could give notice on this place and move in above the shop to save some money.'

His jaw stiffened and he shook his head vigorously. 'You really think that's a good idea? Weren't you just complaining yesterday about not spending enough time with me? How much time do you think we'll spend together if we live above the shop? You'll be working constantly.'

I couldn't argue with that. It would be far too easy to nip downstairs to work on a new idea and lose an entire evening, although I bristled at his use of the word 'complaining'. That wasn't how it had been.

'You're probably right there. I'll have to rent it out instead. Jodie might even be interested if she doesn't change her mind about resigning. But if we're going to continue to rent here, money's going to be tight for a bit so—'

'So you want me to stop going out with my mates to fund your shop?' he snapped.

I reeled back, no idea where the attitude had sprung from. 'I wasn't going to say that. I was going to say I might need you to contribute towards the food and bills until I can get a tenant in.'

He glared at me as he scrambled to his feet, running his hand across his hair. 'Thanks a lot. How do you expect me to pay off my debts if I do that?'

It was on the tip of my tongue to suggest that a little less money wasted on alcohol would help so maybe fewer nights with his mates *would* be a good idea, but I suspected that wouldn't go down well. 'I'm not talking much but I'm paying most of the rent and all of the bills and—'

'Seriously? You're loaded, Charlee! You've got enough money to buy a house *and* a shop and I haven't got a pot to piss in. You've become really stingy recently. I should have stayed at Smurf's. He never charged me rent.'

He slammed the lounge door and, moments later, the flat door and I sank back on the sofa, shaking. Had we just had our first argument? Not that it had been much of an argument – more of a rant from Ricky. Surely it wasn't unreasonable to expect him to contribute financially, especially for food. The man ate like a horse. Smurf might have been happy to let him stay in his spare room rent-free but even the best of friends would expect money for food.

* * *

I should have spent the afternoon celebrating my good news but, instead, spent the next few hours lying on the sofa with the TV on low, thinking that my relationship might be over and it was all my fault. I should have been more understanding about Ricky's financial worries. I could see why he'd be touchy about money when I was flush. Why did I have to be so cautious about everything? If I had to dip into my house fund for the short-term, so be it. If the business went well, I'd be able to replenish what I used so I was worrying unnecessarily. And so what if I had to take out a small mortgage when I was ready to buy? Ricky had bigger money worries than me and I wasn't being fair. It hurt being called 'stingy' but could he be right?

I tried to call him but his phone went to voicemail and I didn't bother leaving a message. One thing I was sure about was how I loved him so much and didn't want to lose him over this. The thought of him returning and packing his stuff filled me with fear. Things had been a bit rocky but only because we'd both experienced so much change. I'd had a bereavement and house sale and we'd both experienced job loss and relocation. Was it any wonder tensions were running high? It would settle down soon.

It was evening before Ricky returned, full of apologies for snapping at me and blaming it on the hangover from hell. 'I'd have bought you some flowers but nice ones would have cost too

much money and you already have some anyway. Then I was
going to get you some chocolates but do you give a master chocolatier chocolates? So can I offer you a kiss instead?'

I smiled at him. 'A kiss from you would be my favourite of the
three anyway.' As I melted into his tender kiss, I was so relieved
we were still together. That had been a close call and I wouldn't
do anything to risk losing him again.

Ronnie was happy for me to visit Oak Bespoke as much as I
wanted during opening hours so I'd been able to take measure-
ments and draw up clear plans. I placed orders for the equipment
and had a good conversation with the Head of Catering and
Hospitality at the local technical college – Whitsborough Bay
TEC – about taking on an apprentice.

My task list seemed never-ending and I could easily have
spent full days and evenings focusing on the business but I vowed
to keep my evenings free for quality time with Ricky. Pinning him
down to that was more of a challenge.

After our big argument, I didn't ask for any more money and
he didn't offer it so I hoped the issue would disappear. It didn't. It
simply wrapped itself up in a different disguise: overtime.

The lads' nights out reduced to once a week but he spent all
his evenings working overtime, making it back to the flat around
half nine. Food lay heavy on my stomach and I couldn't sleep
properly if I ate that late so we didn't even have dinner together. I
hated watching him sitting alone at the small dining table with
his eyes glued to the TV while he shovelled in heated-up food.

On the Wednesday evening ten days after I'd agreed to buy
Oak Bespoke, I placed Ricky's food in front of him and asked if we
could talk when he'd finished.

He raised his eyebrows at me. 'That's what people say when they're about to end things.'

'It's nothing like that. I promise. Eat your dinner.'

'I'm not going to enjoy it now cos you've got me worried.'

I snaked my arms round him from behind and kissed his neck. 'It's your favourite. You *will* enjoy it and everything will be fine.' But even as I said the words, I wasn't so sure. I had a proposal for him which seemed like a win-win solution to me but would he spot a flaw I hadn't considered?

'Hit me with it,' he said, dropping his knife and fork with a clatter onto his empty plate a little later.

I sat down opposite him and switched the TV off to eliminate any distractions. 'We never get any quality time together because you're always working overtime and I'm missing you.'

He rolled his eyes at me as if to say 'not this again' and folded his arms. 'I need to work all the overtime I can get to settle my debts and start to pay my way. I feel bad that I can't help out much at the moment.'

It was the first time he'd said that aloud and I appreciated it. 'What if I had a way of us spending more time together which would also save us some money? I get the shop keys on Monday and there's stacks of work to be done. What if you and I did the work together instead of me paying another contractor? It would mean more money for us.'

His expression hardened. 'It would mean more money for *you*, you mean. Why would I turn down paid work and do the same thing for free?'

'So we can spend some time together. I miss you. I barely ever see you these days.'

'I miss you too but have you heard yourself? Doing up your shop would *not* be quality time together. It would be both of us in the same square footage working our arses off and the only conversation would be about what height you want the shelves at and which wall needs to be what colour. You're better off getting a contractor in.'

'But I'd rather we do it together.' I was in danger of sounding whiney. 'Forget what I said about saving on a contractor. I could pay you what I'd pay a contractor instead.'

His jaw tensed and he shook his head slowly. 'What sort of bloke charges their girlfriend for their time? I'm going for a shower.'

And that was it. Conversation over. He *had* spotted flaws in my proposal after all. I was going to have to go it alone and would just have to accept that time together was going to be rare and precious. My biggest worry was that it could head from rare to non-existent if we weren't careful.

8

Ronnie handed me the keys to the empty premises the following Monday morning. It was the start of the October half term holidays and everything had gone through in the fortnight we'd originally agreed.

'It's all yours now,' he said. 'Thanks for making it all go smoothly.'

'Same to you. I hope you and your wife have an amazing time travelling the world.'

'I'm sure we will.' He shook my hand. 'Good luck with your business. Castle Street's the best and I'm sure you'll do brilliantly.'

With a smile and a wave, he set off down the cobbles and I inserted the key into the lock. This was it! I'd secured my dream premises and Charlee's Chocolates was going to shift from my dreams into reality. Butterflies soared in my stomach as I turned the key and stepped inside.

I locked the door behind me and stood in the middle of the empty shop, grinning from ear to ear, barely able to believe that it was actually happening. I'd hoped Ricky would join me today but he looked at me doubtfully when I suggested it. 'Let me get this right. You want me to take a day off work – losing out on a day's wages – to watch you unlock the door to an empty building when I can see you do that on the evening without taking a day off work?'

When he put it like that, it seemed like a stupid suggestion, especially when money – and more specifically him doing overtime to earn it – had caused so much friction recently. The subject of him helping out hadn't cropped up again. I was going to have to do as much as I could on my own and bring in professional help for anything outside my capabilities. Jodie was joining me for a few days with it being half term although she wasn't going to stay over as she needed the time to pack up her flat in Hull. After half term, she had one more week left to serve on her notice before moving to Whitsborough Bay permanently. She was going to rent the flat above the shop so at least I knew I had a trustworthy tenant although Ricky had rolled his eyes when I mentioned mate's rates. He muttered something about people taking advantage of my good nature. Talk about the pot calling the kettle black!

* * *

I achieved so much over the next fortnight as my business took shape, but I felt like I lost something too: Ricky. He committed to working overtime nearly all week. He said it was because Jodie would be at the shop and he didn't want to get in our way but I'd told him on several occasions that it was only a few days and she wasn't staying over. It seemed to fall on deaf ears. Seeing as he'd agreed to overtime, I put in extra hours at the shop.

It took him until the Thursday evening of the first week to even visit. It was such a brief tour that I couldn't help thinking he'd been lured by the promise of a celebratory meal afterwards instead of a genuine desire to see my shop.

On the Sunday of that week, he did fit the shop counter for me but only because he said the quote I'd been given by a local joiner made his eyes bleed and no way could he let me pay that. I'd been worried he might cut corners because he didn't want to spend his only day off doing joinery but his craftmanship was superb. I told him I wished he was doing all the joinery for me but that was met with a muttered comment about overtime and debts so I let it go. He was beginning to sound like a stuck record.

I was completely on my own for the second week and I felt a cloak of loneliness wrapping round me. I loved Whitsborough Bay and I loved my shop but I felt the lack of friendships. If it hadn't been for the light in the darkness of Jodie moving up at the weekend, I'd probably have spent a lot of the time in tears.

There was so much still to do to be ready for a grand opening at the start of December. I'd known all along that it would be tight, but there was no way I wanted to miss out on the lucrative Christmas trade and risk a flat opening in January when everyone had eaten their fill of Christmas chocolates and made a New Year's resolution to diet. I'd dropped several very unsubtle hints to Ricky that an extra pair of hands would be helpful but he'd mastered the art of changing the subject and I'd become an expert in not rocking the boat.

I couldn't help feeling massively disappointed by his lack of interest. I'd had this romantic vision of us developing Charlee's chocolates together. I'd thought he'd want to be involved in bringing life to the business but I got the impression he couldn't care less which really hurt, especially after it had been his suggestion in the first place. He recommended a few contractors to work in the shop and the flat and probably thought he was being a great help doing that but it wasn't the same.

I didn't want to spend the limited time with Ricky each evening arguing so I did my best to be cheerful and upbeat as I asked him about his day and told him about mine. That approach seemed to work and that short time together felt happy. He picked paint out of my hair, rubbed my aching shoulders and was so attentive towards me that I wondered if it was me being unreasonable. Plenty of couples had phases where their time together was limited and, if they loved each other as much as we did, they made it work.

* * *

'This is it! All my worldly possessions,' Jodie said, getting out of her car on Saturday lunchtime and tapping her hand on the roof. Suitcases, boxes and bags were crammed into every spare inch of space. 'Before I open the boot and everything spills out, are you sure this is okay and you don't want to have the flat above the shop for yourself?'

'I'm sure. I know it would be handy, but I'd never stop working if I lived above the shop. It's all yours and I'm happy to stay where I am. Ooh, I'm so glad you're here.' I flung my arms round her and hugged her tightly, fighting back the tears. There had been far too many moments over the past month where I'd felt lonely but with Jodie here, everything was looking up.

'Me too. This is so exciting.' She stepped back. 'Where's Ricky?'

'Last minute call into work.' He'd surprised me by offering to help Jodie move her belongings in and finally put up the shelving in my storeroom but he'd had a call this morning with some sort of emergency on site. I'd heard his side of the conversation and it hadn't sounded like it was something he could turn down so I'd kissed him goodbye and said we'd manage.

The flat had a large open plan living space across the back with a kitchen and dining area at one end and the lounge at the other. I'd had furniture delivered along with kitchen essentials but was very conscious that it looked sparse and unwelcoming but, after we'd emptied Jodie's car, we unpacked a few of her boxes. The addition of cushions, books, framed photos and a couple of plants instantly transformed it into a more homely space.

We relaxed on the sofa with mugs of tea.

'Here's to new beginnings for both of us,' I said.

We clinked our mugs together and Jodie smiled. 'I can't believe I've finally made the move to Whitsborough Bay after all these years of dreaming about it.'

'Have you had any more thoughts about jobs?' I asked. While helping me last week, she'd told me she didn't want to return to being a teaching assistant, or at least not immediately, but wasn't sure what to do instead.

'I have actually. I know you're taking on a Saturday apprentice but you said you also needed someone full-time. How would you feel about me working for you?'

I widened my eyes at her. 'Are you being serious?'

She nodded. 'I don't know whether becoming a chocolatier is my next career move but it would give me the time and space to decide what is.' She twiddled a strand of hair round her middle finger which I knew meant she was nervous; a rarity for her. 'You don't want me to work for you, do you?'

Realising that my mouth was still open with surprise, I quickly shut it. 'No! I'm just a little stunned. It's only going to be a minimum wage job. Well, until I'm established anyway at which point I'd hope to pay more.'

'That's fine. I wasn't exactly bringing home a six-figure salary as a teaching assistant, was I? I promise I'll respect that you're the boss and that I'm learning. You already know I'm reliable. I'm organised, tidy, great with people and—'

Smiling, I put my hand up to stop her. 'You don't need to sell yourself to me. I lived with you for four years. I know what you're like and what a good work ethic you have. If you're really sure this is what you want, the job's yours. I'd have suggested it myself ages ago but I'd never imagined you'd be interested.' I couldn't think of a more perfect scenario. It would give her time and space, as she said, but it would do the same for me. I'd have an employee I trusted who would be as passionate about my business and as committed to making a success as I was and I'd get to work alongside my best friend every day.

Jodie stopped twirling her hair and grinned. 'Really? It's not too much, me moving up here, living in your flat, and demanding a job from you, is it? Oh God, when I say it like that, it sounds like I'm trying to copy your whole life.'

'As long as you don't start sleeping with my boyfriend, I think we're good.'

She spluttered on her tea. 'Ew! No offence, Charlee, but Ricky really doesn't do it for me, probably because he reminds me too much of Karl. I've decided that older men are the way forward, rather than silly boys who can't keep it in their pants. Not that Ricky can't keep it in his pants, of course... I'm going to stop talking, clamber out of that hole I'm digging, and take a shower because I'm a bit sweaty and smelly.'

I laughed. 'No offence taken and I knew what you meant.' I picked up her mug and took it to the kitchen area with mine. 'And the shower's a good idea.' I playfully wafted my hand under my nose. 'I'm going downstairs so come down when you're ready but there's no rush. If you want to unpack some more stuff, feel free to do that first.'

* * *

Ten minutes later, as I was leaning on the new shop counter updating my enormous jobs list, I jumped and put my hand up to my head. What the hell was that? Another droplet hit me and I looked up at the ceiling.

'No!' I dashed into the workshop, grabbed a large mixing bowl, and held it under the rapidly growing pool. 'Jodie!' I yelled. 'Turn the shower off!'

There was no way she'd be able to hear me, though. The ceiling was extra thick to stop noise passing between the floors. Placing the bowl under the drip, I ran out the shop and let myself into the flat, sprinting up the stairs.

'Jodie!' I banged on the bathroom door. 'Turn it off! The water's coming through the ceiling.'

'Shit! Just a sec.'

More than 'just a sec' passed and I could still hear running water.

'Jodie!'

'It won't turn off!' she cried. 'Help!'

I burst through the bathroom door.

'I've tried it both ways but nothing's happening.'

'Try it again.'

I watched through the screen as she wriggled the lever in all directions before pushing open the shower screen. 'You'd better try.'

I let her past me so she could grab a towel then thrust my hand into the water flow. I turned the lever in the direction that was meant to shut down the water, then the other way, but to no avail.

'Sorry,' Jodie said.

'It's not your fault,' I assured her. 'Can you keep trying? I'll ring Ricky.'

I grabbed the washing up bowl and a bucket from the kitchen before running back down to the shop. I pushed the washing up bowl under the steady flow of water now coming through the ceiling, poured the contents of the mixing bowl into the bucket, and ran through to the kitchen to empty it. Returning to the shop to keep watch, I dialled Ricky.

'Please answer,' I pleaded as I waited for the call to connect. Voicemail. Crap! 'Ricky! It's me. Disaster! The shower's leaking into the shop and it won't switch off. I don't know what to do. Can you ring me as soon as you get this?'

I sent him a text too. Looking up at the ceiling again, my heart skipped a beat. No! There was another pool forming about a foot away from the original one. I thrust the bucket under that one.

The door opened and Jodie appeared in the clothes she'd been wearing earlier with wet hair stuck out in all directions. 'It still won't switch off. I've looked everywhere and I can't find a stopcock. Oh my God! Is it coming through in two places?'

'It wasn't but it is now. Can you do me a favour? Go to the pound shop round the corner and get me a load of buckets. We might need them if it spreads.'

Jodie grabbed the £10 note I thrust at her and ran out of the shop.

Feeling sick with panic, I dialled Ricky's number again but to no avail. Biting my lip, I scrolled through my contacts. Ah! Smurf! Ricky had given me Smurf's number when he'd first moved up to Whitsborough Bay and was staying with him.

The call connected after three rings. 'Hello. Mike Smurthwaite.'

'Smurf? Thank God! It's Charlee. I've got an emergency and I can't get hold of Ricky.'

'What sort of emergency?'

'The shower in the flat is leaking into the shop and it won't switch off.'

'You'll need to find the stopcock.'

'We've tried but we can't find it. Are you at work?'

'Yeah.'

'Is Ricky with you?'

There was a pause.

'Smurf? Are you still there? Ricky said he was working this morning. Is he with you?'

'He's not with me this morning. Sorry, Charlee.'

'If you see him, can you ask him to call me?'

'Will do. I'd offer to help but I can't leave the site. Who put the shower in for you? Was it Toadie?'

'Yes. I don't have his number, though.'

'I do. I'll send you it.'

When I'd thanked him and hung up, I looked up to see another pool forming. I thrust the original mixing bowl under that and hoped it wouldn't fill before Jodie returned.

A moment later, Toadie's number appeared on my phone and I immediately dialled it but he was on voicemail too.

Jodie burst through the door with a pile of plastic buckets as I finished leaving Toadie a message. 'How's it going?'

'Three leaks now.'

'Aw, Charlee. That's rubbish.'

'I know. Still can't get hold of Ricky or Toadie.'

'Toadie?'

'The plumber who fitted it. I don't know what to do. I don't know anyone else. Can you keep an eye on the leaks while I see if Sarah over the road knows anyone who can help?'

I ran across the cobbles to Seaside Blooms. Sarah looked up

from the bouquet she was arranging and smiled. 'Charlee! How's it going?'

'Disaster! Do you know a reliable plumber?'

'What's happened?'

'The shower I've just had fitted in the flat is leaking into the shop and it won't switch off. I can't get hold of the plumber who did it, or my boyfriend.'

'Cathy! Can you finish this off?' An older woman appeared through an archway at the back of the shop. They exchanged a few words then Sarah signalled to me to join her through the archway. She stood by a large desk and ran her finger down a list of names and numbers on a cork notice board behind it before picking up the handset of a phone on the desk.

'I'm in this group called Bay Trade. It's all small local businesses. We had a plumber join us recently and he's lovely. I'm trying him but don't panic if he doesn't answer. I know a couple of others I can try.'

'Thank you.' I crossed my fingers and tried not to think about the damage the water was doing back at Charlee's Chocolates.

'Matt? Hi, it's Sarah from Bay Trade. How are you?' She gave me a thumbs up. 'Sorry to bother you on a weekend but I have my friend, Charlee, with me and she's got an emergency...'

'Great news,' she said, hanging up the phone a few moments later. 'He's in town right now with his fiancée so they'll be with you any minute. He doesn't have any tools with him but says he should be able to switch off the water for you.'

'Sarah, you're a lifesaver.'

She smiled. 'It's no problem. His name's Matt Richards. Let me know how you get on.'

'Thank you. I owe you one.'

* * *

There was a knock on the door less than a minute after I'd returned to the shop. I yanked it open and was momentarily rendered speechless by the dreamy, good looks of the man standing there. He was a little taller than Ricky – I reckoned about six foot two – with dark curly hair, smouldering dark eyes, and facial hair, just like one of my celebrity crushes: Kit Harrington from *Game of Thrones*. My stomach did an unexpected backflip.

'Charlee?' he asked, snapping me out of my trance.

'Yes! You must be Matt. That was quick.'

'We were in town so it wasn't a problem, was it Libby?' He turned to the bored-looking woman beside him who crossed her arms, raised her eyebrows and sighed. Clearly it *was* a problem for her. The sparkle in his warm dark eyes faded, as did his smile. I'd obviously started a domestic.

'I'm sorry for ruining your plans.'

He turned back to me. 'You didn't. You've temporarily saved me from a long and painful cushion-purchasing decision.'

'Oh for God's sake,' Libby snapped. 'You say you want to be involved in decisions and when I get you involved, you don't give a shit.'

Matt grimaced. 'I meant big decisions like room sizes and furniture. Cushions aren't really my thing, are they?'

Libby gave him a hard stare; the sort that could wither a plant at fifty paces. 'Thanks for the support, Matt. I'm off to Gina's. I'll see you at the caravan later.' With a toss of her long blonde hair, she stormed off down the street.

'Libby! Don't be like that,' he called after her.

She stuck one finger up at him and continued walking. Charming.

'Sorry about that,' Matt said. 'We've just started work on a barn conversion at my parents' farm and I think the stress of living in a caravan on site is taking its toll, which doesn't bode well because we've only been in the van for a week. But you don't need to know all about my domestic arrangements, do you? You need a leak sorting. Where is it?'

'Upstairs. Follow me.'

* * *

Relief flowed through me as the sound of silence engulfed the flat, followed a moment later by Matt's voice. 'All done.'

I poked my head round the bathroom door. 'I can't thank you enough.'

Matt stood up and wiped his hands. 'It's a pleasure. Can I ask you a question, though? Who fitted the shower?'

'Toadie.'

'Toadie?'

'I don't know his proper name. He's a friend of my boyfriend's.'

Matt wrinkled his nose. 'I hate to say this but your boyfriend's friend has made what we call in the trade a dog's arse of it.'

My shoulders drooped. 'Really? Ricky said he knew what he was doing.'

'Sorry, Charlee, but he hadn't a clue. The finish looks great but the behind-the-scenes stuff is shocking. I'd guess that this Toadie is a fitter – a good one too – but I'm afraid he doesn't know his arse from his elbow when it comes to plumbing.'

I sighed. 'Great. Is it something you can sort out for me?'

He smiled. 'Happy to. I'll need to go home and get my tools and a few parts, but I can have this sorted out for you today.'

'Today? Are you sure? I thought you had plans.'

'Nope. Libby had plans and now she's gone to her friend's. They'll spend the afternoon in the pub slagging me off and she'll roll in drunk at some point tonight, cushion-gate completely forgotten.'

'Oh.' I didn't know how to respond to that.

He cocked his head onto one side. 'You're a female.'

I laughed. 'I was last time I looked in the mirror.'

'Would you pick out cushions before you'd chosen a sofa or bedding?'

'No.'

'Why?'

'Because they might not match.'

He nodded slowly. 'Yeah, that's what I thought. Oh well. Let me check your drips downstairs, then I'll get my tools and some supplies. I'll be back within the hour.'

9

'He was yummy,' Jodie said, returning to the shop after emptying the final bucket of water down the sink out the back.

'Matt?'

'Unless you're hiding any other hunky plumbers behind these boxes.'

I felt my cheeks colour as my stomach did another backflip. 'I'll admit that he was pretty easy on the eye.'

'You're blushing.'

'I am not.'

Jodie placed two fingers against my cheek and made a fizzing noise. 'Matt and Charlee, sitting in a tree...' she chanted.

'Give over! I've got a boyfriend and Matt's got a fiancée.'

'An evil fiancée.'

'True, but still a fiancée.'

'There's no harm in a little window-shopping, though, is there? Just don't try the goods. Unless your name is Karl, of course, in which case you shag everything that moves.'

'Have you heard from him lately?' Every so often, Karl

emailed or texted Jodie, begging her to forgive and forget, but she always ignored him.

Jodie didn't answer. She stacked the buckets together and moved them against the wall.

'Jodie...?'

She turned towards me, shoulders slumped. 'I did something *really* stupid.'

'What sort of something stupid?'

'I went out with him.'

'Oh my God! When?'

'Last weekend. He rang me when I was back in Hull packing up my stuff. He'd heard that I was leaving and asked if I wanted to go out for a drink for old time's sake. I was about to say no but then I thought that it might be a good way to get closure before I moved away.'

I cringed inwardly. That had definitely *not* been a good idea and from Jodie's frown and the flatness to her tone, it clearly hadn't gone well.

'Why didn't you tell me he'd made contact?' I asked gently.

'Because you'd have tried to talk me out of it.'

'Probably, but I understand the need for absolute closure so I'd have supported you if you'd still wanted to meet him. You know that, don't you? And why didn't you tell me afterwards?'

She lowered her eyes and my heart sank.

'Jodie! Please don't tell me you slept with him.'

She slid down the wall and slumped onto the floor, legs crossed. 'We spent all weekend in bed, but there wasn't a lot of sleeping.'

I crossed the shop, sat down beside her and gave her an affectionate nudge. 'I'm listening.'

'It was the best weekend of my life. And the absolute worst.'

'What happened?'

'I already knew that I was going to sleep with him as soon as I agreed to a drink. I told myself it was my final goodbye and that it was *my* choice and not something he'd talked me into.' She sighed. 'It was amazing, Charlee. Not just the sex, although that was pretty spectacular. He'd certainly learned some stuff. The amazing thing was the connection. We talked loads. *Really* talked. We laughed, we cried, we talked about the future. It was just like old times but better. By Sunday morning, he'd all but convinced me to stay in Hull and give things another go.' A tear slipped down her cheek. Poor Jodie. Getting back with Karl wouldn't have been the right thing for her at all.

'But Karl conveniently forgot to tell me he already had a girl-friend.' Jodie wiped at another tear. 'A girlfriend who he lived with who conveniently happened to be away that weekend.'

'The idiot! Dare I ask how you found out?'

'She walked in on us.'

'Having sex?'

'Worse than that. Oh, God! It was awful. As I said, Karl's learned a thing or two and he asked if I'd be up for something a bit different. He'd...' She coughed slightly. 'He'd er... he'd hand-cuffed me to the bed, hands and feet, and blindfolded me.'

I clapped my hand across my mouth, mortified for her.

'Oh my God, Charlee, it was the most erotic thing I've ever experienced. You and Ricky should try it.'

I blushed as I thought of our afternoon on the sofa. He'd barely touched me since then, though. I couldn't fathom him out. But I needed to stop thinking about my problems and focus back on Jodie. 'And his girlfriend caught you like that?'

'The poor woman. That's a sight you *really* don't want to arrive home to. I lay there, handcuffed and blindfolded while they yelled at each other. She knew who I was. Apparently he was "obsessed" with me. Karl told her that she shouldn't be surprised and that she'd always known he was still in love with me and was only with her for a bit of fun.' Jodie shook her head. 'He was so nasty to her, Charlee. It was like listening to a stranger. He told her she could come back later and get her stuff because I was going to be moving in instead. She ran off sobbing.'

I put my arm round Jodie's shoulders and gave her a gentle squeeze. 'You weren't to know it would end up like that. I take it you told Karl where to go?'

She giggled through her tears. 'In a roundabout way.'

'What did you do?'

'Well, you know how actions speak louder than words? He tried to make out that she wasn't really living with him, that she meant nothing, and that I'd always been the only one for him. I just smiled and said, "No more talking. I understand what's happened." I told him that he'd given me what *I* needed and it was my turn to give him what *he* needed. I handcuffed him to the bed and blindfolded him. I got dressed, telling him that I was going to get some chocolate spread from the corner shop, but I'd squirt some cream on him ready for my return. I wrote WANKER across his body with the cream, took a photo of him, then left.'

'You didn't!'

She took her phone out of her jeans pocket and I squealed at the image. 'Did you just leave him there?'

'I was tempted, but I called his brother and suggested that Karl might need a hand, and that he should approach him with caution, preferably with his eyes closed.'

I looked at her phone again, giggling.

'If I ever find myself thinking fondly of my time with Karl, I can look at this picture and remind myself who he really is.'

I hugged her to me again. 'I'm so proud of you.'

'It's only taken four years, eh? I've finally got my closure, though. I just wish I hadn't been so weak to fall for his charms again.'

'You wouldn't have got your closure without that slight lapse in judgement. And you wouldn't have had the best sex you've ever had.'

Jodie laughed. 'Every cloud...' She stretched her arms out and yawned. 'Karl and Hull are firmly behind me and we have a shop to get ready. What's first, now that Niagara Falls has stopped?'

'I need to get my store cupboard sorted out. Ricky's been promising help all week and was finally going to do it today after you moved in but he's abandoned ship again so it's down to us. I've got some power tools and I know how to use them. Are you up for it?'

'I certainly am.'

I stood up and pulled Jodie to her feet. 'Thanks,' she said.

'What for?'

'For not having a go at me for getting back with Karl, albeit temporarily.'

'It would have been your decision to make and I'd have supported you whatever you'd decided to do.'

'Speaking of support, what's going on with Ricky?'

'What do you mean?'

'I'm sensing trouble in paradise. You don't talk about him as much as you used to and, when you do, there's an edge to your voice.'

'That's probably because I'm seriously pissed off with him today. He went to work when he'd promised he'd do the shelving and help you move in, he recommended some incompetent muppet to do my plumbing, and he hasn't returned my calls.' I counted each point off on my fingers, very much aware that Jodie was right and there was a definite edge to my voice.

She gave me a gentle smile. 'Tell you what, let's get on with the shelving and save the man-bashing for a bottle of wine later.'

'Sounds good.' I pointed Jodie towards the drill that I'd put on to charge that morning while I picked up a box of wall plugs. Was she right? Was there trouble in paradise? I hated to admit it, but there probably was.

10

'Charlee!'

I stopped drilling and turned to see Matt. Butterflies fluttered in my stomach yet again and I frowned. Why was I having that sort of reaction to a complete stranger?

'I knocked but there was no answer,' he said.

'Sorry, Matt. I'm on a shelf-fitting frenzy.' I put the drill down on the floor. 'My friend Jodie's nipped out to get some cold drinks or she'd have heard you.'

'You've got dust on your cheek,' he said.

I wiped at my left cheek.

'The other cheek.'

I wiped at that one. 'Got it?'

He smiled, revealing really cute dimples. I love dimples on a man. 'Not quite. Do you want me to...?'

'Go ahead.' I held my breath as he gently swept his hand across my cheek a couple of times. Wow! Serious belly flop moment!

His eyes met mine. 'It's gone.'

'Thank you.' I had to pull my gaze away before I melted into those chocolate eyes of his. 'So, er, thanks for coming back to sort out my dodgy plumbing.'

'Pleasure. Do you need a hand with the shelving first?'

'It's slow-going but I think we're okay. Thank you.'

'Looks like you're doing a great job. I'll go upstairs, then, and fix that mess but do shout if you need another pair of hands down here.'

I tried Ricky's phone several times across the afternoon, feeling more and more frustrated with him each time my call connected to his voicemail. What the hell was he doing? He was only meant to be working this morning.

Shortly after four, Matt reappeared in the shop. 'You're all sorted now,' he said. 'I've soaked up the water that had leaked and everything's now properly connected. I checked your kitchen sink too which is just as well because that was also bodged but it's all fixed now.'

'I never even thought about checking the kitchen. Wait till I get my hands on Toadie. Thanks so much for checking it.'

'I could tell you'd had a full refurb so I figured the kitchen sink could be at risk. I've run the shower, both sinks, and flushed the toilet. Everything's running perfectly now.' He glanced up at the ceiling where there were a couple of brownish stains. 'That should paint over easily once its dried.'

'Coffee?' I asked.

'That would be great. How's the shelving going?'

I wrinkled my nose. 'Still very slowly and there may be one or two holes where there shouldn't be any, but I keep telling myself that it's a storeroom so it's not like customers will see them.'

'I could finish it for you if you want.'

I was going to protest that he'd done enough already but Jodie had obviously been listening and came through from the back.

'Yes please!' she said. 'My arms are killing me. How about I make the drinks and you two finish the shelves?'

I swear the little minx winked at me when Matt wasn't looking. I'd filled her in on a couple of the incidents with Ricky between drilling holes. She hadn't said much, but I could tell that she wasn't particularly impressed with his recent behaviour. As I spoke, I realised that I wasn't either. Jodie had evidently decided that Matt was a more worthy candidate for my affections and that was before she'd even heard the full story.

After Jodie made the drinks, I suggested she might like to return to the flat to properly unpack. She gave me a look and I knew exactly what it meant: *you're deliberately trying to get rid of me so you can be alone with Matt.* That absolutely wasn't the case. I had a boyfriend and he had a fiancée so nothing was going to happen. I was thinking of her. That was all.

'So, what sort of shop are you opening?' Matt asked after he'd put up the next shelving unit frame with ease and, it has to be said, in about a tenth of the time it had taken Jodie and me to put up one. Although, to be fair to us, it had been our first time and he'd probably done it before.

I passed a shelf up to him as he rested on the stepladder. 'A chocolate shop.'

His expression suggested that he was impressed. 'Are you a chocolatier?'

I grinned. 'No. I'm a *master* chocolatier.'

'Get you! What's the difference?'

'The word "master".'

Matt laughed. 'Very funny. There must be some other difference like qualifications or something.'

I shook my head. 'Not really. Officially, a chocolatier makes confectionery from chocolate. A master chocolatier does that too but is also more creative with chocolate, making figures and structures, for example. It's kind of down to experience and talent.'

He placed the shelf in position and twisted round to receive another. 'Have you always wanted to be a chocolatier... sorry, *master* chocolatier.'

'Yes and no. I was brought up by my grandparents and my Grandpa had a chocolate shop so I learned the craft from him when I was quite young. I worked part-time in his shop throughout school and the plan was for me to take over eventually but I stupidly decided I wanted to become a pastry chef instead...'

I continued to pass shelves to Matt as he listened to me talking about how I'd loved being a pastry chef but had felt like something was missing. By the time I'd realised that the missing piece of the puzzle was the interaction with customers that I'd had at the shop, it was too late. Grandpa had taken early retirement and sold the shop to Pierre.

'What about you?' I asked. 'Have you always wanted to be a plumber?'

He nodded. 'A bit like you, it was the family business. My dad's a builder, joiner and qualified electrician. When my brother, Tim, and I were kids, we went onto building sites with Dad and helped out. We both loved it. Tim trained as a plasterer, painter and decorator and I trained as a plumber and gas safe engineer. The three of us formed a company about a decade ago and it's doing really well because, between us, we can tackle pretty much anything. I couldn't imagine working in an office and I couldn't imagine working with anyone but my family.'

'I know what you mean. I loved working with Grandpa. He was so talented and he had such an easy way with customers. He taught me everything I know. I thought you said earlier that your parents lived on a farm, though.'

'You're a good listener. Yes, they do, and I was brought up on the farm. It was my granddad's and he expected Dad to take over, but Dad wasn't interested in farming. When Granddad retired, he passed the farm to Dad, hoping he'd change his mind when his hand was forced, but Dad appointed a farm manager instead. Mum helps out a bit and Dad, Tim, and I do any maintenance needed, but the animals and crops are left to the farm manager, Nigel. It suits everyone and even Granddad admitted he probably should have taken that approach himself. Far less stressful.'

The warmth in his voice conveyed how much his family and the business meant to him. 'Sounds ideal,' I said. 'Do you have any other siblings?'

'Just Tim. Mum wanted a girl but she joked that she wouldn't have been able to cope with the testosterone if she had another boy so they stopped at two. Tim has two little girls, though. Mum's in her element being a grandparent to them although she keeps going on that she wants a grandson and staring pointedly at me. Never gonna happen.'

'You and Libby can't have children?' I put my hand over my mouth, realising how intrusive that had been.

Thankfully, Matt didn't look bothered. 'I don't know whether we can or can't. It's more of a case of won't. Libby doesn't want kids. Reckons the expense, hassle, lack of sleep when they're babies, and attitude when they're teenagers isn't worth the occasional "aw moment" so I guess that's the decision made.'

'Is that what you want, though?' I put my hand over my mouth again. 'Sorry. That's absolutely none of my business.'

Matt smiled. 'It's fine. I don't mind talking about it. To be honest, I always assumed that I *would* have kids but, when Libby said she didn't want any, it didn't feel like something that I wanted to fight her for.' His face took on a wistful expression for a moment, then he smiled again. 'Although on days like today when she's being massively high maintenance, I do question my choices.'

I didn't like the sound of Libby at all and I certainly hadn't felt any positive vibes from our brief meeting at the door. Matt, on the other hand, seemed to be the exact opposite to Libby: incredibly warm, friendly and laid back. Perhaps that was what made their relationship work; his relaxed approach balanced out her frenzied one.

* * *

'How's it going?' Jodie asked, returning to the shop and poking her head round the stockroom door a little later. 'Wow! You've nearly finished.'

'Last one,' Matt said.

'I'm impressed. Do you want another coffee?'

'Or there are some lagers in the fridge upstairs,' I suggested. 'Can I tempt you with one when we're done?'

'I was going to say yes to the coffee but a lager's even better. I've got the van, but I'm okay with one. Thanks.'

Twenty minutes later, I unplugged the vacuum cleaner and stepped back to admire our work. Tall racks of dark grey metal shelving ran round the perimeter of the large storeroom and four sets of shelves stood back-to-back in the middle of the room, making the most of the floor space.

'I'd have been here all night finishing that off,' I said. 'I can't thank you enough for everything you've done today, Matt. Beer o'clock?'

He nodded. 'Definitely.'

Jodie was waiting for us upstairs. Two opened bottles of lager sat on the kitchen worktop, and she was already halfway down hers. I noticed that she'd plonked herself down on the single chair, which meant that Matt and I would need to share the two-seater sofa. She'd done that deliberately. I indicated that Matt should take a seat and sat beside him, feeling quite hot at being in such close proximity. Ridiculous! He was attached and so was I.

'So, Matt,' Jodie said. 'You're a plumber. I'm guessing you've encountered some pretty rancid toilets in your time.'

'Jesus, yes! I swear I've lost some of my sense of smell now and I can pinpoint it down to the time when I got called to an incident in a hotel in town...'

Matt regaled us with tale after tale. He had a gift for story-telling, full of dramatic pauses, accents, and acting out customers' mannerisms. Tears rolled down Jodie's cheeks and I got the hiccups from laughing so much, which set us all off even more.

'What's going on here?'

We'd been laughing so hard that we hadn't heard the door open or his footsteps on the stairs.

'Ricky! Where've you been? I've been trying to get hold of you all day.'

'Working. I left my phone at the flat and I got back to a million missed calls from you. I called you but there was no answer.'

I felt like I was being told off, despite it being him and his useless mate who should have been the ones in trouble. 'I might have left my phone in the shop,' I said, trying to keep my tone light as I noticed Jodie and Matt squirming.

'That's helpful,' Ricky said.

'About as helpful as you leaving your phone at the flat,' I muttered.

Ricky flashed his eyes at me then nodded his head towards Matt. 'Who's he?'

'My new friend, Matt.' I could have said 'the emergency plumber' but the words slipped out and I was aware that I'd said them to get a reaction. 'He managed to sort out the bodge job that your mate Toadie did on the shower and the kitchen sink, flooding my shop.'

'Toadie did a great job.'

'Yes he did... if the job had been to create a water feature, or rather several water features, in the shop. But given that the job was to properly plumb in the bathroom and kitchen, not so much.'

Matt stood up. 'I'd better go. Thanks for the drink, Charlee.' He headed over to the kitchen area with his unfinished bottle.

I stood up too. 'You don't have to leave.'

He walked back towards me, smiling. 'It's fine. My nieces are having a sleepover at the farm and my bedtime story duties will be required.'

'I bet you tell an amazing bedtime story,' I said, realising too late that it might have sounded flirty.

Matt seemed to take it as the latter too because his eyes sparkled as he said in a teasing tone, 'Maybe one day I'll tell you one.'

'And maybe you won't.' Ricky grabbed me roughly by the shoulders and yanked me towards him, as though staking his claim on me. I tried to shrug him off but he spun me round and lunged at me, forcing his tongue into my mouth as he aggressively kissed me. What the hell had got into him? He was hurting me and he was humiliating me in front of my friends although I couldn't help wondering if that was his intention.

I pushed him away and glared at him as I wiped my mouth with the back of my hand in disgust. I couldn't even begin to find words to convey what I thought of him at that moment but I'd find some later when we were alone. Nobody manhandled me like that and got away with it.

I swallowed down my anger and turned to Matt, fighting to

keep my voice steady. 'I'll let you back into the shop so you can get your stuff, Matt.'

'Okay. Thanks.'

I glared at Ricky. '*You* can wait here. If Jodie's okay with that.'

Jodie nodded. 'It's fine. You go.'

As I set off down the stairs with Matt following me, I heard her snarl, 'What the bloody hell was that all about, you stupid twat?' Yay, Jodie! She'd never been one to mince her words.

'I'm so sorry about that,' I said to Matt when we were in the shop and out of earshot.

'He wouldn't...?'

'God, no! He's not violent. He's not normally full of attitude like that, either.' But I thought about how he'd been with Neil Winters. It would appear that my boyfriend had a nasty jealous streak and, although I'd found it quite sweet that he felt so insecure around Neil, there was nothing sweet about what had just happened. He'd left me with a very bitter taste in my mouth.

'Glad to hear it because you deserve better than that.' Matt rolled his eyes ruefully. 'Says the man whose fiancée stropped off down the street earlier and stuck her finger up at him.'

I smiled at him. 'We do pick 'em, eh? Looks like we've both got our work cut out for this evening, placating our stroppy other halves.'

'Tell me about it.' Matt paused and looked deep into my eyes. 'You've got my number. If he does get nasty with you tonight or any other time, please call me and I'll be there.'

I was genuinely touched that he cared. 'Thank you. I'm sure it won't come to that, but I really appreciate it and everything you've done today.'

'That's what *new friends* are for,' he said, referencing my earlier comment. 'And I'm happy to be one of yours which means we need to get together again at some point. Maybe we could go on a double date.' He laughed. 'Maybe not. I'd happily do beers with you and Jodie, though, if you'd be up for that.'

'Definitely.' I walked him to the door. 'Oh my God! I haven't paid you! What do I owe you?'

He shook his head. 'Nothing.'

'Matt! You've been here for hours. I can't not pay you.'

He paused for a moment, put his tools down, then nodded. 'Tell you what. You said you were going to be running chocolate-making events when the shop's up and running. How about you let my nieces be your first customers, free of charge?'

'Of course they can, but that's nothing compared to what you've done.'

'I'm not taking your money. You have a new business and you'll need every penny.'

'At least let me pay you for the parts, even if you won't take money for your labour.'

He shook his head. 'Spares I had at the farm.'

'Matt!'

'Okay. Two places on your first chocolate-making event, and a slab of the first bar of chocolate you make. That's my final offer. And if you don't accept it, I'll go back upstairs and dismantle it all.'

'You drive a hard bargain, but okay.' I put my hand out to shake on the deal and, as his skin touched mine, a jolt of electricity fizzed through me. I swear he felt it too because he quickly dropped my hand and muttered something about his nieces and bedtime stories. He bashed into his toolbox and then the door-frame in his haste to leave.

I watched him hurrying down Castle Street and bit my lip. Oh crap! What just happened?

11

After Matt left, I needed a few minutes to compose myself before I returned to the flat otherwise Ricky and I were likely to have a blazing row in front of Jodie. Moving to Whitsborough Bay was her long-held dream and no way did I want her lasting memory of her first day to be blighted by us fighting.

I was vacuuming in the storeroom when Jodie appeared and pressed the 'stop' button. 'You don't need to hide out in here,' she said gently. 'He's gone. I told him he was a twat and he stormed out.'

'I'm sorry you had to see that and even more sorry about leaving you with him.'

'Don't worry about that. I can handle myself. And you're not the one who needs to apologise. That was all Ricky. I know I said earlier that I smelled trouble in paradise but is that how it's been between you since you moved here?' Her brow was furrowed with obvious concern.

I shrugged and sighed. 'That little show upstairs was something new, but it hasn't been great. I told you some of it earlier, but there's more.'

'I think we'd better go back upstairs and crack open another bottle each while you tell me all about it.'

* * *

After telling Jodie everything that had happened, I felt a lot more positive. The thing I'd always loved about her was that she recognised when it was appropriate to dish out advice and when it was best to listen and, today, I'd needed her to listen, empathise and help me find a way forward which was exactly what she'd done.

Feeling ready to face the music, I stood up. 'Best get this over with. Thanks for listening.'

'Any time. If you want to talk again or even stay the night, I'm here for you.'

We hugged goodbye and I headed back to Coral Court, feeling steadily more nervous with each step I took. There'd been no calls or texts from Ricky and I had no idea whether that was a good or bad sign.

When I unlocked the door to number twenty-four shortly after seven, I was met with silence. The lack of footwear in the middle of the hall suggested he wasn't home. A quick look round the flat – still as tidy as I'd left it – confirmed he hadn't been back all day.

I texted Jodie to confirm I was home with no sign of Ricky and I poised my fingers over my phone to text Ricky but what would I say? I didn't want to start an argument by text and there was no way I was going to apologise when I'd done nothing wrong. Hopefully he'd stay over at Smurf's, giving us both a chance to calm down.

Twenty minutes later, I was tucking into a cheese toastie when I heard his key in the lock and my stomach flopped to the floor. Appetite gone, I put the plate on the floor and waited. I heard him crashing around in the bathroom and then the bedroom, opening and slamming closed the wardrobe doors and drawers. I remained silent and rigid on the sofa, wondering if he might be packing his stuff ready to leave me. Right now, the thought wasn't altogether unappealing.

Next minute, the lounge door burst open and he stopped dead when he clocked me. He was wearing a fresh shirt and jeans suggesting he'd come home to change rather than to pack to leave.

'Wasn't expecting to see you here,' he snarled. 'Thought you'd be out with your new man.'

My jaw tightened. 'What new man?'

'The one with the girly hair.'

'He does not have girly hair and why would I be out with him?'

'I don't know. Er, maybe because you were all over him earlier.' He put on a high-pitched voice which was presumably meant to be me. 'Ooh, Matt, thank you for sorting out my emergency plumbing. You're my hero. You can read me a bedtime story anytime.'

'I didn't say any of those things.' Although the bedtime story thing hadn't been far off. Why had I said that? I could understand why that particular comment might have inflamed him but he was being childish about the rest of it.

'You were the same with that bloody Neil Winters. All over each other.' He adopted another silly accent. 'Ooh, stop it Charlee. You're such a naughty girl calling me Mr Winters when you really *must* call me Neil. Giggle, giggle, simper, simper.'

'That's pathetic.'

'Is it now? I'll tell you what's pathetic. It's that every time you're around another man, it's like I cease to exist. You were the same with Badger.'

I stared at him, wide-eyed. 'Your mate Badger?'

'Yes! It's bad enough you flirting with neighbours and strangers but to try it on with one of my mates while I'm right there in the pub... that's just low.'

I could barely believe what I was hearing. 'I spoke to Badger for five minutes, if that. Once. ONCE! He asked me what sort of shop I was planning to open which is more conversation than I've ever managed out of any of your bitchy female friends.'

'Yeah, that's right. Flirt round the lads and insult the lasses. You needn't think I'm asking you to join us again.'

'Good, because I don't want to. And don't you ever manhandle me like that again. I'm not your possession.'

'But you are my girlfriend and you weren't behaving like it.'

I glared at him but I'd run out of steam. How could you reason with someone who was being so unreasonable?

'And another thing...' he cried.

He paced up and down and shouted at me while I sank further into the sofa clinging onto a cushion, as though it was my armour against the verbal punches he kept throwing. He moved on from my alleged flirting to rehash the same old, tired story about money and how I expected him to support me with hours of unpaid labour yet I expected him to go halves on the rent and bills. There were so many lies in his rants that I stopped listening.

The beep of a text arriving on his phone cut him off mid-flow. He looked down at his screen and, whatever he saw, it amused him. The frown disappeared, the hunched shoulders softened and I saw a glimpse of the man I fell in love with. It was reassuring to see he was still in there. It stopped me from spilling out the words that were circling round my mind: *If I annoy you that much, why don't you do us both a favour and leave?*

'I'm going out with Smurf,' he said, his gruff tone back. 'I'll be late.'

He'd slammed the lounge door behind him before I could speak which was probably just as well as I couldn't bring myself to wish him a good evening.

With a sigh, I rolled off the sofa, tipped the remnants of my toasties into the kitchen bin and made a mug of tea. My mind was reeling with where this left us. I was still fuming with Ricky's earlier behaviour and he hadn't endeared himself to me just now either. So much seemed to have been strained since we'd moved to Whitsborough Bay and what I had to try to work out was whether it was the stress of all the changes we were going through or whether it was us who'd changed and that was what was causing the tension.

I picked up my phone and scrolled through the photos I'd taken of Ricky and the two of us together in the early days before Nanna received her prognosis. We'd been so happy then. After Nanna died, he was so thoughtful and caring. When he told me he loved me, I really thought my future was mapped out. Could we find our way back to that? I wasn't sure.

If I hadn't been still awake when Ricky crashed into the flat shortly after half two in the morning, he'd definitely have woken me up. I lay on my side in the darkness listening to him stumbling about and dropping things.

He burst into the bedroom and I gagged at the stench of drink emanating from him as he undressed.

'You awake?' he slurred.

I ignored him.

'I'm sorry, Charlee. Love you.'

I kept my eyes tightly closed, the duvet clutched against my chest as he snuggled up to me, his arm thrust over me, his erection pressing against my back. After that disgraceful display, he seriously expected sex?

Moments later, I relaxed as I heard his piggy snores. I shoved him off me and curled up on the sofa instead with a throw for warmth.

* * *

At 7.00 a.m. I quietly closed the door behind me and walked to the shop, the lack of sleep making me feel lightheaded. I hadn't made any decisions about our future. If I was still seeking business premises and if Jodie hadn't moved to Whitsborough Bay, I might have put my uncertainty down to fear of being alone but I didn't feel that way anymore. I was in a good position to build a new life without Ricky in it. The question was whether I wanted to.

I wondered whether his change in behaviour was the bad influence of his old school friends. I'd seen what they were like: loud and immature. Would he get it out of his system and go back to the Ricky I fell in love with or was this who he really was? I didn't like this version of Ricky and there was no future for us if this version was here to stay.

* * *

When I arrived back at the Coral Court that evening, having ignored a barrage of texts from Ricky across the day, I was surprised to find him in the kitchen and even more shocked that he'd cooked a lasagne. I'm not quite sure how he created so much mess given that the tomato sauce and cheese sauce both came out of a jar, but I pushed that thought aside and gave him credit for making an effort.

'I bought you a peace offering,' he said, handing me a paper bag with a dollop of tomato sauce on it. 'I know I'm not meant to be spending money but you were worth it to show how sorry I am.'

I removed an A5 sketchpad with a cupcake on the front and a pretty rose gold retractable pencil.

'I thought you could use it to draw some more of your chocolate ideas,' he suggested.

It was a lovely gift and thoughtful too but I wasn't going to fling my arms round him and instantly forgive him. I needed words to accompany the gift.

'Thank you,' I said, my voice flat, my eyebrows raised.

'I'm really sorry about yesterday. I don't know what came over me.'

'Neither do I and I didn't like it one little bit.'

He looked momentarily taken aback at my sharp tone and I wondered if he was going to turn it back on me again but, instead, he nodded. 'I probably haven't been the best boyfriend since you moved here. I've spent too much time with the lads and at work and not enough time with you. I should have helped you more at the shop. I forgot how much I struggled to settle when I first moved to Hull so it can't have been easy for you moving here. I love you so much, Charlee. Can we forget about the past month and go back to how things used to be?'

It was everything I'd hoped he'd say but I didn't feel entirely convinced. The words were good, but it sounded more like he was trying to convince himself than me.

I put the pad and pencil back in the paper bag and lay them down on the worktop. 'Thank you for the gift. It's very thoughtful. And thank you for the apology. I'd like to go back to how things were but I don't know whether we can. You've shown me a side of you that I didn't know existed and I really didn't like it.'

'I'm sorry. That's not who I am. I'm just shattered with doing so much overtime. Please don't say it's over.'

I studied his face, noting how lost and vulnerable he looked at that moment and my heart won the argument with my head. 'It's not over but—'

'Thank you.' He rushed towards me as though he was going to hug or kiss me but I stepped back.

'I haven't finished. I have conditions.'

'Okay.'

'It's not over yet but if you ever grab me like you did yesterday, it will be. If you ever accuse me of flirting with another man, it will be. And if you spend every night working or out with the lads and make no quality time for us, it will be. Do I make myself clear?' My voice had a hard edge to it but it was necessary to ensure he was in no doubt as to how precarious our future together was. I don't like to think of it as a threat but I suppose it was.

'That all sounds reasonable. Thank you.'

I nodded. 'The lasagne smells good. Do I have time for a shower before we eat?'

'It'll be ready in twenty minutes.' He must have noticed my eyes flicking round the mess because he added, 'And I'll use that time to clear up.'

* * *

Over the next four evenings, I'd never known Ricky to be so attentive. He still worked late – the financial worries hadn't gone away – but he promised me he'd finish at seven and he did. I made sure I didn't work beyond seven either. It had to work both ways.

I felt bad leaving Jodie on her own each evening but she joked she'd had enough of my company by then and was happy to relax in the flat in front of the TV. She had it looking lovely now that she'd hung pictures on the walls and all those lovely personal details like books and candles that made somewhere feel homely.

Each evening, Ricky and I cooked together then curled up on the sofa after we'd eaten. He showed an interest in my chocolate designs and flavours and even made a few good suggestions of his own.

There was no mention of nights out with the lads but there was also no mention of helping me out at the shop and that was fine. Jodie and I had it under control and now that she was going to be working for me, it felt like it was our project rather than mine and Ricky's.

On Thursday night, I suggested that he might like to go out with Smurf and the lads the following night and I'd go out with Jodie. I'd never wanted to stop him seeing his mates; I just wanted him to find a balance and he'd done that.

But the following week, the overtime slipped to finishing at eight and there was a mid-week night out with the lads. The week after, it was the same and, by the final week in November, we were back to how it had been before the bust-up. I should have made an issue of it but the truth was it worked out well for me. I'd set Saturday 3rd December as opening day and I was way behind so I needed every hour I could grab because it wasn't just getting the shop ready and making the stock; it was getting the shop Christmas-ready.

12

'It's beginning to look a lot like Christmas,' Jodie sang. 'Ta-dah! Charlee's Chocolates now has a beautiful tree.' She stepped back to admire her handiwork. The shop had double-fronted bay windows which meant plenty of space to create two large window displays. We'd decided to put an artificial tree in one and decorate it with a combination of orange, gold, and brown baubles, courtesy of Nanna and her many colour schemes, with wrapped chocolates either dangling from the branches or nestling between them.

I grinned. 'It looks stunning. Thanks, Jodie.'

'Not as stunning as your display, but I'm pleased with it.'

We both looked towards the other window. I'd moulded a giant chocolate Santa and snowman as my centre pieces, standing in front of a wooden fireplace that Matt had helped me build and paint. Empty gift-wrapped boxes were piled up either side of the fire and there were some spilling out of a hessian Santa sack. Samples of the Christmas chocolates I'd created filled the space in front of the chocolate figures, nestled among crumpled pieces of red, gold and green tissue paper.

'You're so talented,' Sarah said, coming down from the stepladder from which she'd been stringing fairy lights across my wooden display units and dressers. 'Some of those designs are so intricate. I don't know how you manage it without snapping the chocolate. Or eating it all.'

I laughed. 'Years of practice and a huge amount of willpower! Speaking of talented, what about you? I've seen some of those giant displays you do for The Ramparts Hotel. That's not flower arranging. That's art!'

Over the past few weeks, Jodie and I had become good friends with Sarah from Seaside Blooms. Despite having her own business to run, she'd been exceptionally generous with her time, regularly stopping off before she went home to help us get ready for opening day. Last Saturday, I had a bit of a meltdown about all the work still needed before tomorrow's grand opening. The following day, she turned up with her entire family and several friends to help. There were people everywhere. You couldn't move without tripping over someone. But there was laughter everywhere too and, despite the frenzied activity, I'd never felt more relaxed.

Sarah had introduced me to several of the other shop owners who'd all given me advice and encouragement, and a helping hand where possible. For the first time since I was a child, I felt part of a community and I absolutely loved it. Those feelings of loneliness had ebbed away and Whitsborough Bay definitely felt like home.

'I can't believe it's opening day tomorrow,' Jodie said. 'How do you feel?'

'Nervous. What if nobody comes?'

'They will.'

'But what if they don't?'

'I remember feeling the exact same way when I took over

Seaside Blooms,' Sarah said. 'I never stopped all day, though. People love new shops and December is a great time of year to open. I reckon you'll barely pause for breath all day.'

'That would be amazing.'

'It'll happen. You have the only chocolate shop in town and I think you're exactly what we need. I bet your chocolate-making events will be fully booked by the end of the day too and you'll be scheduling in new dates.' Sarah paused to answer her phone while Jodie and I continued tweaking the window displays.

'I've got to go,' Sarah said when she hung up. 'I'll pop over at some point tomorrow to see how it's going, but I'll be watching those queues from my window.'

She collected her bag and coat from the back and wrapped her scarf round her neck. Giving us both a hug and wishing us luck, she left.

'She's amazing,' Jodie said when the door had closed. 'I can't believe how helpful she's been in getting things ready.'

'I know. I'm so glad I met her.'

'Shall I tell you who I *don't* think is amazing and who *hasn't* been very helpful?'

She didn't need to. Ricky.

'What's his excuse this time?' she asked.

'It's not his fault. The build's behind schedule and they're all having to put in overtime to catch up. His boss told him that if he wasn't willing to do it, there were plenty of others who'd welcome a well-paid job with regular overtime. What could he do?'

'Do the overtime. Can't say I blame him for that. But he should have spent his spare time fitting out his girlfriend's shop instead of going out on the lash with his mates. That spending time together agreement barely lasted five minutes.'

'I hear you and I hate that I've turned into one of those women who says "but" all the time but I have too much going on right now to deal with another argument or a potential break-up. Let's get opening day done and the first week out the way and then I'll take stock.'

'And then it will be Christmas and who wants to break up with their boyfriend at Christmas?'

'I don't know that I *do* want to break up with him. I know we don't get much time together but the time we do have is better than ever.'

She shook her head. 'I just hope you know what you're doing.'

I turned back to adjust my display. That was the problem. I *didn't* know what I was doing anymore but I didn't have the headspace to work through it. Yes, the time together had been better than ever but only because I never raised my building list of niggles. A bunch of strangers should not have had to come to my rescue. Ricky should have been helping. My boyfriend should have been the one creating the wooden fireplace for me instead of Matt, especially when he was a joiner and could have knocked it up in no time.

Matt had even apologised for not being able to help out as often as he'd have liked and he'd already put in way more hours than Ricky. Matt told Jodie and me that Libby was very insecure and didn't like him having female friends. He wasn't going to let her dictate who he was friends with but he was careful not to push things. Jodie suggested that he lie about where he was because, unless Libby actually came to the shop to check, she'd never know. His response was that he believed in complete honesty in a relationship and, if he was going to be the sort of man who lied to his partner, then he was the sort of man who didn't deserve to have a partner. My stomach did a little backflip when he said that. I, on the other hand, didn't so much lie to Ricky as omit to mention Matt's presence. It was easier that way given the blazing row we'd had the night of the plumbing emergency.

While Jodie took the empty Christmas baubles crates through to the storeroom, I gazed round the room, pride bursting in me. We'd done it and it looked better than I'd ever imagined. On one side of the room was the serving counter with a glass display unit containing individual white, milk and plain chocolates. There were truffles, caramels and fondants in a variety of shapes, textures, flavours and colours. Customers could have a bag or box made up of their favourites and I had pre-prepared collections of the most popular ones.

Along the back and far wall were two dressers and several tall shelving units, each made from sturdy painted grey oak to convey a homely feeling rather than having a posh and unaffordable chocolate shop vibe. It was important for customers to feel comfortable in the shop. Comfortable customers spent more money and they came back!

The cupboards and drawers at the bottom of each piece of furniture provided storage space for boxes and spare stock. The small drawers at eye-height on the dressers had bags of chocolates sticking out of them, begging customers to take them home. Wicker baskets displayed other products, all beautifully arranged.

A tiered plinth on a round wooden table at that side of the shop displayed seasonal products and there was a carousel unit with a cheaper – but still delicious – range of chocolates than those in the glass display unit.

Saloon doors into the workshop allowed customers to see into the area if they were interested in a chocolate-making party but gave a clear signal the area was closed to the public otherwise. We could hook the doors back when we needed easy access like now.

I took several photos on my phone.

'Are those to send to Pierre?' Jodie asked, returning to the shop side.

'Yes. And social media. And for me to gaze at tonight when I can't sleep.'

She took my phone from me. 'Pierre will want to see some of you.'

'My hair's a mess and my cheeks are probably glowing red.'

'The only thing that's glowing is how happy you look right now. I'm so damn proud of you.'

Tears rushed to my eyes and I blinked them back. 'Don't! You'll set me off.'

Jodie took several photos and then we posed for a couple of selfies.

'Is there anything else to do?' she asked.

I checked the list on my phone. 'Sarah's put the lights up, you've done the tree, I've done the other window, the shelves are fully stocked, the fliers are out, the chocolate-making booking forms are printed and just need adding to the clipboard. The free samples are ready and I've got plenty of spares. Business cards! I've got a packet of them somewhere that I need to put under the till. And I think that's it!'

'I'll put the booking forms on the clipboard and you sort the business cards,' Jodie said, disappearing into the workshop.

'Anything else?' she asked when she returned, clipboard in hand.

I scanned down my list again and shook my head. 'All done. Oh my God, Jodie! I've got my very own chocolate shop and we open for business tomorrow. I can't believe it.'

She grinned at me. 'I can imagine your Nanna and Grandpa looking down on you right now and doing a happy jig.'

'I can imagine that too.'

'Charlee's Chocolates is going to be an amazing success. I know it.'

'And I couldn't have done it without you. I hope you know how grateful I am for the phenomenal number of hours and aching muscles you've put into getting it to this point.' Jodie really had been a Godsend. In exchange for helping me get the shop ready, I'd refused to accept any rent from her or money towards bills, although I'd chosen not to mention that to Ricky. She'd tried her hand at making some chocolate drops and, after a few miss-shaped trays, had got the hang of it, but her real strength was in packaging and displaying. She was exceptionally neat and seemed to have an eye for how to present stock in the best possible way, so she was going to be a definite asset.

'Hey, it's me who should be grateful,' Jodie said. 'You've given me a home and a job in the place I've always dreamed of living. Best early Christmas presents ever!' We hugged each other.

'How about a celebratory drink?' I suggested. 'We've more than earned it.'

'Now you're talking. I'll grab our bags.'

A knock on the door made me jump and I spotted Matt and Libby were outside.

'I wasn't sure I'd catch you,' he said when I opened the door and ushered them both in from the cold. 'That window display looks amazing, doesn't it Libby?'

Libby smiled sweetly at me and I got the distinct impression that she was under strict instructions from Matt to be nice. 'It's very impressive. Wish I could arrange a couple of chocolate statues like that.'

Matt frowned. 'Libby! Charlee didn't just arrange them. She made them from scratch.'

'Clever Charlee.' Libby's sing-song tone suggested that she thought I was anything but clever. 'I'll wait outside.' If she could have, I'm convinced she'd have banged the door on her way out but the soft-close mechanism prevented it.

'Sorry, Charlee,' Matt said, watching Libby wander down the street with her phone pressed to her ear. 'One day you'll meet her and I won't have to apologise for her behaviour. She's not normally like this.'

'I seem to remember saying something very similar to you about Ricky.'

'Hi, Matt,' Jodie said, coming back through to the shop with our bags and coats. 'How's it going?'

'Good, thanks. I'm sure you both have loads to do but I wanted to drop something off for Charlee. He lifted up a plain paper carrier bag. 'Libby was meant to get me some wrapping paper today but, perhaps conveniently, she forgot. I suppose it's the gift that's important, and not the packaging.' He handed me the bag. 'This is for you to say good luck on opening day.'

'Aw, thank you. You didn't have to get me anything.'

'What is it?' Jodie asked, stepping forward.

I lifted out a wooden picture frame and, for a moment, I was speechless. Various words were arranged on the image to create a large four-leaf clover. As I looked more closely, I spotted the name of the shop, the street, Whitsborough Bay, my name and Jodie's, and various words connected with chocolate and the process of making it like tempering, moulding, cocoa, truffle, chocolatier.

'Oh, Matt,' I whispered. 'It's amazing.' My eyes darted from word to word, then tears pricked my eyes and I looked up at him again. 'You've got my grandparents' names in there and the name of Grandpa's shop. How did you know?'

He glanced towards Jodie. 'I did a bit of sleuthing.'

'Thank you. Thank you so much. This is so kind and thoughtful. I'd hug you, but I don't want to start a domestic.'

Matt glanced towards the window. 'She's on her phone. She'll be yakking to Gina as usual so I doubt she'll notice. And if she does, so what? We're friends.'

I passed Jodie the picture and hugged Matt tightly. 'Thank you,' I whispered into his ear.

'You deserve it. I'm so proud of what you've achieved.'

As I clung to him, heart racing, I closed my eyes. An image of kissing him filled my mind and, for a moment, I wished it wasn't just in my imagination. Shocked at my unfaithful thoughts, I stepped back.

'Good luck tomorrow,' Matt said. 'My nieces can't wait to meet the chocolate lady, as they call you. I've got a job on during the morning, but I'll be down with them at some point in the afternoon.'

A loud rap on the door signalled Libby's growing impatience.

'I'd better go,' he said. He gave me another brief hug, and gave Jodie one too, then left.

'You lurve him,' Jodie said, in a singsong voice.

I touched my burning cheeks with my fingertips. 'I don't! I just—'

'You just seriously have the hots for him.'

I bit my lip. 'Okay. I admit it. I've got a teeny tiny soft spot for him. Who wouldn't? He's gorgeous and he's so lovely. Do you think he knows?'

She shook her head. 'Your secret's safe. For now.'

Looking out the window, my heart sank as I watched him put his arms round Libby and gently kiss her. He said something that made her laugh then they headed off down Castle Street, arm in arm. They both looked relaxed and happy, like a perfectly-matched couple. I obviously brought out the worst in her but Matt brought out the best and that was why they were together.

'Shame he doesn't feel the same way,' I said, turning back to Jodie, feeling quite deflated.

'Oh, he does. He just isn't prepared to admit it yet.'

'Who turned you into a clairvoyant?'

She laughed. 'It's not clairvoyancy. I'm just great at reading people. Well, everyone except that knobhead Karl, that is. My "gift" obviously doesn't work on my own love life.'

I sighed. 'How can I have a crush on Matt when I love Ricky?'

'Simple,' she said. 'You don't really love Ricky.'

13

'There's a queue!' I squealed the following morning, tying my chocolate brown apron behind my back in the dimly-lit shop. 'There's actually a queue! Do you think we should open early?'

'No!' Jodie cried. 'We should open at nine as planned. It's only seven more minutes. Let the excitement build. There'll be an even bigger queue by then.'

I shook my head. 'I can't believe there's a queue.' Taking a deep breath, I turned to my new sixteen-year-old apprentice, Ashleigh Denholm. 'Are you all set? You know how to use the till?'

She smiled. 'It's the same one as we had at the farm shop so I'm all good.'

Ashleigh had been a brilliant find. A first year student studying catering at Whitsborough Bay TEC, her dream was to become a chocolatier. She already had valuable retail experience and confidence round customers having worked in her uncle's farm shop for the past two years. She'd work Saturdays and after college if I needed her for parties or events. In return, I'd train her in chocolate-making twice a week.

'I need to give you my gift,' Jodie said. 'It's not quite as amazing as Matt's but I think you'll like it.'

'Jodie! There was no need, especially after all the work you've done already.'

She reached behind the counter and handed me a bright pink gift bag.

I pulled out a wooden sign with the phrase, 'She believed she could, so she did,' written on it. It was one of my favourite sayings. 'Thanks, Jodie. I love it.'

'You're welcome. It seemed very apt for what you've achieved in such a short space of time. It's been inspiring watching it all come together.'

'I'll have to put this up in the workshop later with Matt's picture. They'll look great on the wall. I've been so spoilt. When I got home last night, there was a huge bouquet of flowers and a good luck teddy bear waiting from Pierre.'

'Aw. He's so adorable. What did Ricky get you?'

I busied myself putting the sign back in the bag.

'Charlee?' she prompted.

'Ricky gave me a card.'

'Ooh, a card. How very thoughtful and generous of him.'

'He's a bit skint. I was surprised he even got me a card.'

'How's he skint when he does so much overtime?'

It was a good question and one I'd often wondered myself. 'He built up a lot of credit card debt when he was living in Hull so he's working hard to clear it.'

'I'm surprised he hasn't asked you to use your inheritance to clear it.' She shook her head when I didn't respond. 'The cheeky git has, hasn't he?'

'I'm just going to nip to the loo before we open,' Ashleigh said, hurrying out the back, obviously uncomfortable about the turn in the conversation.

'Charlee?' Jodie demanded.

I bit my lip again. 'Sort of. He hasn't directly come out with it but he's dropped a few very unsubtle hints. A couple of weeks ago, I actually said to him, "I'd love to pay off your debts for you but, until I know how well the shop's going to do, I need to hang onto every penny I have". He tried to make out that he'd never have expected me to give him any money, but I could tell he was lying. Am I being mean for not helping him out?'

'No! Don't do it, Charlee.'

'But I could afford to.'

'That's beside the point. If it was the other way round, would you expect him to settle *your* debts?'

'Of course not.'

'There you go, then. *Don't* settle his. It would be different if you'd been together for years or you were married, but it's been less than nine months and we both know you've been having problems. Make sure he does a free balance transfer thingy so his debt doesn't keep rising and, if you're still together this time next year, maybe you could help him out a bit. Except you won't be together because you'll be with Matt.'

I couldn't help smiling at her persistence.

'Should I switch the shop lights on?' Ashleigh asked, returning from the toilet.

I looked at my watch. 'Eek! It's time! Yes, please, Ashleigh.'

Wiping my sweaty palms down my apron, I turned round the sign to 'open' and unlocked the door. I grinned when I saw that the first people in the queue were Sarah, her husband, her two best friends, Clare and Elise, and their partners. She'd said she'd pop over at some point so it was a lovely surprise and very touching to see her right at the front.

Behind her group were half a dozen people I'd never seen before, all smiling at me. How exciting.

'You're my very first customers,' I said to the small crowd. 'Thank you. I'm Charlee. Welcome to Charlee's Chocolates.'

* * *

Sarah had been right about opening day. I hardly paused for breath as we received a steady stream of customers. Some purchased an inexpensive treat, some were browsing, but others spent a small fortune, gushing about how I'd helped them tick several people off their Christmas present lists.

One of the most popular products was small squares of milk and dark chocolate with a white chocolate letter moulded on the top. I had various sized boxes in which the chocolates could be arranged to spell out a name or message. I'd convinced Pierre to stock them back in La Chocolaterie, but Gabby had vetoed the order, like she'd done with so many of my suggestions. I therefore felt very smug to see them flying out the door.

Chocolate drops in bags of different flavours like mint crisp, salted caramel, peanut brittle, and orange fizz sold extremely well, helped by an enticing 3 for 2 offer; yet another product idea that Gabby had refused to consider.

And, of course, my Christmas stocking fillers like moulded snowmen, Santas, reindeer, elves, angels and penguins were really popular. I'd done an opening day discount of 25 per cent off them, which proved very successful.

Sarah popped back over later that morning to see how it was going but we were so busy, we could barely exchange a few words. She left calling, 'I told you so!'

As the morning turned to afternoon, I found myself looking up every time the door opened, eager to see Matt. I was therefore a bit stunned when I looked up at about half two to see Ricky stepping through the door. He paused and looked round, taking it all in, before his eyes rested on me.

'You've done well. This place looks good.'

It was on the tip of my tongue to snap, 'No thanks to you', but I smiled instead and said, 'I had lots of help from some very good friends.'

'Jodie?'

'Among others. What are you doing here? I thought you were working.'

'I was but we weren't needed all day so I thought I'd come down and see how your opening day was going. Been busy?'

'Very,' I nodded towards the queue at the till.

'I'd better let you get on. Get earning that money so that—'

'So that what...?' I interrupted, thinking about the conversation I'd had earlier with Jodie.

He looked surprised at my sharp tone. 'So that we can retire and travel the world, of course.'

'Of course.' But I knew that wasn't what he meant. He definitely wanted some money out of me. Should I just give him it? We loved each other. We were living together. We hadn't talked about marriage, but we'd certainly talked about the future. All the arguments we'd had since we moved to Whitsborough Bay about Ricky working so much overtime, us barely seeing each other, me paying the rent and most of the bills, and him not helping get Charlee's Chocolates ready all led back to one thing: money. Or lack of it on Ricky's part. I could easily resolve that. I could dip into my house fund, settle his debts, insist he cut up his credit cards and eliminate all our problems. So what was stopping me?

* * *

About forty minutes later, I looked up to see Matt with the cutest pair of little girls all wrapped up in bright red puffer jackets, green scarves, and purple bobble hats. My heart raced at the sight of Matt and it struck me that I hadn't reacted that way when Ricky had unexpectedly visited earlier. That wasn't good.

'You came!' I said, walking over to them.

'I always keep my promises.' He bent down and said to his nieces, 'This is Charlee. She's the lovely chocolate lady I was telling you about. Would you like to tell her your name and age?'

'I'm Lucy and I'm seven-and-a-half,' said the taller girl.

'I'm Erin and I'm nearly six,' said her sister. 'Are you going to show us how to make choc-lat.'

The way she said chocolate was adorable, as though it was two words.

'I am. I can't do it today because the shop only opened for the first time ever this morning and we're really busy, but your Uncle Matt said he'll bring you to my first special chocolate-making event next week. I have your names on my list. Would you like to see?'

I produced the already-full list and pointed at their names in the first and second slots. 'Uncle Matt will bring you after school on Thursday and you'll make a chocolate lollipop each. Would you like that?'

The girls giggled as they nodded enthusiastically.

'I've got something for you,' I said to Matt. I dipped behind the counter and produced a large navy gift bag full of chocolate goodies.

'What's this?'

'Payment for my plumbing emergency. It's the first bar of chocolate I produced, as agreed. And the first bag of buttons. And the first of a few other things. Share them with your family. I'll be offended if you don't take them.'

Matt hugged me. 'My mum is going to love you. She's a serious chocoholic. Thank you.'

'Absolute pleasure.' We stood there for a moment, grinning inanely at each other, while my stomach did somersaults.

'I'd better let you get back to your customers,' Matt said, as a customer knocked into him. 'You've created something brilliant here.' He gently touched my arm and held my gaze for a moment as fireworks exploded in my stomach.

'Uncle Matt?'

He looked away and I took a deep breath. Wow! There was no denying I had one massive crush on that man. I had to seriously get over it. Quickly.

'Yes, Lucy?' Matt asked.

'Can I have a chocolate snowman?'

'Tell you what, girls. Let's have a good look round and I'll let you pick something each for yourselves, and something for Mummy and Daddy as a little present. Does that sound like a good idea?'

'Can we get something for Grandma and Granddad and Great Granddad too?' Erin asked. 'Can we get them a Santa?'

'No!' Lucy cried. 'A snowman.'

'But *you* want a snowman. You can't have the same.'

'I can!'

Matt smiled at me and my stomach did a somersault once more. 'We might be some time. I'll see you at the till in a couple of hours.'

* * *

'You need to dump Ricky and tell Matt that he can fiddle with your plumbing any time he wants,' Jodie whispered after I'd waved goodbye to Matt and the girls, giggling like a love-struck teenager.

'Jodie! Stop it!'

'You know you want to,' she said.

'I'll admit that the thought of Matt, erm… fiddling with my plumbing as you say, isn't an unappealing thought, but I love Ricky and I'm not about to ditch him because I've got a silly crush that will soon blow over.'

'Are you trying to convince yourself, or me?' she asked, before turning her attention to a customer. 'Is that everything? Have you seen our 3 for 2 offers on these?'

I watched Jodie as she talked the customer into spending even more money. Who knew she had a gift for sales? If she decided to stick with the shop instead of returning to her role as a teaching assistant or finding a new career, I'd be very lucky.

14

By the time 5.30 p.m. arrived, my feet throbbed and my cheeks ached from smiling. I flipped the door sign round to 'closed' and swiftly turned the lock.

'Quick, Ashleigh, hit the lights. I can't cope with anymore customers today.'

Ashleigh flicked the switches, leaving only the spotlights over the till.

'So, how was your first day, both of you?' I asked.

'Exhausting!' they both chimed.

'I can't believe how quickly it went,' Ashleigh said. 'I really enjoyed it, though. Thanks for the opportunity, Charlee.'

'Absolute pleasure. Thank you for all your hard work and for being so amazing with customers.' I stretched my arms and rolled my head. 'I'll see you next week.'

I let Ashleigh out and Jodie cleared away the sample trays and disposed of the spare chocolates while I ran off the sales report. I did a double take at the total sales and had to check I'd actually done it right, but I had. Wow! I couldn't recall a day at Pierre's anywhere close to that. Granted, it had been opening day, a Saturday, and the start of the Christmas trade, but it was still seriously impressive. I knew it wouldn't continue but if I could even make a quarter of that level of sales on other days, I'd be thrilled.

There was a knock on the door and I looked up to see Sarah and her husband, Nick, waving at me.

'Hi,' I said, opening the door. 'Thank you again for being my first customers this morning.'

'You're welcome,' Sarah said. 'But I need to thank *you*. Oh my God, Charlee! Your chocolates are absolutely divine. That bag of salted caramel drops somehow fell open this afternoon—'

'Yeah, right,' Nick interrupted.

'You think I opened it deliberately? How could you? It was a complete and utter accident. Anyway, it barely lasted ten minutes. Cathy and I were actually salivating. One of my regulars came in and I felt I had to offer her one. You should have seen the three of us sucking on the drops, in absolute raptures. She came straight over and bought some herself.'

'Fortunately I took my bag home,' Nick said. 'And I'm going to have them all to myself tonight.'

Sarah gave him a look that suggested there was no way he was getting away with that. 'Anyway, Charlee, that's not why we came over,' she said. 'With you being new to Whitsborough Bay, it struck me that you probably don't know about the Christmas lights switch-on.'

'Half six by the tree outside the shopping centre? Jodie and I are wandering up in a bit.'

Sarah shook her head. 'That's the official one and that's where most people go, but that triggers all the other lights in town and... no, I don't want to spoil it for you. You've got to see it for yourself. All the traders from Castle Street gather round the tree in Castle Park at the end of the street to watch it. Tara from The Chocolate Pot supplies hot drinks and Carly from Carly's Cupcakes brings cakes. It's a lovely atmosphere. Much cosier than the big switch-on. Nick and I are heading there now to help Tara with the drinks. Do you fancy joining us later?'

'It sounds perfect. Thank you.'

* * *

'Would you mind if I rang Ricky to see if he wants to join us?' I asked Jodie when I'd told her about Sarah's invitation. 'He might be interested in a smaller gathering.'

I'd invited him to the main switch-on but hadn't held out much hope of him saying yes. He can't stand being in a huge crowd, saying it makes him feel claustrophobic. We'd never been to a gig because of it. Sure enough, he'd said no to the big lights switch-on tonight but he might be up for the smaller traders' event instead.

'Go for it,' Jodie said.

His phone rang for ages before it was answered.

'Hello?' I said, when he didn't speak. 'Ricky?' I looked at my screen to check I hadn't called someone else by mistake. 'Hello? Can you hear me?'

I'm sure I heard a woman giggling before the phone went dead. I rang it again but it went straight to voicemail so I left a brief message telling him where we'd be if he wanted to join us.

A text came through as we neared the end of Castle Street:

✉ From Ricky
Got your message. I'm at Smurf & BJ's and we've just ordered pizza so I'll give it a miss. Have fun. See you later xx

That explained the woman giggling. I wouldn't put it past BJ to have done that deliberately when Ricky was out of the room, just to wind me up.

'Looks like you've got my company for dinner, too,' I said to Jodie. 'I've been blown out.'

She linked my arm. 'Here was me thinking he'd have had a lovely celebratory meal planned for you. His loss is my gain. Over dinner, we can hatch a plan for Exit Ricky, Enter Matt.'

'How many times do I have to tell you that I'm happy with Ricky?'

'Until you realise you're lying to yourself,' she said gently. 'Come on, or we'll miss it.'

She tugged me towards the park, her eyes sparkling with excitement. I didn't feel excited anymore, though. Her words kept spinning around my mind. Was I lying to myself? Yes, I'd admit that our relationship was far from perfect at the moment, but was it bad enough to call it a day? A scary thought struck me. Had I turned him into my safety blanket: someone to cling onto as I embarked on a new business venture, in a new town, while still grieving for the loss of my grandparents? No! I loved him. Didn't I?

* * *

Sarah was right. Obviously, I hadn't been to the big Christmas lights switch-on before with being new to Whitsborough Bay, but I couldn't imagine the atmosphere outside the shopping centre being as friendly and cosy as the traders' event. They couldn't have done more to make Jodie and me feel welcome. They were all eager to hear how the first day had gone and several of them said they'd sent friends and family in to support my fledgling business. At Jodie's suggestion, I'd distributed some sample bags to all the traders over the past few days, which had clearly been a good tactic for garnering support.

At 6.30 p.m., a hush descended on the group and all eyes turned towards Castle Street. A cheer in the distance indicated the switch-on of the main tree.

'Look down to the end of Castle Street,' Sarah whispered.

I looked towards the end where our shops were. Earlier in the week, I'd watched the council string lights in a tight zigzag from one side of the street to the other, but I hadn't imagined the effect to be quite so spectacular. Gradually, sections of white lights illuminated, like a Mexican wave rippling along the street. The traders made appreciative 'ooh' and 'aah' noises as each section lit up. When it reached the end of Castle Street, an arch with the words 'Welcome to Castle Street' and a series of stars illuminated followed by a little explosion of firework-effect lights.

As one, the crowd turned and watched as the star on the top of the tree glowed, then lit up white, red, and green lights, one colour at a time. Spontaneous applause broke out followed by a chorus of, 'We Wish You a Merry Christmas.'

'What did you think?' asked Sarah when the singing stopped.

I couldn't speak. Tears welled in my eyes and a lump blocked my throat. It had to be the most beautiful thing I'd ever seen. I loved fairy lights all year round and how magical they made everything feel, but this was something else. Perhaps it was all the more emotional because of how welcome and part of the community I felt, and how much my grandparents would have loved it.

Sarah squeezed my hand. 'I know. Pretty special, eh?'

She turned to Nick who hugged and kissed her. What a romantic moment to be caught in a kiss, and what a stunning setting for it too, with the tree behind them and the inky sea beyond that in South Bay below. Lucky Sarah. If only Matt was here... Oh, my God! What had I just thought? Ricky! If only Ricky was here!

'You look like someone who needs a drink,' Jodie said, obviously clocking my stricken expression.

'Yes. A very large one!'

15

Over the next couple of weeks, life settled into a routine. Three mornings a week, I arrived at Charlee's Chocolates an hour before opening to temper chocolate and make different ranges of products, alternating between drops, lettered squares, moulded figures and luxury chocolates. On a Wednesday and Thursday, I trained Ashleigh in a variety of products and techniques and was thrilled to see that she was a quick learner with a natural aptitude for the craft.

My favourite part of the day was about 4.00 p.m. when dusk settled and the Christmas lights came on. Standing under Castle Street's white lights was like standing under a blanket of stars. If I wasn't serving anyone, I'd nip out of the shop for a moment and drink in the atmosphere, saying a silent thank you to my wonderful grandparents who'd given me the means to open my business in this beautiful place.

At home, things had thankfully picked up again. It turned out that Ricky was like an excitable little kid when it came to Christmas. He was desperate to put a tree up at the end of the first week in December. He picked out a real tree that was way too big for the flat – paid for by me, of course – but we'd had such a lovely time decorating it while sharing a bottle of red, that I couldn't be mad with him for his over-the-top choice and the dent in my bank balance.

From Nanna's crates of decorations, I'd chosen the red, cream, and gold colour scheme. Even though Ricky took the mickey out of me, demanding to know what was Christmassy about a gingham elephant, he did admit that the finished effect looked pretty spectacular.

As we made love on the sofa again with red and white fairy lights softly illuminating the room, I felt truly content. The only worrying thing was how much my heart had raced the whole time that Matt had been at my first chocolate-making event with his nieces. I told myself it was nerves at my first workshop for my new business but chocolate-making didn't make me nervous. Matt's presence did. It didn't mean anything, though. As I'd repeatedly told Jodie, it was a silly crush and I would get over it soon. It was Ricky who I loved – not Matt – and our relationship was finally back on track.

On Tuesday evening, five days before Christmas, I joined Jodie in her flat after work so I could wrap Ricky's Christmas gifts. He'd admitted that he and his brother had been terrible for searching for gifts when they were little and, as their parents weren't very good at hiding them, they usually knew everything they were getting a couple of weeks before Christmas Day. With nowhere to hide anything in the flat and with online deliveries directed to the shop anyway, I'd kept everything in Jodie's spare bedroom.

'What's he getting you?' Jodie looked up from writing her Christmas cards at the opposite side of the dining table and nodded towards the growing pile of gifts that I'd painstakingly spent the last couple of hours wrapping.

'I'm not sure. I'm hoping for a pair of Ugg boots.'

'Ugg boots? From Ricky? I thought he was skint.'

'He is, but I said I've always wanted a pair and that they'd be perfect for work for the colder weather. He said, "We'll have to see what Santa brings," with a twinkle in his eyes, so I think I'm going to be in luck.'

Jodie raised an eyebrow.

'Don't look at me like that. He's not completely unreliable, you know.'

'Given the small fortune you've spent on him, I hope he doesn't disappoint you with a biro and a box of cheap chocolates.'

'He's never bought me chocolates and the last gift was thoughtful.'

'The sketchpad and pencil?' she asked. 'Yeah, they were lovely... until you spotted them in the pound shop last week.'

My shoulders sagged. That had been an unexpected discovery, made even worse by the pencil being sold in a pack of four. Presumably he'd decided the packaging looked cheap – which it did – and one pencil on its own created the illusion of more expense. I hadn't mentioned it to Ricky. It seemed churlish to bring it up after several weeks had passed and while things were going so well. The value of the gift hadn't bothered me at all. The lies about me being worth the expense had. I'd struggled to sleep that night wondering if that had been some sort of message that my value to him was £1.25 and what that said about our relationship.

'It's not the money he spends, it's the thought that counts.' Even as I said the words, I wasn't convinced. I genuinely didn't want him to spend a fortune on me but he was living practically rent-free with very few expenses and masses of overtime. It wasn't unreasonable to anticipate a little treat.

'Yes, it is,' Jodie agreed, 'but one biro from a multipack and a box of chocolates doesn't exactly scream, "I saw this and thought of you", does it?'

She was right about that but, cost aside, the sketchpad and pencil had been thoughtful gifts. I didn't need to worry about Christmas. He was *definitely* going to get me some Ugg boots. They weren't cheap so I didn't anticipate anything else, but that was fine as the boots were all I wanted.

I continued wrapping his gifts. Okay, so I had gone a bit overboard, but I'd felt a bit lost when it came to Christmas shopping, realising that I no longer had a family to buy for. I'd missed shopping for a new cardigan for Nanna; one of our many Christmas traditions. I'd missed buying her a new pair of slippers, a bottle of Opium Eau de Toilette, a selection of romance novels, and some Yardley Lily of the Valley bubble bath, which she adored. My first Christmas without her. My first Christmas in Whitsborough Bay. My first Christmas with Ricky. It was certainly going to be different.

'God, I'm so bored!' Jodie flung her pen down. 'I hate writing Christmas cards.'

'Then take a break.'

'But I'll only have to do them another time.'

'Then don't take a break.'

'But I've got writer's cramp.'

'THEN TAKE A BREAK!'

Jodie laughed. 'I'll check my emails,' she said, picking up her tablet.

'Oh my God!' she said ten minutes later. 'Stop what you're doing right now. You have *got* to see this! Let me stop it and go back to the start.'

'What is it? Cats opening doors? Parkour fails?' Jodie had an obsession with watching clips like that.

'No. My old colleague Vix sent me it. It's CCTV of a couple in Dice Pizza in Whitsborough Bay. They're... no, I don't want to spoil it for you. I'm shocked, though.'

Intrigued, I pushed aside the box I'd just wrapped. 'Let's see, then.'

She crouched beside me with her iPad. 'Apparently the staff in the takeaway suspected that a drunk couple were getting a bit amorous a few weeks ago and, when they checked CCTV, this is what they found.'

Slightly grainy footage filled the screen, showing a male and female staggering into the pizza shop. I recognised the interior from ordering takeout there a couple of times. They paused at the counter. While the woman must have been giving their order to the server, the man ground into her from behind, and fondled her breasts right in front of the server.

'Ew! Get a room! That's gross.'

'That's nothing compared to what happens next,' Jodie said.

Order presumably placed, they moved into the far corner of the waiting area, out of sight of the serving staff and started kissing passionately, hands all over each other. I squirmed, feeling very uncomfortable watching it. The couple changed position.

'What's she doing on her knees?' I said, realising exactly what she was doing as soon as the words left my mouth. 'No! She never is!'

'She is,' Jodie said. 'Classy or what? Pizza and a blow job. And look! She doesn't even stop when someone else comes in.' Sure enough, a woman walked up to the counter, was handed a few pizzas and left, either oblivious to or deliberately ignoring the floorshow.

The clip must have been edited because it flickered, then the couple were back at the counter. The woman was at the front again. Whatever she was saying to the server had him going back and forth a few times with different boxes which meant they were at the counter for a while. And the whole time they were there, her skirt was hitched up and her companion was thrusting into her from behind.

'Her turn now,' Jodie said, giggling.

'I can't believe they're doing that,' I cried. 'It must be against hygiene standards.'

We both giggled. 'I hope they don't fancy any chocolate,' Jodie said. 'Could you imagine that happening downstairs?'

A few more urgent thrusts and the mystery man was obviously spent. He stepped back and zipped up his flies. Jodie and I both squealed as the woman put one of her hands between her legs, then wiped it down her skirt, before wriggling her skirt back into position. She took the pizza from the server and turned round, flicking her long blonde hair out of her face. At that moment, the camera had a really clear view of her face and I gasped.

'Shit! That's BJ!'

'No! The dirty cow. Looks like I was right about what BJ stands for. Is that Smurf, then?'

I shook my head, my eyes glued to the screen. 'No. Smurf's huge. That's not him.' Her companion was wearing a baseball cap so I couldn't see his face. 'I don't know who that...'

But as he passed the camera, he removed his cap and my stomach dropped down a six foot well. 'Yes I do. That's Ricky.'

16

'Oh, God, Charlee! I'm so sorry!' Jodie slapped the tablet cover closed. 'I hadn't watched it till the end. If I'd seen it was him...'

She looked as though she might burst into tears at any point whereas I felt surprisingly calm. I'd never have had Ricky pegged as a cheater but now I wondered why I hadn't considered it. All that overtime but no money? It seemed so blindingly obvious now.

I patted Jodie on the shoulder. 'It's not your fault. You weren't to know it was him.' I grabbed the gift I'd just wrapped and ripped the paper off it. 'Looks like I'll be returning all of these. Lucky I found out before Christmas.'

Jodie straightened up. 'Can I?'

'Be my guest.'

For the next ten minutes, we furiously ripped the paper off all the gifts, dropped it onto the floor and stamped on it, adding a few select adjectives to describe Ricky and BJ.

When we were finished, Jodie cracked open a couple of bottles of lager and handed me one. 'What happens now?'

'I'm not sure.'

'You're not thinking of staying with him?'

I smiled at her shocked expression. 'No chance. I just mean I'm not sure how best to end it. I can't face him tonight.'

'Then stay here. I can lend you something to sleep in and a fresh T-shirt for the morning.'

'You're on. Let me text him.'

✉ To Ricky
Lots of planning to do so staying above the shop tonight xx

I was loathe to add the kisses but I always signed off texts that way and I didn't want to do anything to arouse his suspicions. I could have hurled my phone at the wall in disgust at his response:

✉ From Ricky
I'm out with Smurf and BJ. Will probably stay at theirs. See you later xx

'How long do you reckon it's been going on?' Jodie asked after I read his text out to her.

'I dread to think. He's been putting in alleged overtime since I moved here so my guess is the moment he moved back and was staying with Smurf.' My heart sank for Smurf, presumably just as much in the dark as I'd been. 'He's stayed over there so often. Do you think he could have been having sex with BJ while Smurf was asleep in the next room?'

'Having seen that video, I think Ricky's capable of anything.'

'How could he do that to his best mate? He's always banged on about how much Smurf meant to him. Said he was more like a brother to him than his real brother.'

'I'll never understand how anyone can treat another person with such a lack of respect,' Jodie said, and I knew from the distant look in her eyes that she was thinking about Karl. She shrugged and took another swig of her drink. 'So what's the plan? Revenge?'

Over a couple more drinks, we discussed all sorts of crazy revenge strategies but concluded they weren't my style. I was going for the dignified approach: changing the locks, dumping his stuff at his mum's, and sending him the footage of his evening of fun. I texted Matt:

✉ To Matt
I don't suppose you, your dad or your brother can include a locksmith among the huge range of talents you have?

My phone rang seconds later.

'Has he hurt you?' Matt asked, his voice full of concern. I knew he was thinking about the incident after the flooding.

'Yes, but not in the way you think. He's been seeing someone else but he doesn't know I know so I want to change the locks before I tell him.'

He sighed. 'I'm so sorry, Charlee. Are you okay?'

'I will be when I'm shot of him.'

We arranged to meet at Coral Court at 7.30 a.m. so Matt could check the type of lock and pick up a new one from the builder's merchant. Hopefully that would give enough time for him to fit it and for me to drop Ricky's stuff at his mum's before the shop got busy. Ashleigh was now on her Christmas break from college so was working full-time for the next four days so at least Jodie wouldn't be on her own if things took a little longer than hoped.

Feeling drained, I headed to bed shortly after nine, assuring

Jodie that I wasn't going to spend the night sobbing into my pillow.

As it happens, I didn't cry at all that night. I didn't sleep either. Every time I closed my eyes, all I could see was Ricky and BJ together in Dice Pizza. I thought about the couple of times that I'd been out with the group and remembered that they'd gone to the toilets at the same time. I'd thought nothing of it until now.

What about that time when I'd phoned Ricky to invite him to the Castle Street lights switch-on? A woman had answered his phone, giggling. He'd said Smurf was there but had that been a lie? Had he been alone with BJ and I'd phoned them mid-shag?

What about that time before I'd found the premises, when he'd arrived home for lunch later than expected, jumped straight in the shower, and initially resisted my advances? Had he seen her after work and was that why he was late? Had he jumped in the shower knowing he reeked of her knock-off perfume? We'd made love on the sofa after that and it had been incredible, but had he been with us both that same day? Ew! Images of them together in pub toilets, at Smurf's flat, and even in our flat wouldn't leave me.

My mind whirred with doubts about what else Ricky had lied to me about. Jodie had asked, 'How's he skint when he does so much overtime?' What if doing overtime had been a lie? What if it had been an excuse to be with her? All those times when he'd avoided helping in the shop, had he been with her too?

I thought about my plumbing emergency and how I hadn't been able to get hold of Ricky that day. When I phoned Smurf, he'd seemed surprised when I asked if he'd seen Ricky. Had he known what was going on? No! BJ was his girlfriend. He'd have thrown her out if he'd thought that something was going on between them. Maybe he'd thought that Ricky could be playing away with someone else, though. Poor Smurf. He was going to get a hell of a shock. Should I tell him? He had a right to know, but did I have the right to break that news?

17

I gave up trying to sleep a little after five. Both bedrooms were front-facing and I padded over to the window in my bare feet, the duvet wrapped round me for warmth as the central heating hadn't yet clicked on.

Opening one of the curtains and peering out into the darkness, I smiled to myself. Castle Street looked like a scene from a fairy tale. A heavy frost had settled overnight coating the cobbles in tiny crystals which sparkled in the gentle golden light from the Victorian lampposts. I gazed up and down the street, mesmerised. I could almost hear and feel the delicious crunch of frost underfoot and how romantic it would be to... I yanked the curtain back into place and stepped away from the window shaking my head. No romance. No Ricky. The anxious knot returned to my stomach. Today was going to be difficult.

I checked my phone but there were no further messages from him, not that I'd expected there to be. The anger had eased a little now that the shock had worn off but it wasn't replaced by tears. My overriding emotion at the moment – aside from nerves – was humiliation. I felt so naïve for not considering, even for a split second, that he might be seeing someone else. He'd played a blinder with the whole 'being back with the lads' thing that I'd never suspected his nights out were anything other than that. As for working late. Oldest trick in the book and I'd fallen for it hook, line and sinker.

In the kitchen area, I filled the kettle as quietly as I could but Jodie shuffled out of her bedroom, rubbing her eyes.

'I'm so sorry. I tried not to wake you.'

'I've been awake for a while anyway. If you give me ten minutes to get sorted, we can drive over to yours and I can help you pack up his crap.'

'That would be amazing, thank you. I just want it to be over.'

It didn't take long to pack up Ricky's stuff because he didn't have much. His clothes filled one suitcase and two binbags and there were several well-used cardboard storage boxes stacked up in one corner of the lounge containing a mishmash of belongings.

'I'll be glad to see the back of "the cardboard tower",' I said to Jodie after we'd piled the last of the boxes up in the hall and settled down with a coffee while waiting for Matt.

'Why didn't he unpack the boxes?' she asked.

'No idea. He kept promising he would. I can't help wondering now whether he saw no point unpacking properly because he was only staying with me as a temporary thing until he ran off with BJ.'

'Or until you agreed to settle his debts.'

I gasped. 'You don't think...? He wouldn't! That's so...' I couldn't find the words but Jodie could.

'Cold? Calculated? Devious? Manipulative?'

I stared into my coffee as I played the words over in my mind.

Yes, all of the above! How had I not realised? His disappointment when I didn't want to buy somewhere. The arguments about overtime and lack of money. His objection to contributing towards the bills because he was so skint. Sometimes he'd tugged on my heart strings and other times he'd frustrated me but both tactics had nearly worked. When I'd started thinking about Christmas gifts for Ricky, I'd wondered about paying off his credit card bills. I'd even started designing a certificate on my laptop that I'd give him as his gift, then changed my mind. It was far too generous.

I looked up at Jodie and nodded. 'Lucky escape eh?'

'Doesn't make it hurt any less.'

The buzzer sounded and my heart leapt. Matt to the rescue! He seemed to be making a habit of that.

I opened the door and was immediately enveloped in a hug. I rested my head against his chest, my heart thumping. When he stepped back, I felt disappointed. I could have stayed like that for hours feeling warm and comforted but he had a fiancée. I knew the hug was one of friendship and nothing else as both Jodie and I had received several hugs from him since we'd met him. He was a hugger. That's all there was to it.

'How are you feeling this morning?' he asked.

'Nervous. Ask me again when the deed is done.'

'Let's get my part done then.' He bent down and checked the lock. 'Should be a straightforward swap. I'll be back in about twenty minutes.'

And then he was gone and my heart was still thumping.

'I know the last thing on your mind right now is another man,' Jodie said, leaning against the lounge doorframe with her hands wrapped round her drink. 'But I think you two would be perfect together.'

'He's engaged. It's never going to happen.' Tears unexpectedly rushed to my eyes as I said it and I blinked them back, conflicted. How was it that I hadn't yet cried about it being over with Ricky but the thought of it never happening with Matt made me tearful?

'But you'd like it to if he wasn't seeing Libby?' Jodie suggested.

'It doesn't matter whether I would or wouldn't. He *is* seeing Libby and I would never make a play for someone who's attached, especially after being on the receiving end of how that feels.'

18

'It's him,' I whispered to Jodie as Ricky's name flashed up on my phone later that morning. My heart was racing and my stomach was in knots.

We both glanced over to where Ashleigh was filling a box with luxury chocolates for a customer. I'd decided it was unprofessional and unnecessary to involve her in my personal situation so I'd simply told her I was expecting an important call at some point that morning and would dip outside when it came through.

'You know what to do,' she whispered back.

I turned down Ricky's call request, removed my apron and grabbed my coat from the workshop.

'Wish me luck,' I said, as I pushed open the external door.

Jodie crossed her fingers on both hands and held them up. 'Luck. Be strong.'

The earlier frost had melted away but it was still chilly and my breath hung in the air as I headed down the cobbles towards Castle Park, texting Ricky as I walked:

✉ To Ricky

```
WhatsApp me

⊠ From Ricky
WTF! Why?

⊠ To Ricky
Just do it!
```

Moments later, I perched on the edge of a damp wooden bench overlooking the sea and connected to WhatsApp. Even though I didn't want to see him in person ever again, I wanted the satisfaction of seeing his face when I told him where to go.

'Ricky,' I said in a flat voice as I flashed him a sarcastic smile. 'I wondered when I'd hear from you.'

His face was red and I could feel the fury emanating from the scrunch of his forehead and eyes. 'Why've you dumped all my stuff at my mum's? What the hell's going on?'

'I could ask you the same question.'

'What?'

'You heard me. What the hell's going on, Ricky?' I have no idea how I managed to sound so cool and collected when I felt anything but that.

'I don't have time to play games. I'm at work. Seriously, Charlee, why's my stuff at my mum's?'

'Why do you think?'

'I haven't a bloody clue.'

'Really? Have you had any good takeaways lately?'

There was a pause and a flicker of something across his face. Guilt?

'What's that got to do with anything?' Ricky's tone had gone from angry to hesitant. I could imagine his mind racing. He'd know what I was alluding to, but he wouldn't be able to work out how I knew.

'It's got everything to do with it. One of your recent visits to a takeaway is the reason why your stuff's at your mum's and why I've had the lock at Coral Court changed.'

'You're not making any sense.' But his face and the lack of conviction in his voice told me I was making perfect sense.

'Seeing as it's so close to Christmas, there's a little gift in one of your bags,' I added, smiling sweetly at him. Inspired by Jodie's tale of what she'd written in cream across Karl's chest, I'd put together one of my boxes of chocolate squares spelling out the word 'WANKER'. And I'd used dark chocolate which Ricky detested so he couldn't even eat it.

I'd specifically chosen WhatsApp so I could stay connected and see his reaction to the video but I couldn't bear to look at him for a moment longer. The *I've no idea what you're talking about* routine was a disgrace and it made me wonder if anything he'd ever said to me had been the truth.

'Goodbye, Ricky. Happy Christmas!' I disconnected.

He called back immediately, but I ignored it and switched the phone to silent then typed in:

You wanted to know why. This is why. I don't think I need to clarify further, do I? GOODBYE

I added the Dice Pizza clip.

* * *

Charlee's Chocolates was busy when I returned. As soon as it cleared, I asked Ashleigh to make us all a drink and quickly filled Jodie in on the conversation while she was gone.

'I'm so sorry,' she said, giving me a hug.

'Please stop apologising. It wasn't your fault. This was all Ricky. Well, Ricky and that dirty little slapper, BJ.'

'Yeah, but I showed you the video.'

'Which you hadn't watched through to the end so you had no idea it was Ricky.'

'I can't believe how calm you're being about it all.'

I shrugged. 'I think I'm still in shock. It'll probably catch up with me later.'

'Do you want to stay with me again tonight?'

'Thanks, but I'll be fine. I could do with a long, hot bath and an early night.'

'The offer's there if you change your mind,' she said, her eyes full of sympathy.

* * *

We were busy for the rest of the day, which was exactly what I needed to take my mind off Ricky. I'd texted Smurf to say that I needed to talk to him about something to do with Ricky and could he meet me at Coral Court at six. I'd gone back and forth on whether I should be the one to tell Smurf or not but he had the right to know and I wasn't convinced Ricky would be honest with him. Videos like that had a tendency to go viral and I wouldn't want him to be blindsided like I'd been. I owed it to Smurf to warn him.

I felt sick as I buzzed Smurf into the building that evening. My legs were actually shaking as I answered the flat door and led him into the lounge. Between customers, Jodie and I had role-played how to approach the conversation, but the big unknown was how Smurf would react. What if he was livid and he had a go at me?

'Are you okay?' he asked once he'd sat down beside me on the sofa. 'Your text was a bit cryptic and you don't look so good.'

I took a deep breath. Here goes... 'I've ended it with Ricky.'

'I know. He's at ours now. Said you'd kicked him out although he wouldn't say why.'

'He's been seeing someone behind my back.'

'No! The little fu...' Smurf shook his head. 'I'm sorry, Charlee. He swore to me that he wasn't doing the dirty on you.'

My eyes widened. 'You suspected?'

'Remember when you had a leak at the shop and you phoned me? I felt awful. Ricky wasn't at work that day. If he had been, he'd have been working with me. I confronted him about it and he swore that he wasn't messing you about. He reckoned you'd misheard him about the overtime.'

'I didn't. Did Ricky *ever* work overtime on weekends?'

Smurf grimaced. 'Once or twice. He was offered it, but he couldn't do it cos he was helping you get the shop set up.'

Another lie. 'He barely lifted a finger to help me.'

'Seriously?' Smurf ran his hand through his hair. 'He does work with you now on a Saturday morning? No? So that's when he's been seeing her. What a tosser! Do you know who she is?'

My cheeks burned. Awkward. 'I'm really sorry, Smurf, but he's been see—'

'It's BJ, isn't it?' he interrupted, his shocked tone suggesting he'd just had a lightbulb moment.

I nodded slowly.

'Shit!' He hung his head.

'I'm really sorry. I hate being the one to tell you, but I didn't want you to see it online like I did.'

Smurf's head snapped up. 'Online?'

'There's a video...'

Smurf listened, mouth open, while I told him about the

footage, shuddering as I pictured it. He insisted on watching it. I tried to talk him out of it, but he said that he had to see for himself otherwise he'd manage to convince himself it wasn't them. Closing his eyes at the end, he took a deep breath, opened them again, then handed me back my phone.

'Can you forward that to me?'

'I'll do it now.' I sent it over and listened for the beep as he received it.

'Did Ricky tell you that BJ used to be his girlfriend?'

My stomach sank. 'He somehow omitted that little detail.'

Smurf nodded. 'They were together for about three years, on and off, when we were in our early twenties. They argued constantly so none of us were surprised when they called it a day. Ricky always said that me and BJ were better suited. He was actually the one who pushed us together.' He ran his hand across his stubble and shook his head. 'Six years down the toilet. I was going to ask her to marry me at Christmas.'

'No! Oh, Smurf, I'm sorry. Did I do the right thing telling you?'

'Definitely. Cheers for doing it face to face, too. That took guts and it was decent of you.'

'As I said, I didn't want you to stumble across the video and discover the truth that way. What will you do?'

'Kick her out and hope that Castle Jewellery will give me a refund on the engagement ring. What about you?'

'I've changed the locks and dumped his stuff at his mum's. He phoned me up demanding to know why so I sent him the video.'

Smurf sank back into the cushions, pale-faced and looking defeated. 'So he knows that you know about him and BJ, yet he's brazening it out at my place, the cheeky git. I'd better get back and confront them. Jesus! I can't believe they're together right now, probably...' He shook his head. 'I can't bear to think about it.'

'Do they know you're here?'

'No. I told BJ I was working late, which I often do so she didn't question it. She's done this before, you know, although not quite so publicly. I stupidly forgave her, but not this time.'

'Was that with Ricky?' I asked, bracing myself against the answer.

'No. Some bloke she knew from work. Big mistake, they were drunk, it meant nothing, she really loves me, blah, blah, blah. Now I'm thinking there were probably others and I've just been the stupid adoring boyfriend, paying all the rent and the bills, while she shagged her way round Whitsborough Bay, laughing at me for being such a pushover.'

'I know how that feels,' I muttered. 'What he contributed would barely keep us in teabags and loo roll.'

'You haven't settled Ricky's debts, have you?'

I shook my head. 'He kept dropping hints, but something stopped me.'

'Good. I told him he was bang out of order when he said he reckoned he could get you to pay them off.'

My stomach lurched. I'd hoped I'd been wrong about that but apparently not. 'Was that all I was to him? A bank balance?'

Smurf shrugged. 'I honestly don't know, Charlee. He didn't... no, it doesn't matter.'

'You've started, so you're going to have to finish. Anything you say can't be worse than what's in that video.'

Smurf grimaced. 'Okay. This is going to hurt, but you might as well know what he's like. He didn't talk about you much but, when he did, it was usually negative. He said you expected him to do loads of work in the shop but you never paid him for it, that you nagged him for going out with the lads, and that you were really high maintenance, constantly whining about moving to Whitsborough Bay away from your friends and family.'

My fists clenched. How could he? 'He's a lying little git. I have no family, my best friend lives in the flat above the shop, I love living here, I encourage him to go out with the lads, and he's done about three hours in the shop, very begrudgingly. And he was offered payment for that.'

Silence settled on us. Eventually Smurf stood up. 'I'd better go home and kick them out. Will you be okay?'

'I need to lick my wounds for a bit but I'll get there eventually.'

'He was never good enough for you,' Smurf said. 'You'll be better off without him.'

I walked him to the door. 'Can I ask you a question? I've got my own theory but I'd like your take on it. How long do you think it's being going on?'

'The truth?'

I nodded.

'I swear I hadn't a clue, but now that I'm piecing it together, I reckon it was from the minute he moved back up here.'

'While I was still in Hull?'

'Yeah.'

'That's what I thought. So why was he so keen to get me to move up here?' Smurf looked down at his feet and I realised I'd just asked a really stupid question. 'It was for my money, wasn't it?'

'Sorry, Charlee.'

'Wow! I am *such* an idiot,' I muttered, furious with myself for being used like that.

'You and me both.'

I opened the door. 'Good luck with the confrontation and whatever you do afterwards.'

'Thanks. Same to you. I'd say happy Christmas, but under the circumstances...' Smurf gave me a quick hug. 'Look after yourself and give me a shout if you ever need anything. You're a good lass, Charlee, and Ricky's a twat. Don't get upset about him cos he's not worth it. Neither of them are. Learn from it and move on. I'm going to.' He smiled ruefully and his eyes glazed with tears. 'Well, I'm certainly going to try to.'

The moment I closed the door, the tears started. I'd been fine until Smurf's last few words, but the hurt in his eyes and the wobble in his voice tipped me over the edge.

Curling up on the sofa, clinging onto a fluffy cushion, hot tears streamed down my cheeks and dribbled down my neck. Yes, we'd had some rough moments when I first set up the shop, but the past month or so had been really good. Our combined excitement about Christmas had made the world seem magical. We'd driven through to York one evening and had giggled as we'd clung onto each other, trying to keep our balance as we ice-skated at the Winter Wonderland. We'd cooked a romantic meal together and had slow-danced in the lounge in front of the Christmas tree. I thought that Ricky and I were building the sort of relationship my grandparents had enjoyed. I'd loved and trusted Ricky and I'd genuinely believed that he loved me too. Turns out that the only thing he'd loved about me was my inheritance.

Last night, I'd wondered whether all that attention and intimacy had been as a result of his guilt, or perhaps to keep me off the scent but now it hit me what it had really been: Ricky's final attempt to butter me up to pay off his debts, before he left me for BJ. As soon as that thought popped into my head, it wouldn't go. He'd used me good and proper, hadn't he?

19

Matt rang about thirty minutes after Smurf left to check how things had gone with Ricky and to make sure he hadn't tried to get into the flat.

'I don't think I'll hear from him again,' I said. I hadn't heard a peep out of Ricky since I sent the video. I don't think he'd have dared to offer any excuses although he could have had the decency to say sorry. He probably wasn't, though. His only regret would be that he was still saddled with debt up to the eyeballs although it probably amused him that he'd managed to live rent-free for a few months.

'Good. But if he does turn up, even if it's the early hours, call me.'

'Thanks, Matt. You've been so helpful.'

A couple of hours later, Smurf rang. 'I just wanted to thank you again for being honest with me earlier,' he said.

'How did it go?'

'It was grim. I parked round the corner from our house and watched that video again, hoping there'd been a mistake and it was really another couple who looked like them because no way would they do that to me. I sent BJ a text saying I'd be back in half an hour, waited in the car for another five minutes then slipped into the house.'

The crack in Smurf's voice told me what he'd found. 'You found them together?' I prompted.

'It was painful but I needed to see it with my own eyes.' He sighed. 'I ordered them to get dressed, hand over their keys and get out. She started crying and I thought for the briefest moment that she was upset it was over. Then do you know what she said? "Where am I supposed to live now?" As if that was *my* problem.'

'I'm sorry.'

'Then she had a hissy fit about wanting time to gather her clothes and make-up together but I wanted her out. Shoved her crap into binbags and left it in the yard. They've just collected it. She saw me watching from the bedroom window. You'd think I'd seen enough but she rammed her tongue down Ricky's throat while giving me the finger.'

My heart broke for Smurf as his voice cracked again. I'd known Ricky for less than a year but he'd just lost his partner of six years and his childhood best friend. It would impact on all his other friendships. Would the lads take sides? If so, I hoped they'd support Smurf and ostracise Ricky.

'You said earlier that Ricky wasn't good enough for me. BJ wasn't good enough for you either.'

'You know what's weird? Right now, I'm more gutted about Ricky than her. I thought I knew him well.'

'Me too. Seems we were both duped.'

'One more thing,' Smurf added. 'I got BJ to admit how long it had been going on and she clearly took great delight in telling me. Do you want to know?'

I drew in a deep breath knowing that, from the hard edge to his tone, I wasn't going to like the answer. 'Hit me with it.'

There was a pause. 'It never ended.'

My stomach lurched. 'What do you mean?'

'I mean that before he moved to Hull, they'd still get together every so often. When he moved to Hull, they'd meet up halfway for... I don't need to spell it out to you. I'm sorry, Charlee. They've been lying to us both the whole time.'

* * *

Jodie's great grandma had arranged for her large family – seventy-nine of them – to go on a Christmas cruise together, departing on Thursday evening. She'd offered to drop out to spend Christmas with me but I wouldn't hear of it. Her great grandma had been planning it for years and, until things ended with Ricky, Jodie had been really excited about being part of such a huge family gathering. I did, however, feel very tearful as I hugged her goodbye on Thursday morning and gulped back the lump in my throat as I reassured her I'd be absolutely fine and it was only one day. I was dreading it but no way was I going to pull a guilt-trip on my best friend.

Even before I'd found out about Ricky and BJ, I'd had mixed emotions about Christmas. On the one hand, I was excited about the shop and my first Christmas with Ricky, but there were occasions when I felt like I was caught in a riptide, dragging me into a cold and lonely place. Christmas without Nanna and Grandpa filled me with dread. I ached for my tiny family. Neither of my grandparents had siblings so it had always been just the three of us, then the two of us. And now it was only me.

Every time I'd felt like I was drowning, though, Charlee's Chocolates seemed to throw me a lifeline. The shop was always full of fun and laughter and we already had several regular customers who felt like friends. Jodie had been amazing, as always, understanding my whirr of emotions when I'd drift into a moment of melancholy about Christmases past.

Ricky had also been a lifeline. When we'd put the tree up, we'd chatted about childhood Christmases and I'd shed a few tears. He'd been so lovely, acknowledging how hard my first Christmas without my family was going to be. He'd reassured me that he'd always be there for me; that he was my new family and we'd face everything together. What a joke that had turned out to be.

He'd promised to spoil me in the run-up to Christmas so that I wouldn't feel so sad, and he had done. I'd arrived home from work on a couple of occasions to find a candlelit bath ready for me. He'd organised dinner a few times, too. Granted, it was a ready meal twice and fish and chips from the local takeaway on the other occasion, but it was the thought that counted. The ice-skating had been a complete surprise too, although I'd ended up paying for that, of course. What I'd appreciated even more than all those things was how attentive he'd been towards me, always hugging, kissing me and telling me how much he loved me.

And all that time, he'd been shagging BJ.

* * *

I opened the door to let Ashleigh out after a busy day and was surprised to see Matt outside.

'Libby's gone to a gig in Leeds with Gina and, with Jodie being away, I thought you might be at a loose end too. Fancy a drink?'

I stepped back to let him in. 'Sounds great. I need to get cleared up a bit. I can meet you in the pub—'

'Or I can help if I won't be under your feet.'

'Some help would be great.'

Twenty minutes later, we sat in Minty's – a bar at the top of town – with a couple of lagers. It was tastefully decorated with an elegant tree hung with black, silver and pale blue baubles, and garlands swathed across the bar in a matching colour scheme. Ricky had never liked Minty's, saying it was pretentious. It wasn't. It just wasn't rough like the pubs the lads favoured; the same ones they'd frequented for years.

'How are you holding up?' Matt asked gently.

'I've been better. I'm annoyed more than anything.'

'Has he said sorry yet?'

'Not a word. In his twisted mind, he probably thinks I'm the one who owes him an apology for spilling the beans to Smurf...'

Matt listened as I told him about the lies Ricky had spun Smurf about me and what Smurf had discovered about how long it had been going on.

'It sounds like Ricky and this BJ woman deserve each other,' he said. 'I hope they'll be very miserable together.'

'I'll drink to that,' I said, clinking my bottle against his.

'Does this mean you're on your own for Christmas?' he asked.

'For the first time ever, yes.'

'Then you're invited to the farm for Christmas dinner with my family.'

I shook my head. 'That's very kind of you but I can't accept.'

'Why not?'

I raised my eyebrows at him and he shook his head. 'Libby won't be there. She goes to her grandma's for lunch.'

'Even so, I won't be the cause of any niggles between you, especially not on Christmas Day. Thanks but no thanks. It's just one day and it'll soon be over.'

'But Charlee, you can't—'

'I can and I will,' I said firmly. 'And I don't want us to niggle about it so let's drop the subject. Tell me about Christmas in the

Richards house when you were kids. Was it exciting having Christmas on a farm?'

For the next couple of hours, we reminisced about Christmases past and the best and worst gifts we'd received and it was lovely. My heart felt warm again as I spoke about my grandparents and told Matt about the photo album I'd found in the attic. But my heart also felt warm because of my present company. That crush was still there and, without Ricky in my life, it had sprouted wings. I just hoped the wings would grow big enough for it to fly away because all Matt could offer me was friendship and, so long as Libby was in his life, I needed to make sure I never said or did anything to make him believe I'd like something more.

20

One of the things I've always loved about Christmas is that moment when I wake up and it sinks in that Christmas morning has finally arrived. Every year, I dash to the window to see if it has snowed because, to me, nothing feels more magical than a white Christmas. I don't remember many of them, but having even a slight sprinkling of snow on Christmas Day or Christmas Eve would make me believe that magic could happen.

Not this year, though. When Christmas morning arrived, I didn't believe in magic. Having spent all night on the sofa, wrapped in my duvet, unable to sleep, there wasn't that special waking up moment. Instead, I had a vague acknowledgement that it was 6.00 a.m. and that, all round the country, people would be celebrating. Not me.

I found myself wondering how Smurf would be spending today now that he wouldn't be getting down on bended knee. I hoped he had family he could be around and wasn't all alone.

Sighing, I shifted position on the sofa. 'Happy Christmas,' I muttered to myself, pulling the duvet more tightly round me. 'It's going to be a fun one.'

My phone beeped with a text from Jodie:

⊠ From Jodie
How are you holding up? Feel so guilty being
away. Thinking of you xxx

⊠ To Jodie
I'm fine, thanks. Hope you're having an amazing
time. Happy Christmas xx

⊠ From Jodie
Why don't I believe you? I repeat my first
question: How are you holding up?

Did she really want to know? To be fair to her, she could probably guess the truth:

⊠ To Jodie
My arse is welded to the sofa and has been
since I got home yesterday. If I watch another
Christmas film, my head might explode, and
there are no tissues left in the corner shop.
Other than that, it's all good ;-)

A WhatsApp message and photo came through a few minutes
later of Jodie with her head inside an enormous turkey. The
turkey was wearing a party hat and giant sunglasses. The caption
read:

And you thought you had problems? xx

I had to give Jodie her due; that really made me smile. I could always rely on her to brighten my darkest moments.

Tossing back the duvet, I decided I might feel better after a shower and a coffee. It didn't work. I felt fresher, but still lonely and still miserable. I'm usually content in my own company but Christmas Day was not a day to be spent alone. My heart went out to anyone else who was on their own today and wished they weren't.

Matt rang shortly after 8 a.m. I toyed with ignoring his call in case I turned into a blubbering mess.

'Hi, Matt, happy Christmas!' I hoped I'd managed to pull off bright and breezy instead of hysterical.

'Same to you. I bet you can guess why I've called.'

'Christmas dinner?'

'Come on, Charlee. Please say yes. I can't bear the thought of you spending the day on your own.'

'It's still a no. Sorry. I don't want Libby to—'

'I've already told you she won't be there,' he interrupted.

'I know, but I don't want Libby to hear that I've been there and get funny about it. I'm not having your Christmas ruined by an argument caused by me. And don't say you won't tell her because that's not you. You'll confess and there'll be consequences. Am I right?'

There was a moment's silence. 'I'm happy to face those consequences, though. Please come.'

I thought about it for a moment, but the reality was that Libby was an easy excuse. I wasn't in the mood for faking joviality and I didn't want to be the person who got over-emotional after a couple of drinks and ruin everyone's day. 'It's still a no, but thanks for trying. You're a good friend.'

Matt sighed. 'What will you do?'

'There's a cheeky bottle of red with my name on it, a chilled turkey dinner for one, and Netflix. What more can I girl ask for?'

'Call me if you change your mind. I can come and pick you up. I don't drink on Christmas Day because we give Nigel the day off while Dad and I see to the animals, so I can collect you even if you've already necked that cheeky bottle of red.'

'Thanks, Matt, but I won't change my mind. Have a fantastic day and maybe we can meet up in the New Year.'

'I'd like that. Take care, Charlee.'

I hadn't realised that I'd started crying again at some point during the conversation. Looking round the flat at the soggy tissues strewn everywhere, I shook my head. What the hell was I going to do all day? Paperwork. Accounts. Tidying. Hardly Christmas Day activities, but ideal for taking my mind off how lost and lonely I was. Plus, it would stop me opening that bottle of red and drowning my sorrows.

* * *

By lunchtime, a pile of Charlee's Chocolates paperwork had been dealt with and/or filed and my accounts were up to date. I'd ordered Valentine's Day and Easter moulds and a couple of extra pieces of equipment for the shop. All that remained was tidying.

The bedroom had fitted wardrobes stretching wall to wall across one side of the room with the bed nestled between them. Ricky's belongings had barely filled half the wardrobe on his side of the bed so I'd filled the rest of the space. With his stuff gone, it was time to spread my clothes out. I could be super organised and have winter clothes in one wardrobe and summer in the other.

I put on some loud non-Christmas music and spent the next hour or so reorganising my clothes, trying not to even think about what day it was. When I'd finished, I looked at the cupboards above the bed. I hadn't actually opened them since moving in which suggested that, whatever I'd stored in there, I probably didn't need anymore. Standing in the middle of the bed, I pulled out carrier bags and small boxes, checking their contents. There was a bag of flip flops and sandals and another containing swimwear and suntan lotion, which I pushed to the back. I dropped a carrier bag full of stationery items onto the bed to sort through. Standing on my tiptoes, I reached for another bag and my heart leapt. Crudely wrapped in thin Christmas paper was what felt like a large cardboard box. Could it be the Ugg boots that Ricky had hinted he'd bought me? Ripping off the paper, my heart sank again. Yes, it was a pair of boots. Cheap imitation Ugg-style boots with a large sale sticker across the box. £15 reduced to £7.50. I used to have a pair just like them and they'd been more like expensive fluffy slippers than boots, providing no support to my feet, soaking up even the slightest drop of rain, and ripping at the seams. I'd specifically told Ricky about that pair of boots and why it had to be Uggs instead. I knew Uggs were expensive but with all that overtime … I shook my head. He hadn't done any overtime, had he? I knew that now.

I pulled out another bag containing more gifts. Sighing, I sat down on the bed and ripped off the paper one by one. It looked like Ricky had gone on a shopping spree in the pound shop: talc (when had I *ever* used talc?), a memo block, a pack of cheap biros, a chocolate orange, a pair of plain sports socks, and a very basic desk calendar with no pictures on it. I stared at the random selection of gifts spread across the duvet, blinking back the tears. I wasn't one for extravagance, I really wasn't, but as Jodie had predicted, what the hell said, 'I saw this and thought of you,' about Ricky's choices? It wasn't the money as much as the lack of thought. I'd rather he hadn't bought me anything or that he'd bought me one gift for a fiver that really showed consideration, like the sketchpad and pencil (if it hadn't been accompanied by the lies). It was probably just as well it was over with Ricky because this morning would have been an awkward gift exchange otherwise. With the refunds on everything I'd bought for him, I could buy myself a lovely pair of Uggs and a few other treats in the January sales.

Grabbing the chocolate orange, I ripped off the outer wrapping, gave it a few hard taps against the bedside drawers, then shoved a piece into my mouth. Of all the gifts, it was probably the best. It might be mass-produced but I was quite partial to a chocolate orange.

I shivered suddenly. The heating had switched off and a chill had settled in the flat. Opening one of the wardrobes, I pulled on the cream fluffy cardigan I'd given to Nanna, stroking the fabric and trying to smell her perfume, but there wasn't any trace left. My throat burned, making it hard to swallow the remnants of chocolate, and my eyes stung. I couldn't start crying again. Got to keep busy.

Standing on the bed once more, I continued my rummage, pulling out a bag of paperbacks and a couple of soft toys. Ricky hadn't liked cuddlies round the flat. Tough. He wasn't here anymore so my cuddly Eeyore and Pipkin the bear were coming out of hiding and would keep me warm at night. My throat burned once more as I looked at them. Pipkin had been my christening gift from Nanna and Grandpa, and Eeyore had been a gift for passing my GCSEs as I was obsessed with classic Winnie the Pooh characters at the time. A tear slipped down my cheek as I hugged them to me. *Stop crying! Be strong!* Cuddling them under one of my arms, I reached into the cupboard again, and pulled out the red Christmas album Nanna had made. I slumped onto the bed, sobbing. I couldn't be strong anymore.

* * *

A noise woke me up. I gazed round the gloomy room, feeling completely disorientated. The curtains were wide open and I could see that it was dark outside, so it had to be at least late afternoon. I reached my hand out and flicked the switch on the bedside light, squinting at the clock. 6.10 p.m. Nanna's Christmas album lay beside me on the bed, open, surrounded by crumpled tissues. A couple of pieces of chocolate orange were part smeared across the duvet suggesting that I'd rolled onto them at some point and my head felt fuzzy. I remembered opening that bottle of red after I dug out the album, drinking it straight from the bottle, flicking through the photographs and crying. A lot. I put my hand to my aching head. It felt strange. I rubbed at my forehead then looked at my fingers. Chocolate. Ew!

I heard the noise again. Was that someone knocking on my door? On the flat door? It couldn't be. I'd just been asleep so I certainly hadn't buzzed anyone up. But the knocking came again.

I staggered into the hallway. 'Who's there?'

'It's me.'

'Ricky?'

'No. Matt. Will you open the door?'

I squinted at the peephole to make sure and my heart leapt. Even the distorted version of Matt through the glass was downright gorgeous.

I opened the door and smiled as I clocked his Christmas jumper; a pug wearing illuminated antlers.

'Happy... oh.' His face fell.

'What's up?'

'What's that on your top?'

I glanced down. 'Shit! Chocolate orange.'

Matt laughed. 'That's a relief. For a moment, it looked like the first thing you said.'

I pulled the cardigan across my chest to hide the mess. 'How did you get in?'

'Someone was leaving as I was about to buzz you so they let me in. Can I come in?'

'Why?'

'Because I've brought you something.' I noticed he was holding a carrier bag.

'I didn't get you a present.'

'It's not a present.'

I sighed and stood back. 'Go through. I need the loo.'

I had the fright of my life when I looked in the mirror. My eyes were red and puffy, I had red wine stains round my mouth, my hair was sticking up on end and was that ...? Yep, I'd got chocolate in my hair. Attractive. No wonder Matt's face had fallen. I tried my best to run a brush through my hair but I was going to need a shower to dislodge the chocolate properly so it would have to do. I brushed my teeth, wiped the chocolate from my forehead, splashed some cold water onto my face, squirted myself with deodorant and nipped into the bedroom to change my top before joining Matt.

He was in the kitchen, removing plastic food containers from the bag. The kettle was on and mugs were at the ready.

'I've changed my top but I still have chocolate in my hair. I might have got drunk and fallen asleep on a chocolate orange.'

He laughed. 'It happens to the best of us at Christmas.'

'What's in the containers?'

'Your Christmas dinner. You wouldn't come to us so it's come to you.'

It smelled delicious and my stomach growled in anticipation.

A bottle of Merlot and three quarters of a chocolate orange weren't exactly filling. 'You didn't have to.'

'I wanted to. And my mum insisted as a thank you for all those chocolates you gave me when the shop first opened. How about I make the drinks and you plate up whatever you want? I don't know if you're a sprout person or not.'

I shuddered. 'Not!'

'Me neither. Evil little buggers. Mum, Dad and Tim all love them. I don't get it.'

'Grandpa loved them but Nanna hated them.' I smiled wistfully, recalling the hilarious debate they had about them every Christmas. 'I think it was the only thing they ever disagreed on.'

'When we were kids, Tim and I went through this phase of daring each other to do stupid things. He challenged me to a sprout-eating contest. I couldn't refuse because he'd met my challenge of eating dog food. I remember sitting there with about eight of them in my mouth, the smell and taste making me retch. It was the worst thing I've ever done.'

I screwed my face up. 'That's disgusting. Did you swallow them?'

'I couldn't. I'd rather have eaten the dog food.'

'Me too.'

'Do you know what our Tim bought me for Christmas the next year? A bag of sprouts.'

'No!'

'They reeked. He'd wrapped them about a week before Christmas and put them under the tree, but they gradually got shoved closer to the radiator as other gifts were added so they were seriously minging when I opened them.'

His eyes had sparkled throughout the story and the affection he had for his brother radiated from him. It was such a contrast to Ricky talking about his brother. 'Our kid's a stupid twat,' and phrases along those lines were all I heard from him. Whenever I expressed envy that he had a brother, he'd just laughed and said having a sibling was crap. Matt clearly had the relationship with his brother that I'd have loved if I'd had a sibling.

The kettle boiled and he busied himself making the drinks. I loved how at ease he seemed and how, in the space of five minutes, he'd instantly brightened my dismal day.

I picked up the separate sprout tub. 'Let's pop these bad boys in the bin, eh? Thanks for keeping them apart from the rest of the food.'

'They can contaminate, you know. Mum told me I was being daft, but I refused to risk it until I knew your stance.'

'My body is a sprout-free zone so thank you for understanding.'

The food looked delicious and tasted even better, despite it being microwaved. We sat on the sofa together and Matt chatted about his day as a farmhand while I eagerly tucked in, trying not to focus on how shocked Nanna would be at the sight of Christmas dinner not being consumed at the dining table. Every time I ate a TV dinner, I imagined her and Grandpa looking down on me, tutting.

'Emotional day?' he asked after I declared myself stuffed and took the remnants into the kitchen.

I curled up on the sofa beside him again. 'What gave it away? The red eyes, the snotty tissues everywhere, the stench of wine, or the chocolate mess?'

He smiled. 'I'm no Poirot but I think they were all pretty good clues. Better or worse than you thought?'

'Worse. A lot worse.' I pulled Nanna's cardigan across me for comfort and told Matt how I'd already been in an emotional mess but the discovery of Ricky's Christmas gifts for me, followed by a trip down Memory Lane with the album had finished me off.

Matt gently touched my arm, making my heart race. 'I wish you'd have come up to the farm. I hate to think of you spending the day here all alone, getting so upset.'

'I'd have been horrendous company. I love that you offered, though. Maybe next year?'

'We have a New Year's Eve party at the farm each year...?'

I shook my head. 'Thanks, but I have another date with a bottle of wine and a box of tissues.' I started giggling as I realised what I'd just said. 'It sounds like one of Ricky and BJ's dates.'

Matt laughed with me but my giggles quickly turned to tears and Matt cuddled me to his side.

'I'm sorry,' I said. 'I can't believe I've got any tears left.'

He didn't say anything; just held me close. We sat like that for a good half an hour or so until his mobile phone rang.

'Sorry,' he said as he answered it. 'Hi Libby... yeah... Well, you didn't say you'd be back this early or I'd have been there ... With a friend ... Come on, Libby, I'm allowed to have friends ... Don't be like that!... Okay, I'll be home soon. Bye.'

I grimaced. 'Are you in trouble?'

'No more than usual. I'd better go.'

'Of course.' I jumped up. 'I'll see you out. Ooh. Your tubs. I haven't washed them.'

'Shove them in the bag and I'll do it at home.'

At the door, Matt turned to me. 'I'm so sorry to shoot off like this. Will you be okay?'

I nodded. 'I've made it through the worst. You get back to Libby and your family. Thank your mum for dinner.'

'If you change your mind about New Year's Eve...'

'I'll let you know.'

Matt gave me another hug and a kiss on the cheek before setting off down the stairwell. He turned at the corner and gave me a smile, then disappeared out of sight.

I closed the door, my heart thumping, still feeling the touch of his soft lips against my skin. Crap! No matter how much I tried to convince myself that I had a stupid crush on Matt which would eventually go away, it kept deepening. Why did he have to be so gorgeous and lovely?

Returning to the lounge, I slumped onto the sofa. What now? I flicked the TV on and discovered that *The Vicar of Dibley Christmas Special* was on. Surely watching the wonderful Dawn French would take my mind off Ricky, Matt, and being alone, but it didn't. Nanna and Grandpa had adored the programme so it reminded me of them, and the image of the vicar ramming sprouts down her neck made me think of Matt and I really didn't want to go down that road. Ricky had already broken my heart. I certainly didn't need Matt to crush the remaining pieces.

I closed my eyes for a moment and took a deep breath. My first Christmas without my grandparents was always going to be tough and the emotions had been escalated this year because of a combination of Stacey infiltrating my thoughts thanks to those Christmas albums, and Ricky's humiliating infidelity. I'd almost made it through the day and next year wouldn't be nearly so bad … hopefully. All I needed to do now was make it past New Year and I'd be fine. At least the shop would be open after Boxing Day so I'd have plenty to occupy me during the day. The nights were going to be harder, especially with Jodie away, and New Year's Eve would be the hardest of them all.

I'd always preferred to spend New Year's Eve at home. Nanna, Grandpa and I, and then just Nanna and I, would stay in, order a Chinese, and watch the TV coverage of the different cities round the world seeing the New Year in. We'd loved watching the excitement and fireworks from the warmth and comfort of the sofa instead of being jostled by large crowds. This year, keen to do something completely different to take my mind away from my usual family New Year, I'd booked for Ricky and me to go away for a two-night romantic break in a log cabin in Kittrig Forest, just outside Whitsborough Bay. We'd have enjoyed a hot tub on the balcony, and relaxed as a romantic meal was prepared and served to us on New Year's Eve. It was too late to get my money back, but I certainly wasn't going to go on my own, so it looked like I'd be in the flat, watching the TV coverage alone. So very alone.

ONE YEAR LATER

November

21

'And now for the final Best of the Bay Award for the evening. This one's for the best new independent retailer, a category which includes cafés and bars as well as shops. The shortlist is: Charlee's Chocolates, Glitter and Glitz, Heart and Home, Pink Mist, and Snackies.'

My heart thudded as the compère read out the company names and I glanced round the table which my team were sharing with Sarah and the staff from Seaside Blooms.

'It's yours,' Sarah mouthed to me.

I shook my head. No way. The shortlist had been announced on Thursday and Jodie and I had nipped to the pub after work to celebrate and analyse the other businesses. She was convinced we had it in the bag, but I wasn't so sure. They were all impressive and most of them had huge followings on social media, which was where half of the vote was coming from, with the other half coming from the independent traders in town. The Castle Street traders were an exceptionally supportive bunch and, as I was the only shortlisted business on Castle Street, I was fairly sure I had their votes. Would it be enough? I wasn't local; something I was very aware could stand against me.

'And the winner is...'

Jodie squeezed my hand as the compère opened a silver envelope.

'... Charlee's Chocolates.'

It was only when everyone at my table got to their feet, clapping and cheering, that I registered that I'd won. Me! In a daze, I was pulled to my feet and pushed towards the stage. Self-consciously, I tugged down the skirt of my short, flared, navy cocktail dress and prayed that I wouldn't go splat, unaccustomed as I was to wearing heels.

'Go Charlee!' someone yelled as I ascended the few steps to the stage, blinking in the spotlights.

The compère shook my hand, kissed me on both cheeks and signalled towards the podium.

'You want me to make a speech?' I asked.

'Just a short one.'

Still feeling dazed, I stood in front of the microphone as the applause settled. 'Er, evening everyone. I should probably have taken the advice of my assistant manager, Jodie, and prepared a speech but I didn't dream for one moment that I'd actually win! Don't panic! I've watched the Oscars before so I can probably blag something.'

I paused while I tried to get my brain into gear and was surprised to hear the crowd laughing. Had I made a joke? 'They said short so I won't upset them because they still have my prize...' More laughter. 'I'd like to thank my best friend Jodie and our apprentice Ashleigh who've been with me since day one. You two are amazing and this award is as much for you as it is for me. I didn't think I'd find anyone else as enthusiastic and devoted as you two but our new apprentice, Kieran, is already following in your footsteps so thank you to Kieran too.

'I opened Charlee's Chocolates almost a year ago and have been quite overwhelmed by the friendship, encouragement and support of all the Castle Street traders. You guys are mint. It would *not* be a short speech if I name-checked everyone so I hope you'll forgive me for just mentioning Sarah Derbyshire from Seaside Blooms. Sarah, I'll always be grateful for your help last October in helping out a complete stranger. Thanks to you, I found my dream premises and also a friend for life.'

I looked across to Sarah and she blew me a kiss. 'Thank you to my other new family at Bay Trade. I'll be gagged if I name you all too, but I have to name-check Matt Richards of Richards & Sons because, without him rushing to avert my flood disaster, I might have had a ceiling cave-in and missed my first Christmas.'

I pointed towards the table where Matt was with his dad and brother, having received an award themselves earlier that evening for Best Trade Provider. My eyes filled with tears as my gaze connected with the man I'd been helplessly in love with – unrequited love – for the past year. I blinked rapidly and gulped down the lump in my throat. No way could I lose it on the stage in front of all these people.

'Finally, congratulations to the other nominees. In my eyes, you're all worthy winners. In a retail world where it's so challenging to compete with high street chains, supermarkets, and the Internet, we're so lucky to have a town filled with thriving, unique, independent businesses. Apologies if this sounds really cheesy, but Whitsborough Bay rocks! Thank you.'

As I stepped away from the podium, I was stunned to see everyone in the room standing and applauding.

'Amazing speech,' the compère said, grinning. 'And you say you hadn't prepared anything.'

'I hadn't. That was completely off the cuff, but from the heart.'

'I loved it. Stay on the stage for a moment for photos.' I moved aside as the compère stepped up to the podium and made some closing remarks followed by more applause then there were photos. It all felt like a dream. I was still shaking when I stepped off the stage, clutching my engraved glass plaque, a framed certificate and an envelope which the compère had said contained a cheque.

I hadn't even made it halfway to the table before Jodie grabbed me in a huge bear hug. Thankfully somebody took the plaque and frame out of my hands before I dropped them. Ashleigh was next, mopping her eyes. Kieran went for an awkward limp handshake. We'd make a hugger out of him eventually. Then it was Sarah, her husband Nick, her team, and other members of Bay Trade, a business club that Nick had set up several years earlier with his two best friends. It sounded geeky but it was a group of business owners who met once a month for a few drinks, lots of laughter and banter, and some exchanging of ideas and services. Sarah had asked at the start of the year if I wanted to join them. I already knew that Matt was a member so it was a no-brainer for me.

Matt. My heart thumped as I spotted him hovering nearby waiting for his moment to congratulate me. I felt shaky all over again as he stepped forward, wrapped his arms round me and held me close. 'I knew you could do it. Congratulations,' he whispered. 'How do you feel?'

How did I feel? About what? About winning the award or about being held in the arms of the man I absolutely adored but who was marrying another? About how every photo he showed me of his barn conversion had me wishing I was the one picking out soft furnishings and paint colours instead of Libby? About how I'd pointed out my dream kitchen in his catalogue and had immediately pictured Matt and me cooking together as we chatted about our day at work?

'Overwhelmed,' I said, truthfully. 'I feel overwhelmed.'

Matt's dad called his name so he said we'd catch up later. I watched him cross the room, cursing the event for being black tie because Matt in a tux had floored me. From the moment I met him, I was attracted to him but never had a man looked hotter than Matt did tonight.

I returned to my chair and gulped down the remnants of my glass of wine – half a large glass. Grabbing the bottle from the centre of the table, I refilled it, sloshing wine onto the crisp white tablecloth. I gulped down several more mouthfuls then put my glass down and closed my eyes for a moment.

'Right you, you're coming with me.' Jodie grabbed my hand and pulled me to my feet.

'Where are we going?'

Without answering, she power-walked me across the hotel lobby, past an enormous Christmas tree, and to a pair of high-backed leather armchairs in a darkened corner of the bar. 'Sit.'

Feeling a little intimidated at Scary Assertive Jodie, I did as I was told.

'Charlee! This has to stop,' she said, her tone soft yet insistent.

'What has?'

'You and Matt.'

'There is no me and Matt.'

'Exactly. And there never will be if you don't tell him how you feel. So you need to be honest with him, get him to end it with Libby, move into his gorgeous barn conversion and live happily ever after. Or you need to accept it's never going to happen and get over him. I know that's easier said than done but, seriously Charlee, you can't waste another year head over heels in love with him like this. Look at you! You're shaking and I've just watched you neck back a huge glass of wine. And don't try to tell me it was because of the shock of winning the award when I just watched you and Matt together. I know it was the effect he has on you.'

I hung my head. She was right about it all.

She sighed and leaned a little closer. 'I hate to lecture you but this should be a special night for you and you deserve it so much but I wouldn't be your best friend if I let you ruin it by getting hideously drunk over a man. Even a man as lovely as Matt. So which is it going to be?'

I held my head in my hands. 'I can't tell him how I feel.'

'Why not?'

'Because he's engaged. I can't and won't steal someone else's man. I know how that feels, don't I?' I looked up at her. 'I can't put someone else through what I went through.'

'I'm not proposing you get down and dirty with him in full public view,' Jodie said. 'I'm just suggesting that you let him know that Libby isn't his only option.'

'It's still stealing someone else's man.'

'It isn't. It's giving him a little encouragement. If he doesn't take it, then it's his decision. You won't have actually done anything.'

'You can package it up however you want, but it's *still* stealing someone else's man.'

Jodie sat back in her chair, clearly frustrated with me. 'Do you really think that Matt's living the dream with Libby?'

'All relationships have ups and downs.'

'Yes, they do, but they mainly have ups which is why the couple work through the downs. I know he's not constantly bitching and moaning about her because he's too lovely, but most of what Matt says about Libby is negative, isn't it? He usually laughs about it but there's no denying that the woman is seriously high maintenance and we both know that first-hand from meeting her several times.'

I shrugged. 'Maybe he likes it that way.'

'Maybe he does, and maybe he's just putting up with it because he doesn't think he has another choice.'

'And you think he'd jump at the chance to be with me instead?' I asked, doubt hanging off every word.

'Yes!' Jodie sat forward again. 'I said it from the start and I haven't changed my mind. I'm convinced he feels the same way about you but you've stupidly got yourselves into the classic friend zone and you're both too scared to say anything in case the friendship is ruined.'

She was right about the friend zone and it was a tricky place to be because I absolutely didn't want to do anything to jeopardise my friendship with Matt. I loved spending time with him, and couldn't bear the thought of not having him around.

The moment I'd met Matt, I'd felt an instant connection, as though I'd known him for years. That initial click had developed into a friendship, which had strengthened as he'd helped me get through the aftermath of *that* video. I'd been really touched by his strength and support changing the locks, turning up after work to take me out for a drink, and bringing me dinner on Christmas Day. Even though I'd repeatedly refused his invitation to join him at the farm on New Year's Eve, he'd turned up again on New Year's Day with a tub full of party food, some party poppers, and a bottle of bubbly, insisting that we toast to a fresh start and a happy New Year.

After that, Matt and I had seen each other fairly regularly. We met up at monthly Bay Trade meetings and he brought his nieces into the shop once a month to pick out a chocolatey treat. We went out for a meal or drinks with Jodie on several occasions, and sometimes it was just the two of us although, in some ways, I preferred it when Jodie was with us. When Matt and I were alone, it took considerable restraint not to gaze lovingly into his eyes, reach across the table to hold his hand, or to kiss him goodnight.

In the early part of the year, I came very close to doing what Jodie had just suggested and telling Matt how I felt but, every time I saw an opportunity, I bottled it. At first, I worried that my feelings for Matt could be a rebound thing so it didn't seem appropriate to broach the subject. When I was sure that I genuinely had fallen for him, I quickly talked myself out of saying anything because, let's face it, he wasn't available and, even though I didn't like the woman, I couldn't show such a lack of respect towards Libby.

There were several occasions during the year when Matt and Libby had major arguments and I found myself desperately hoping that one of those would signal the end of their relationship. I'd lost count of the number of times that Libby had stormed out and stayed the night with her best friend, Gina. Unfortunately for me, they always seemed to kiss and make up. They'd then go through a really good patch, suggesting to me that they were one of those couples who could ride out any storm and nothing would break them apart.

In early August, they had a huge bust-up over something to do with the house and Libby took off to Gina's for a few days. It got really nasty and Jodie and I were convinced the end had finally arrived. I think it might actually have been over if it hadn't been for Matt's granddad having a massive stroke while out walking the dogs on the farm. His granddad died the following day and it seemed that the bereavement brought out Libby's softer side because she'd rushed back to support Matt and his family. Since then, he'd mainly spoken positively about her. Instead of expecting (and hoping for) an announcement that they were over for good, I kept expecting (and dreading) an announce-ment that they'd set a date for their wedding.

'I want you to do something for me,' Jodie said. 'When the clock strikes midnight on New Year's Eve – just over six weeks away – I want you to be either kissing Matt Richards or kissing goodbye to your little fantasies about him. Next year, you're his new girlfriend, or you're just his friend and will have come to terms with it never being anything more. What do you say? Do we have a deal?'

I leaned back in my chair and focused on a huge Christmas tree in the corner of the bar, behind Jodie, mesmerised for a moment by the twinkling blue lights. Matt had helped me put up the tree in the shop this year after Jodie reluctantly accepted that she had the flu and needed her bed. We'd giggled each time we reached for the same branch, our fingers touching. I found myself imagining that we were putting up a tree in our own home rather than the shop one, and had to make an excuse to check on Jodie before I started believing the dream and moved in for a kiss.

'Okay,' I said. 'You're right. I can't go on like this. It's a deal.'

She reached out her hand and I shook it. 'You're doing the right thing.'

Was I? So why did I feel like I'd lost him? For me, the choices were to be as bad as BJ, which I absolutely couldn't do, or to push him away because spending time with him as nothing more than friends was killing me.

22

When Jodie and I returned to the function room, the lights had been dimmed and a disco was in full swing. There'd been a balloon release and there must have been some confetti canons as shiny squares were scattered across the dance floor. The volume of excited chatter had significantly increased to compete with the music.

'You could always tell him tonight,' Jodie said, as we set off in search of our table, which had been moved aside to clear the dance floor.

I could. But I wasn't going to. Although, if I had some Dutch courage inside me...

* * *

Too much to drink. Definitely too much to drink. I did some sort of hiccup giggle as the arm I'd been leaning on gave way and I managed to only just stop myself from face-planting the table.

'Are you okay?' Matt asked, reaching across to steady me.

'Bit pissed,' I muttered, hiccupping again.

'You deserve to be. Tonight's your night.'

I raised my wine glass as a toast to myself, then frowned when I realised it was empty. 'Who drank that?'

Matt laughed. 'You.'

'I did not.'

'You did too.'

He could be right. Might be why I was so drunk. Oh well, it was nearly the end of the evening. It wouldn't be right to end it sober.

The DJ announced that he was going to slow things down for the last few songs, starting with a track from the early noughties.

'Aw, I absolutely love this song,' I gushed as I recognised one of my all-time favourite ballads: 'If You're Not the One' by Daniel Bedingfield. It came out when Jodie and I were at college and we'd sit in my bedroom playing the video on repeat as we both had a massive crush on Daniel Bedingfield.

'Do you love it?' I asked Matt.

He held my gaze and for that brief moment, it felt as though there was only the two of us in the room. The music and chatter seemed to fade away as I lost myself in his dark eyes.

'Yes, I do,' he responded, his voice hoarse.

I dared to imagine that he wasn't referring to the song and he meant he loved me instead but, even in my inebriated state, I knew it was wishful thinking.

He cleared his throat, stood up and held his hand out towards me. 'Do you want to dance?'

I widened my eyes. 'With you?'

'No, with the woman in the red dress over there. Of course with me.' Although the words were humorous, his expression was earnest.

Feeling suddenly very sober, I placed my hand in his, my heart racing as he led me onto the dance floor.

We'd hugged on countless occasions and, while the close contact always left me a little flushed and breathless, nothing had prepared me for the overwhelming sensation of being held against Matt's chest while we slowly moved to the rhythm.

The lyrics could have been written for me. 'Unrequited love,' I muttered.

'What's that?'

'This song's about unrequited love. Story of my life.'

I felt Matt's body tense against mine. 'He wasn't worth it,' he muttered.

'Who wasn't?'

'Ricky. That's who you're talking about, isn't it?'

What could I say? *No, Matt, I'm talking about you.* I couldn't do that to him. But if I simply answered 'no', then the obvious question was to ask who I was referring to and how could I respond to that? So I remained silent while we shuffled to another verse, every word dripping with poignancy. I desperately wanted to share how I felt, to hold him tighter, to feel his lips against mine and I needed to push those thoughts away before I acted on them. *Focus on his fiancée. Remember his dad and brother are here. So are your staff and friends and traders and you don't want any of them to witness you making a move on an engaged man because that's not the sort of person you are. Libby. Ask him about Libby.*

'So what was Libby doing tonight?'

'Big night out with Gina and the girls from work to celebrate Gina's divorce. They're all dressed as nurses for some reason.'

'Sounds like fun.'

'Sounds like carnage,' he said. 'He was Gina's first and only boyfriend and, from what Libby tells me, she's making up for the lack of experience. She was up to double figures within three months of them splitting up. I always thought Gina was pretty sensible, but I think she's regressed to her teens.'

We shuffled in silence again.

'Have you heard from Ricky lately?' Matt asked.

'No, thank God, although Smurf came into the shop last weekend and said that Ricky and BJ had split up.'

'Again?'

'I know. Must be, what, third or fourth time? But Smurf thinks it's for good this time although there were kids in the shop so he said he couldn't go into the details. I'm assuming one or both of them have been up to no good.'

'As long as he doesn't come sniffing round you again.'

The words were out before I could stop them: 'Would it bother you if he did?'

He pulled me a little closer and his voice came out all husky like before. 'Of course it would.'

I held my breath as my heart thumped faster and faster. 'Why?'

Silence.

I stepped back and looked up into his eyes. 'Why would it bother you?' I asked again.

He visibly gulped, his eyes fixed on mine, and I was sure he was going to say something meaningful but the track ended and my stomach sank at the track that started playing next: the song Libby wanted for their first dance at their wedding.

Matt glanced towards the DJ, a frown creasing his forehead, then he looked back down at me and smiled as he released his hold on me. 'Because you're my friend and I wouldn't want to see that tosser hurt you again.'

Friends. Yes, that's all we were. I was going to have to spend New Year kissing goodbye to my fantasies about Matt because there was no way I'd be kissing him for real.

23

It was inevitable, really. Deep down, I'd known it would happen as soon as Smurf told me that Ricky had split up with BJ yet again.

'Charlee! How are you? You look amazing.'

I dropped the shop keys in my handbag and looked him up and down. I wished I could return the compliment but he looked terrible. Perhaps it was the gloomy night doing him no favours, casting dark shadows across his face. 'What do you want, Ricky?'

'Don't I even get a "hello"?'

I rolled my eyes. 'Hello. So what do you want?'

'To take the winner of Best Newcomer out for a drink to celebrate her amazing success.'

'You heard about it then?'

He nodded. 'It was on Bay Radio this morning. I'm so proud of you, Charlee.'

'You're not my boyfriend anymore and you haven't been for a long time. You don't get to be proud of me.'

'Aw, don't be like that. I still care about you.'

I set off walking.

'Charlee!' Ricky ran after me. 'Sorry. That was a stupid thing to say. Can I buy you a drink? Please.'

I spun round to face him. 'Why?'

'Because I owe you an apology. What I did to you last year was out of order and I never said sorry.'

'You've just said it so you can ease your conscience and I can go home for my dinner.'

'One drink. Please, Charlee.'

Although going out for a drink with Ricky wasn't a remotely appealing way to spend the evening, neither was going back to an empty flat to eat a ready meal for one. Jodie had gone to Bradford for the day to celebrate her great grandma's ninety-seventh birthday and wouldn't be back till late. Sod it. I was curious to hear his excuses. He'd texted me, emailed me and phoned me intermittently over the past year, but I'd ignored his calls, and deleted all his messages without reading them.

'One drink. But that's it. I mean it.'

* * *

'A pint and a large glass of Merlot,' Ricky said to the barmaid in The Purple Lobster.

I gazed round the pub while we waited, already regretting agreeing to a drink. Someone could have done with a serious lesson in Christmas decorating. It looked like there'd been an explosion in a tinsel factory with gaudy foil garlands and baubles that had seen better days randomly strung across the ceiling, walls, and the bar.

The server told him the price as she placed the drinks on the bar towel.

Ricky patted his pockets and shot me a stricken look. I rolled my eyes. 'Really?'

'Sorry.'

With a sigh, I handed over a note, seething inside as I waited for the change. I'd walked into that one.

'Cheers,' he said, as we sat down. I didn't feel like reciprocating it. Instead, I took a good look at him. It hadn't just been the bad light; he genuinely did look like crap. He'd grown out his buzzcut and his hair was now messy and curling up on the collar of his T-shirt. He needed a good shave and his rumpled clothes looked like they'd been fished out of the bottom of the laundry basket. Unlike Matt, he couldn't carry off the long hair and designer beard thing; it aged him about thirty years.

'Do you remember the last time we came here?' Ricky asked, looking round and nodding.

'Not especially.'

'You must do. It was a great night.'

I sipped on my wine then sighed. 'For you, it probably was. You'll have spent the night flirting with BJ. You probably went out the back for a quickie while your unsuspecting girlfriend here was being ignored by most of your friends and wishing she wasn't there.'

Ricky looked a little shocked. 'It wasn't that bad, was it?'

'Why do you think I only came out with you all twice?'

'Sorry, I didn't realise.'

'No, you wouldn't. Because, as I've already said, you spent all night flirting with BJ although, at the time, I had no idea you were shagging your best mate's girlfriend behind our backs.'

'I'm sorry about what we did to you. I don't know what I was thinking.'

I shrugged. 'Really? Because, from the video, I thought it was pretty obvious what you were thinking both then and the umpteen times before that when the pair of you conveniently forgot you already had partners.'

He winced at my sarcasm. 'I deserved that. It's over with BJ, you know. For good.'

'So Smurf tells me.'

'You've been seeing Smurf?' His eyes flashed.

'Oh for God's sake, don't start that jealousy crap again,' I snapped, incensed that he had the audacity to be jealous after what he'd done. 'Smurf and I are friends. In fact, we're not even that. Acquaintances. He comes into the shop for some chocolates every so often and, last time, he mentioned it was over.'

'I dumped her.'

'I'm not interested in who dumped whom.'

Ricky either didn't hear me or chose to ignore me. 'You know the bloke from the takeaway who posted the video?'

'Not personally.'

'He recognised BJ in the pub one night and asked her if she'd re-enact the video with him. She was pissed off with me because I said I couldn't afford to take her to Paris for her birthday, so she agreed.'

'Not in Dice Pizza again?'

'No. She's not that stupid. We're still struggling with the aftermath from that.' His shoulders slumped. 'It didn't go viral this time but it did make it back to me.'

The aftermath Ricky had referred to went much further than Smurf and me finding out and ending the relationships. When the video went viral, the story was picked up by the tabloids and the 'amorous couple' were identified. Ricky's employers didn't appreciate him bringing the company's name into disrepute so he was given his marching orders. The owners of Dice Pizza hadn't appreciated the undesirable publicity either and alerted the police. Ricky and BJ were arrested and charged with 'outraging public decency contrary to common law'. They were lucky to avoid a prison sentence, getting off with a caution, a fine and community service.

The pained look in Ricky's eyes and his deflated demeanour suggested he was devastated at the break-up with BJ and I felt a flicker of empathy towards him, accompanied by a moment of smug satisfaction. That saying about having a taste of your own medicine had never been more appropriate.

'I suppose you think it serves me right,' he said, as though reading my thoughts.

'I'd be lying if the word "karma" didn't spring to mind. I'm sorry, though, because I know it hurts. What happens now?'

'I'm back at my mum's, sleeping on the sofa. She says I can't have my bedroom back unless I pay rent but work's erratic. Did you know I got sacked?'

'Smurf told me.' He said Ricky had done a mixture of labouring and private work since then but nobody would give him a decent opportunity. I'd initially felt sorry for him but had reminded myself that he hadn't just been having sex with BJ the whole time we'd been living in Whitsborough Bay – which would have been bad enough – but he'd been seeing her while pretending to be the doting boyfriend supporting me through Nanna's prognosis and subsequent death. I didn't feel quite so sorry for him after that.

'I can't find any work,' he continued. 'I've still got my court fine to pay and my debts from before. Mum's not charging me for food but she says I have to move out after Christmas because her boyfriend says I'm cramping their style. I was wondering...'

'No,' I said firmly.

'You don't know what I was going to say.'

'Yes I do. You were going to ask if you could move back in with me and the answer's no.'

'I miss you, Charlee. I still love you.'

I glared at him. How dare he? How dare he come crawling back to me after everything he'd done, turn on the puppy dog eyes, spin me a sad story about his life falling apart, and declare his undying devotion when I believed without a shadow of a doubt that he'd never loved me in the first place?

'Don't spout crap you don't mean, Ricky.'

'But I do mean it! I know I hurt you, but I'd never do that again. We were good together.'

He reached across the table to take my hand but I snatched it away. I knew this had been a mistake.

'"Were" being the operative word,' I hissed at him, jumping to my feet.

'Come on, Charlee. It could be good again. The sex was amazing. We don't have to have a full-on relationship if you don't want. We could be friends with benefits.'

Oh. My. God! I yanked my coat back on. 'Enjoy your drink. You can have mine too if you want.'

Ricky stood up too. 'Please don't go.'

'What possible reason is there for me to stay?' I started counting off the negatives on my fingers. 'You beg me to join you for a drink but then I have to pay for it. You ask if you can move back in with me because your own mother is kicking you out. You want to sleep with me again but really the offer's for an open relationship which is clearly how you like it. I guarantee the next step is to ask me for some money.' The guilty expression on his face answered that one for me. 'I've been single since we split up and I admit that I do miss having someone in my life, but I would rather stay single forever than have you back. I loved you and you lied to me. I trusted you and you let me down. I don't love you now and I don't trust you now. And I'm certain that you never loved me.'

'That's not fair,' he cried. 'I did. I still do.'

'Bollocks! It was all about the money, wasn't it? I was your meal ticket. You even told Smurf you were hoping I'd pay off your debts.' Despite the evidence to the contrary, I had desperately wanted to believe that he couldn't really be that mercenary, but right now he looked like a little kid caught with his hand in the sweetie jar.

I picked up my bag. 'I guess that explains why you put up with the crying and the lack of sex at the start or our relationship. It was worth it because of the financial reward you anticipated when I got my inheritance and sold the house, wasn't it?'

He at least had the decency to gaze downwards.

I stepped away from the table then stopped, grabbed my wine and glugged it down in one. Banging the glass down on the table, I hoisted my bag onto my shoulder. 'You're not getting *anything* from me, Ricky. Not even the dregs of my drink. I'm sorry your girlfriend did the dirty on you, I'm sorry you lost your job, I'm sorry you've got fines and debts to pay, and I'm sorry you're homeless but these are *your* problems; not mine. I don't owe you anything. We're not friends. We'll never be friends again. You're just somebody that I used to know. Good luck in getting your life back on track, but I won't be part of it. Goodbye, Ricky.'

As I walked out of The Purple Lobster, I was shaking with adrenaline. I'd wanted to tell him what I thought for so long and I'd finally had the chance to do it without shouting or crying or crumbling. And it felt so good. I felt liberated.

I'd meant what I said. I would rather stay single and alone than have Ricky back in my life. But what I'd really like was Matt. Sadly, that was never going to happen. Being with Ricky just now had brought those feelings of hurt bubbling to the surface. Libby may not be my favourite person and I might not think she was right for Matt but he was a grown adult and capable of making his own decisions. He obviously loved her and wanted to marry

her and any moments of chemistry between Matt and I had all
been in my imagination. From now on, Matt and I were friends
and that alone. From the New Year, I'd gradually drift away from
him, turning down nights at the pub until all we did was catch up
at the monthly Bay Trade meetings. I could do that. Maybe.

24

'Oh my God, Charlee! What time did you start this morning?' Jodie stared at the workshop table covered in truffles, and the cooling racks full of letter cubes, truffles and chocolate drops a little after half seven the following morning.

I continued piping white chocolate onto some of the truffles, creating Christmassy shapes like holly leaves, stars and trees. 'About four, I think. Did I wake you?'

'No. I can't hear a thing in the flat, but I spotted the light on when I came back from my run so I thought I'd shower then investigate.' She sat down. 'Why 4 a.m.?'

'I couldn't sleep. Too much on my mind.'

I was aware of Jodie watching my frantic piping, but I couldn't look at her. I knew that if I looked into her sympathetic eyes, I'd crumble.

'I think someone needs a strong coffee and a friendly ear,' she said.

* * *

'Coffee,' she said, placing a mug in front of me five minutes later. 'It's time to take a break.' She attempted to extricate the piping bag from my hand.

'The chocolate will set,' I muttered, clinging onto it.

'Then you can make some more. Give me it.'

'No!'

'GIVE ME IT!'

'NO!'

We wrestled with the bag for a moment, but Jodie squeezed it in the wrong place and squealed as warm chocolate squirted all over her face.

'Right! That's it!' She grabbed another piping bag off the table, filled with white chocolate that I'd coloured pink.

'No, Jodie! Don't!'

But she did. As pink chocolate dripped down my nose, I aimed my piping bag towards her like a gun and fired.

A few minutes later, we giggled as we surveyed the chocolatey mess. We were covered in the stuff. I had a paper hat and my apron on so it was only my face and the top of my T-shirt that had suffered but Jodie had it in her hair and all over her clothes.

'I think you might need another shower,' I said, pulling off my hat and apron.

'Not until you've told me what's going on.'

'It's nothing much.'

Jodie shook her head. 'Not buying it.'

I shrugged. 'Help me clear this mess off the floor and walls and I'll tell you.'

With a bucket of soapy water and a cloth each, we started clearing up.

'I went out for a drink with Ricky last night and he asked me to take him back.'

Jodie gasped. 'No! Seriously? After what he did to you?'

'He's split up with BJ and he says he misses me and still loves me.'

She rinsed her cloth in the bucket. 'Do you believe him?'

'About BJ? Yes. I do think it's for good this time. About the rest of it? Not a word. He only wanted me for my money from the very start and that hasn't changed.'

'Please tell me you told him where to go,' Jodie said, sounding hopeful.

I nodded.

She picked up her cloth and squeezed it out. 'So why the sleepless night? You're not regretting saying no, are you?'

I scrubbed at a lump of pink chocolate on the floor while I found the right words. 'I absolutely don't want to get back with Ricky. I actually never even want to lay eyes on the cheating, money-grabbing git again.'

'Good. But this still doesn't explain the sleepless night.'

Rinsing the cloth, I started on another lump. 'I miss being in a relationship.'

'I miss being in a relationship too. It's nice to have someone to snuggle up to at night.'

I shook my head. 'It's more than that. I miss being part of something. I miss being part of a couple but I also miss being part of a family. I miss my grandparents and I started thinking about my birth mum and, well...'

Jodie stopped what she was doing. 'You're not thinking of contacting her, are you?'

'Not just thinking. I've already done it.'

* * *

They say you can't miss what you've never had and I have to agree with that. I'd never had parents yet I'd never felt that I missed out.

From what I could tell from conversations at school, my grandparents had been far better 'parents' to me than many biological ones were towards their children.

Throughout school, I never felt that the absence of parents made me particularly different, probably because I wasn't the only one without a mum and dad at home. Several of the children at primary school lived with a single mum, a single dad, or across two homes. Some had step-parents, step-siblings and/or half-siblings, one of my classmates was fostered, and another had two dads.

It had been meeting Jodie that triggered me questioning my family set-up. She'd moved to the area when we were ten and I was given the proud responsibility of showing the new girl round. She told me that she'd moved from Bradford because her dad had a new job and she was excited about living near the sea, but she was going to miss all her cousins who she'd played with regularly. I vividly remember her saying, 'The best thing about cousins is that it's like having lots of brothers and sisters to play with but it's even better because they aren't mean to you. I've got twenty-three cousins although some of them are a lot older than me so I don't play with those ones. How many cousins do you have?' And for the first time ever, it struck me that I didn't have any cousins. I didn't have any aunties or uncles either, or a second set of grandparents. There were just the three of us and that wasn't very many. Not very many at all.

'You have your thinking face on,' Nanna had said when she picked me up from school that day and we set off walking home.

'Why don't I have any cousins, Nanna?' I asked.

'Because your mum didn't have any brothers or sisters. If she had done, they'd have been your aunties and uncles and, if they'd had children, those children would have been your cousins. Why do you ask?'

'I have a new friend at school called Jodie McAllister and she has twenty-three cousins.'

'Goodness me, lovey. That's a lot of cousins.'

We walked in silence for a while.

'Would you like to go to the swings on the way home?' Nanna asked.

'No thanks.'

I *always* wanted to go to the swings so I imagine that Nanna might have felt a little anxious at this point.

'Why do I never see my mum?' I asked as we passed the entrance to the park. 'Doesn't she like me?'

Nanna drew a sharp intake of breath. I looked up at her but she was looking off into the distance, frowning.

'Nanna?'

She looked down and gave me a gentle smile. 'No, lovey. It's nothing like that.'

'Is she in prison?'

'Oh my goodness. Where did you get an idea like that?'

'Alfie Spencer's stepdad is in prison.'

'Is he? Oh dear. No, your mum isn't in prison. Come on. Let's get home and get those potatoes peeled. We're having your favourite. Bangers and mash.' Nanna's pace quickened and I had to run to keep up with her.

'Is she in hospital, then? Like Elliott Traske's mum?'

Nanna sighed. 'She's not in hospital either. She's...' She stopped and looked around her as though checking nobody was in earshot then she bent down so her face was closer to mine. 'I don't know where she is at this precise moment.'

'Why?'

'We're not in contact, lovey.'

'Why?'

'It's complicated.'

'Is she still in Hull?'

Nanna's eyes started watering and she stood up and dabbed them with a handkerchief from the pocket of her cardigan. 'No. Not Hull. Not England either. She'll be somewhere in Europe, I imagine, but I've no idea where because she moves round a lot.'

'Why?' I knew I'd asked the same question an annoying number of times but Nanna's answers were so vague, it seemed the only question I could ask.

'I don't know, really. She's always been like that, even as a child. She never seemed to be able to settle with one thing or one friend. She was always looking for someone or something new and exciting.'

'Was I not very exciting? Is that why she left?'

She stopped walking and bent down again. 'Oh lovey, it wasn't about you. It was about her.' She pulled me into a sudden hug and kissed the top of my head. 'You were the most wonderful, exciting, amazing thing to happen to any of us.' She let me go but kept hold of my arms while she looked into my eyes. 'Promise me you'll never doubt that.'

I nodded solemnly. 'So why did she leave me?'

Nanna pressed her fingers against her lips. Her hands were shaking and her lip wobbled. She looked up at the skies, as though searching for the answer in the fluffy clouds then straightened up, took my hand, and set off walking again. 'We'll talk at home.'

Back at home, I removed my shoes and sat on the sofa waiting for an explanation. Nanna emerged from the kitchen with a glass of squash for me and a cup of tea for herself and sat down beside me.

'I'll explain this as best as I can,' she said, handing me my drink. 'When some people have children, they are brilliant parents from the start. It's as though they automatically know what to do and they do it really well. Some people find it difficult becoming a parent but they learn every day and they hopefully get better. But there are others who struggle all the way. Not everyone has what it takes to be a parent and your mum was one of those people.'

I frowned at her. 'How did she know? You said she left on the day I was born.'

Nanna closed her eyes and dipped her head, nodding. It was obvious to me how much this conversation was hurting her but I was desperate to know.

She opened her eyes again. 'Long before you were even born, your mum knew that she wouldn't be a good parent and that you wouldn't have the happiest childhood if you stayed with her so she asked if we could look after you instead so that's what happened and we've been very, very lucky to have you in our lives. We were only blessed with one child but we always wanted a big family, so you've been our second chance to be parents, and we've loved every single moment.'

'Why does she never visit?'

'I don't know, lovey. I'm sorry.'

But she did know. And now I did too.

* * *

I'd been surprised to see Neil Winters's name flash up on my mobile a couple of months ago. With the sale of Nanna's house long complete, I hadn't expected to hear from him again.

'We've made a discovery,' he said after we'd exchanged pleasantries. 'My daughter wanted stripped floorboards in the master bedroom so we took up the carpet and found a couple of loose boards. We lifted them and found two bundles of letters and postcards addressed to your Nanna.'

My mouth suddenly felt dry. 'Who are they from?' I asked, the words sounding stilted and distant.

'I haven't opened any of the letters. They're private. But I couldn't help spotting a name on one of the postcards. It was...'

I already knew what he was going to say.

'...Stacey,' he said. 'Do you want me to send them to you?'

Did I? Could anything be gained from reading letters from her, especially when Nanna wasn't around to explain any of the contents. But if I told Neil to shove them in the recycling, would I always be wondering?

'Yes, please. That would be great.' It probably wouldn't be 'great' at all but I didn't have to read them when they came. I told Neil I'd text him my address and thanked him for letting me know.

'No worries. I'm not likely to get to the post office this week but I'll definitely post them next week.'

There was no rush. It gave me time to decide whether I wanted to open them or not. But Neil obviously made it to the post office sooner than expected as I arrived home from work three days later to find a package in my pigeonhole.

My stomach churned as I climbed up the two flights of stairs holding the large, padded envelope, debating what to do with them. By the time I reached my flat, I'd decided to open them. What was the worst that could happen? I was already indifferent towards Stacey so the contents were either going to continue that indifference or make me dislike her. There was nothing she could possibly write that would make me want to track her down.

I sat at the dining table, opened the envelope and removed the two bundles. One was tied with a golden ribbon and the other with a cerise pink one. I took several deep calming breaths then released the golden ribbon. The letters and postcards fanned out on the table and I could immediately see that they were all addressed to Nanna in the same neat, sloping handwriting.

I picked up the item that had been on the top – a postcard – and ground my teeth as I read it:

Loving Paris but those feet are itchy again.
Met a darling Italian.
He's taking me to Milan but I shan't stay long.
So much world, so little time.
Ciao
Stacey

That was it. No enquiring after her parents and absolutely no mention of me. Looking at the clear date stamp, I'd have been eight and was clearly out of sight, out of mind. A spark of anger ignited inside me as I read the words again. How dare she be so carefree and dismissive of her family? I gathered up the items, shoved them back into the envelope along with the pink ribbon bundle and stormed into my bedroom. Standing on the bed, I opened the over-bed wardrobe and tossed the package towards the back where it slid behind the box containing my Christmas boots from Ricky. There the envelope remained, also out of sight but not so much out of mind. I'd come close to reading the rest of the letters several times but had always recoiled, shaking my head, when my fingers touched the padded envelope. Until last night when, disturbed by my interlude with Ricky, I'd retrieved the envelope, tipped the contents onto the bed, and started reading.

Halfway through the open bundle was as far as I managed before I felt compelled to write to her. I thumped out an abusive letter on my laptop, demanding to know what had happened to make her so damned selfish. I have to say, it was very cathartic letting go of my initial flurry of anger towards her, but what was the point in sending her it? I saved it and opened a fresh page. It took me ages to find the right words and tone. After well over an hour, I finally felt as though I had written something that was informative, not too emotional, and which had no suggestion that I wanted her in my life because I really didn't.

Dear Stacey

It feels strange to write that but it doesn't feel appropriate to start this letter with 'dear mum' for obvious reasons.

I've recently discovered that you were intermittently in contact with Nanna over the years so I'm assuming you're aware that your dad died six years ago. However, you probably won't be aware that your mum also passed away in May last year. I had no way of contacting you at the time.

Some letters you wrote to her have come into my possession and the most recent has a UK address on it. I therefore hope this news reaches you. You have, of course, missed the funeral but, considering you didn't attend your dad's, I don't imagine you'd have attended your mum's either.

After Nanna died, I moved to Whitsborough Bay. Grandpa trained me as a master chocolatier and I now run my own chocolate shop. You've never been part of my life and you've barely been part of your parents' lives so I don't know how the news about Nanna will affect you, but I thought it was important that you were aware that she is now with Grandpa.

I've put the shop contact details at the top of this letter. If you do want to ask any questions about how she died, you know where I am.

Charlee

I printed it off, sealed it in an envelope and nipped out in my

PJs to shove the letter in the post box nearest Coral Court before I could change my mind.

After that, any attempts to sleep were fruitless. I kept imagining what I would say if Stacey did turn up at the shop. Would she still be the selfish self-centred woman she came across as in her letters, or would the years have changed her? Would she show any remorse at walking out on me the day I was born? Did I look like her? I'd seen some similarities from our childhood photos in those Christmas albums I'd found in the attic, but had this continued into adulthood?

After two hours of imagining all sorts of scenarios, I decided that I might as well get up, get ready, and go to the shop to lose myself in my creative world, hopefully shoving all thoughts of Stacey out of my mind.

As I filled my first piping bag a little later, I realised that I might have made a huge mistake. Yes, Stacey had a right to know about Nanna dying. I had no idea whether she'd care but surely she'd want to know, but what had possessed me to pass on my contact details? Had I set myself up for weeks or even months of being on tenterhooks, wondering if every dark-haired female who walked into the shop was her? Why hadn't I thought that one through? It wasn't as though I wanted to build a relationship with her after all these years.

Or did I?

I didn't like the idea that there was only me now. Had this made me reach out to the only person left who I could call family? The one person who'd spent the last thirty-one years making it clear that she had no interest in being part of our family and who certainly had no interest in making me part of hers. Oh God, what had I done?

25

'Let me guess,' Jodie said, turning the door sign round to 'closed' after a busy Friday a week later. 'Matt? Ricky perhaps? Santa?' Or is it your mum?'

'What is?'

'The person you keep hoping or expecting to walk through that door.'

I pressed the till button to print off the day's sales report. 'Hopefully not Ricky. I haven't heard from him since last Thursday so I think he's finally got the message and is out of my life for good. Sadly, hoping for Matt is as unrealistic as hoping for Santa.'

'Which just leaves your mum.'

'Stacey,' I said. 'She's *not* my mum.'

'Stacey, then.' Jodie flicked the main shop lights off. 'I hate to say this but, from what you've told me, it's very likely she won't get that letter because she'll have moved on. And if by some miracle she has stayed put for longer than five minutes, she's not the sort of woman who'll turn up for an emotional mother and daughter reunion.'

'I'm not expecting her to do that,' I snapped.

'Then what are you expecting?'

'For her to care enough to want to know how her mum died.'

Jodie shook her head. 'The last time she saw your grandparents was the day you were born. She didn't go to your grandpa's funeral so do you really think she'll care about the details? And, if she does, do you think she'll travel all the way from Dorset to ask you when she could just as easily email you?'

I ripped off the sales report and lifted the money tray out of the till with such ferocity that some of the change bounced onto the floor. 'No. But there's a tiny weeny part of me that wants to believe that she isn't the cold-hearted uncaring individual that I have her pegged as based on her letters. Because, if she really is that horrible, what does that make me?'

Jodie helped me retrieve the coins. 'It makes you Charlee Chambers, of course! It makes you an award-winning business owner, a much-loved granddaughter and the best friend a girl could ever dream of having.' Her voice cracked and she cleared her throat. 'It makes you you, Charlee. You are *not* her. You share some genes but you do *not* share a personality with her. Or a heart.' She swiped at a tear.

'Are you crying?'

'No!'

'You are.'

'I'm not. Well, maybe a bit. It just makes me so mad that you would even think that you could be like that woman. You don't need her in your life. Look at you! You've sent her one letter and you've been off your game all week. Ashleigh's noticed. Even Kieran asked me if you're okay because you snapped at him.'

I dropped the coins into the tray, feeling mortified by my behaviour. I'd been like a bear with a sore head all week because I was angry with Stacey and angry with myself. Jodie, Ashleigh and

Kieran had done nothing to deserve my wrath and I hated the thought of upsetting any of them.

'I didn't mean to snap at him.' I leaned against the counter, my head in my hands.

'I know you didn't and it's so unlike you,' Jodie said gently. 'And that worries me. Don't do this to yourself. Please. We've got an amazing weekend coming up with our one-year anniversary and the Christmas lights switch-on. There's so much to look forward to after that with Christmas approaching and you know it's your favourite time of year.'

It was but I couldn't seem to muster my usual excitement although that was mainly because Christmas had been ruined last year by Ricky's floorshow going viral and the aftermath of that.

'Come upstairs,' Jodie said. 'I'll let you decorate my tree if you like.'

'But you don't like putting it up until a week before Christmas.'

'And you would put it up in September if you had your own way so the first day of December is a reasonable compromise, don't you think?'

'Did you get some new decorations?'

'Yes.'

'Do they match?'

'Yes. Would I dare get anything that didn't when my landlady's Chief of the Christmas Tree Theme Police?'

I smiled. 'Okay. You know how to win me over.'

* * *

Ninety minutes later, listening to a soothing Michael Bublé Christmas album on repeat, the tree in Jodie's flat was decorated in silver, blue and white baubles, stars, and a few felt animals. We sat down with a glass of wine and a takeaway pizza (not one from Dice Pizza!)

'You look a lot happier now,' Jodie said.

'Bublé, Christmas, wine and pizza. It doesn't get much better than this.'

'You know what I mean. At the risk of breaking the good mood, what will you do if your mu... if Stacey gets in touch? Do you want a relationship with her?'

I took a sip of wine as I mulled it over. Downstairs earlier, I'd have snapped an immediate 'no' but now that I'd relaxed, it wasn't that straightforward.

'No. And yes.'

'Well, I'm glad we cleared that up.'

I shook my head. 'Sorry, Jodie. I know that doesn't make much sense. It's a no because I've read half of her letters and, to be honest, I don't like her based on those. But it's a yes because she's the only family I've got and, as I said, I feel like something's missing.'

Jodie stared at me for a moment, frowning. Then she smiled. 'If she does reappear, I hope you find what you're looking for. Whatever that is.'

'So do I.'

Jodie stared at me again. She looked as though she was going to say something, but then she yawned. 'Would it be rude if I kicked you out so I can get to bed?'

I stood up. 'I need to head off anyway. Big day tomorrow. Thanks for letting me decorate your tree.' I gave her a hug. 'See you in the morning.'

As I left the flat, I felt relaxed and content, but by the time I returned to Coral Court, my shoulders felt tense again because I knew what I was going to do. I was going to read the rest of Stacey's letters and I probably wasn't going to like what I read, but I needed to get over it then hopefully I could forget about her and move on.

26

I nearly slept in the following morning, exhausted after being up until the early hours reading through the pink-ribboned bundle of correspondence from Stacey and working myself into a sobbing mess.

There was no sense of date order within the bundles but it seemed the contents of the second bundle were from much earlier. Several letters from before and shortly after I was born conveyed exactly how she felt about me. At some point, my eyes burning with tears and tiredness, I'd fallen asleep among the scattered items and failed to set my alarm. If it hadn't been for Jodie ringing me shortly after 7.30 a.m., asking if she could borrow one of my tops for the evening's pub crawl, goodness knows what time I'd have awoken.

Showering quickly and tying my damp hair into a loose pony-tail, I grabbed my bag and dashed to work, cursing myself for letting Stacey get to me again. How was it that somebody I didn't know and had never met could have such an effect on my emotions? Well, I wasn't going to let her ruin my day. Although it was officially our one-year anniversary tomorrow, it made sense to run a full weekend of celebrations. We had various promotions planned and competitions running across each day. After work, we'd be joining the traders' celebration of the lights switch-on followed by a pub crawl. It would be an amazing day and a fabulous night and I wasn't going to give *her* a second thought. Hopefully.

Tears welled in my eyes as I approached Castle Street and clocked the large banner hanging up outside the shop, which Jodie had obviously sneakily ordered, flanked by two colourful balloon bundles:

CHARLEE'S CHOCOLATES IS ONE!
PLEASE COME IN AND HELP US CELEBRATE!

Unlocking the door, I hoped we had enough time to put up the posters and decorations I'd ordered for inside. I cursed Stacey again. If I'd been thinking straight, I'd have got the shop ready last night instead of needing to decorate Jodie's tree to cheer me up.

'Surprise!'

I jumped as the lights flicked on revealing Jodie, Ashleigh and Kieran, all grinning. I gazed round the shop feeling quite tearful. 'You've decorated!'

Jodie handed me a champagne flute. 'It's Bucks Fizz,' she said. 'I thought it might be a bit early for the hard stuff. Happy anniversary!'

Taking care not to pour my drink down her back, I hugged her, then Ashleigh. I even managed a half-hug with Kieran. He was learning. 'I can't believe you're all here so early and that you've put the decorations up for me. I was panicking that there wouldn't be time. And thank you for the banner outside. It's brilliant.'

'I've got these too,' Jodie said, pointing to a large badge pinned to her apron announcing our first anniversary. 'I've pinned yours to your apron already.'

As Ashleigh and Kieran prepared some trays of samples, I went out the back with my coat and bag.

Jodie followed me. 'How are you feeling this morning?'

I sighed. 'I read the rest of her letters last night.'

'Oh, Charlee. Why?'

I shrugged. 'I'd already opened Pandora's box.'

'And?'

'And I think even less of her than I did after the first batch, if that's possible.'

'Then forget about her and enjoy your day.'

I hung my coat up. 'Don't worry. I intend to.'

'Intend to what? Forget about her or to enjoy your day?'

I smiled. 'Both. Well, sort of. I want to tell you what was in the letters, but not today because, as you say, it's a day to celebrate. And I promise I'm not planning to tell you because I want to dwell on her but because you're my best friend and you know everything so I want you to know this too.'

Jodie gave me another hug. 'Whenever you're ready.'

* * *

Ashleigh and Kieran insisted on back-to-back Christmas music all day and, as they'd declared that Michael Bublé was for 'wrinkly oldies' this pretty much consisted of *Now Christmas* on a continuous loop. Thankfully the shop was busy so I didn't notice the repetition too much although it seemed that, any time there was a lull, it was always the same track.

My apprentices manned the till for most of the day, one of

them ringing through the orders while the other packed bags. Jodie and I restocked the shelves and chatted to new and regular customers. Every hour, I rang a hand bell to signal a new offer. It created a massive buzz of excitement in the shop. We'd set up a blackboard outside which Jodie updated with each new deal, helping entice new customers inside.

Humming along to Slade as I restocked a display of Christmas moulded figures, I felt myself relax for the first time since the interlude with Ricky got me all het up about missing something in my life. I had lots to be thankful for, including more friends and a better social life than I'd had at any other point in my life. I may have no family and no boyfriend, but I wasn't lonely. Not anymore.

I still found myself watching the door anxiously, but I wasn't trying to spot Stacey. Instead, I was watching out for Matt again. He'd texted to wish me a successful anniversary. He had hoped to bring his nieces down but Erin had been off sick from school for a couple of days so it depended on how she was feeling. If she was still poorly, he'd see me later for the pub crawl, providing World War III didn't kick off in the meantime.

It seemed that the good patch with Libby following his grand-dad's death was well and truly over. I'd picked up on a few niggles but nothing serious until now. Libby wanted Matt to go to her work's Christmas party tonight. He'd refused because it clashed with the Christmas lights switch-on and pub crawl. Over the past year, his company's services had been in demand on Castle Street and the traders all loved him. Reliable, friendly and with top quality work at a reasonable price, what wasn't there to love? So he'd been given an exclusive invite for tonight. Libby, however, wasn't impressed that he'd chosen us over her. Gina had managed to calm her down, reminding her that most of their colleagues weren't taking partners, but Matt suspected he hadn't heard the last of it because Libby didn't let go of things easily.

Yet they were still together. I didn't get it. A glimmer of hope was that they'd still made no plans for their wedding, but it was the faintest of faint glimmers on a dark day because building and furnishing their new home was their current priority and that was as big a commitment as getting married. Matt and I were obviously destined only to be friends and I was going to have to hope that I'd wake up one day and be over him. Was that a pig flying past my window?

* * *

By the time the shop closed for the day, Matt hadn't appeared. Either Erin was too poorly or it had kicked off with Libby again, as he'd predicted.

The team and I had some time to kill before the lights switch-on so I decided to run a 'Charlee's Chocolates Challenge'; something I'd introduced earlier in the year for a bit of fun. This one was a pairs challenge that involved throwing chocolate elves into each other's mouths with points awarded depending on throwing distance. I paired up with Kieran and Ashleigh was with Jodie but our two apprentices were ridiculously competitive, determined to win, pushing and shoving each other. Their expressions were so serious which Jodie and I found hilarious because we didn't take any of the challenges seriously at all, especially when the prizes were damaged stock.

Somehow Kieran and I won. He was rewarded with a decapitated snowman and I was rewarded with a stitch for laughing so much.

We stepped out of the shop onto the cobbles and I took a moment to look up and gaze at the unlit lights strung between the buildings, recalling how magical they'd looked last Christmas. I couldn't wait to see it again.

As we ambled along Castle Street towards the park, admiring the lit windows with their Christmassy brilliance, we were still giggling. Charlee's Chocolates Challenges had worked brilliantly for building the team and tonight's elf-throwing contest had been exactly what I needed to soothe the emotional wound I'd opened by reading Stacey's letters.

'That must have been the world's best joke,' said a voice behind us.

I turned round, my heart racing. 'Matt!'

He grinned and my heart melted further at the sight of those dimples. 'I could hear you lot giggling as soon as I rounded the corner.'

'We were doing a Charlee's Chocolates Challenge,' Kieran said. 'It was hilarious. I won a headless snowman.'

'Er... congratulations?' Matt suggested.

'It was awesome,' Ashleigh added.

'You know what's awesome?' Jodie asked. 'That I'm twice your age but I can whip your butts in a running race. Race you to the tree.' Without waiting for them, she set off sprinting down the street. With cries of 'cheat', Ashleigh and Kieran sprinted after her. I had to bite my lip to prevent me from smiling at Jodie's blatant tactics to leave Matt and me alone.

'You've managed to secure a get out of jail free card for the evening, then?' I asked.

'Literally. Going to that works do would have been like a prison sentence.'

'No World War III, then?'

Matt grimaced. 'Depends what your definition of war is.'

I tutted. 'What did she do?'

'Tried to talk me into being her taxi service for the evening which makes no sense because her company have already organised and paid for taxis.' He sounded like a defeated man and my heart broke for him. Perhaps his happy ever after wasn't with me but it didn't seem he was heading for one with Libby.

'When I reminded her that I'd been invited out, she gave me *the look*,' he continued. 'Then she packed her bag and stormed off to Gina's, telling me not to expect her home tonight. Her parting shot was something like, "Why do you always put your friends ahead of me?"'

'Oh, Matt, what do you see in her?' I put my hand over my mouth as my cheeks burned. 'Oh my God! Did I say that out loud? I'm so sorry.'

Matt laughed a deep belly laugh. 'Our Erin asked me that the other day after Libby refused to push her on the swing at the farm in case she snapped a nail. I was so shocked to hear it come from a six-year-old that I didn't know how to respond.'

I chewed my lip as I looked deep into his eyes. I had to be brave and push. This wasn't about me telling him how I felt about him; it was about being a friend and challenging him about a relationship that clearly didn't make him happy.

'And do you know how to respond now?' I asked.

He paused and seemed to drink me in causing my stomach to swirl like a washing machine on fast spin. His eyes were so mesmerising: deep brown with little flecks of gold like pools of dark chocolate sprinkled with honeycomb. I longed to touch his face, to run my fingers through his hair, to taste his kiss.

'I don't know anymore, Charlee. We've been together so long that I think it's become a habit and I'm not—'

A loud cheer interrupted him. 'What was that?' he asked spinning round.

'Crap! It's half six. It's the switch-on at the main tree. We're going to miss it.'

Matt grabbed my hand. 'Then we'd better run!'

As we ran down Castle Street, hand in hand, the lights above us sparked into life, as though our steps were activating them. The welcome banner illuminated as we reached the end of Castle Street, setting the stars and fireworks off. A couple of cars passing on the one-way street at the end of the cobbles stopped us in our tracks. We looked up as the star at the top of the tree lit up and sent a ripple of lights cascading down the branches.

Matt turned to me. 'Sorry I made you miss it.'

I shook my head, tears springing in my eyes. 'We didn't miss it. We were in the middle of it and it was beautiful.'

The cheering round the tree seemed to fade as we faced each other. I could hear my heart thumping fast, not from the run, but from the close proximity to the man I loved.

'Happy Christmas, Charlee,' he said.

'Happy Christmas, Matt.'

And then it happened. He bent forward and gently kissed me on the lips. It was brief. A casual observer might say that it was only a peck shared between friends. But, for me, it was a moment of pure heaven and I couldn't help but close my eyes. When I reluctantly opened them again, Matt was looking at me with his head on one side, frowning slightly.

'Are you okay?' I asked.

He nodded slowly. 'I wasn't, but I think I'm going to be. Charlee, I—'

'Charlee! Your hot chocolate's getting cold!' I looked over at Sarah's husband, Nick, and waved. For goodness' sake, what was it with interruptions this evening when Matt was mid-flow?

'I think you're wanted,' Matt said.

'You were about to say something.'

'I was, but we've got all night. We can talk later.'

But we didn't get a chance. Every time we came close to having a moment alone, somebody would appear asking if we wanted a drink, wishing me a happy anniversary, or asking if we were all set for Christmas.

'Can I walk you home later?' Matt asked after yet another interruption. 'There's something I need to talk to you about and I don't think we stand a chance unless we've ditched the crowd.'

'Of course.' I hoped he couldn't see my hands shaking. 'I'd like that.'

But we never got the chance to do that either. Matt's phone rang as the group were moving between The Old Theatre and Minty's. 'It's Gina,' he said, frowning. 'I'd better answer it. Hello? Yeah, hi Gina... Sorry, I didn't hear it... She's done what? ... Slow down! ... What? ... Jesus!... Yeah... yeah. Okay. I'll see you there.'

'That didn't sound good,' I said.

He ran his hand down his facial hair, shaking his head. 'It's Libby. She's taken something. Gina isn't sure what, but she's collapsed. They've rushed her to hospital.'

'Oh my God! Matt!'

His face was grey. 'I'd better go.'

'Do you want me to come?'

'Yes!' Then he shook his head. 'No. Better not. Libby doesn't ... you know.'

I nodded. He didn't need to say the words. The fact that Libby didn't like me had been obvious from the day we met.

'Sorry, Charlee.'

'Will you ring me and let me know how she is? If you can, that is. It doesn't matter what time. I'll keep my phone on.'

'I will if I can.' He gave me a quick hug before turning and sprinting down the pedestrianised precinct, then disappearing round a corner towards the nearest taxi rank. Poor Matt. And poor Libby. She wasn't my favourite person but I hoped she was okay. She'd taken something? What did that mean? Had she taken drugs? Had she overdosed? Whatever it was, if she'd collapsed and been rushed to hospital, it didn't sound good.

27

I peered out of the shop window on Thursday morning, watching the rain bouncing off the cobbles and running down the street in ever-widening streams. It was only 11 a.m. but it was so dark, I could have been fooled into believing it was dusk. What a day!

Across the street, Sarah and Cathy stood in the open doorway of Seaside Blooms, shaking their heads. They waved as they spotted me, then beat a hasty retreat into the shelter of the shop as the downpour intensified.

'Hot chocolate,' Jodie said, handing me a mug with one of my chocolate stirrers sticking out of it. 'It feels like the sort of day where tea and coffee just won't cut it.'

I smiled. 'I think you're right.'

We stood by the window containing this year's chocolate display – a Santa's workshop scene in which the elves were making chocolates instead of toys, supervised by a giant moulded Santa – and watched the rain pelting down, gently swirling our chocolate stirrers. I sighed. 'The last time we had rain like this, we took a grand total of £8. Do you remember?'

She laughed. 'Two customers all day, wasn't it? At least it was nice first thing so we've exceeded that already.'

I turned away from the window. 'Anyone who comes out in this is either desperate or mad. We might as well go into the workshop, have a seat, and enjoy these. I doubt we'll have any customers.' We'd hear the bell if, by some miracle, anyone braved it.

'Any more news from Matt?' Jodie asked when we sat down. Matt had texted me from hospital late on Saturday evening to say that Libby had come round but hadn't wanted to talk about it. Gina had already filled him in and he had some thinking to do and would call me later. He'd then phoned on Sunday night with the details, gleaned from Gina.

Libby and Gina had downed two bottles of wine between them before they'd even left Gina's house and at least another bottle each at the party. Realising that she'd had too much when she went to sit down and landed in a heap on the floor instead, Gina ordered a strong coffee and hoped she hadn't made a fool of herself in front of her manager. When she suggested that Libby might like to do the same, Libby had turned on her, accusing her of sounding like Matt; always out to ruin her fun. She'd stormed off in a huff.

Gina didn't see her for another half an hour or so, but then she clocked her on the dance floor with a couple of men from another company, also out on their works do. Although she hadn't expanded on that, Matt said it was obvious that there'd been more than dancing going on. Gina had watched Libby stagger off the dance floor a couple of songs later and suspected she was going to be sick. She was annoyed with Libby so left her to it but, after about ten minutes, she decided she'd better play the good friend and hold Libby's hair back. She found her collapsed on the floor in one of the toilet cubicles in a pool of vomit.

When the paramedics arrived, they checked Libby's eyes and asked Gina what she'd taken. Gina pointed them in the direction of the men she'd been with and one of them admitted to giving her Ecstasy so at least the paramedics knew what they were dealing with.

'He rang last night,' I told Jodie, 'but he couldn't talk for long because he was going to watch Lucy and Erin in a dance show or something. Libby's staying at Gina's – more comfortable than the caravan – but he says she's doing well and she's going back to work on Monday.'

'And how's Matt?'

'He sounded exhausted.'

'I'm not surprised. What was she thinking? Is it finally over for them?'

'I don't know. Obviously I couldn't ask that on Sunday but it didn't feel appropriate to ask last night either. If she was kissing another man or men, even, I can't see him wanting to stick around, but he's hinted that she's had some problems in the past. I'm worried for him that he feels obligated to look after her. Maybe that's why he's put up with her crap for all these years.'

Jodie slurped on her hot chocolate. 'All you can do is be there for him, whatever he decides.'

'I know. I will be.'

The bell sounded. Jodie went to stand up, but I beat her to it. 'You finish your drink. I'll see to them.'

I pushed through the saloon doors. A tall, slim woman probably in her late forties/early fifties was tentatively leaning a golf umbrella against the wall. She looked extremely stylish in a forest green wool coat, cinched at the waist, and high-heeled brown suede boots.

'Morning!' I said. 'You're brave coming out in this.'

She ran her hands through her dark shoulder-length hair. 'Or mad.'

I laughed. 'I wasn't going to say that.'

'But I bet you're thinking it.' Her voice was confident and refined, reminding me of Nanna's favourite actress, Audrey Hepburn.

'You've got me. Was there anything special you were looking for, or are you just browsing?'

'Just browsing, if that's okay.'

'It certainly is. Take your time and let me know if you have any questions.'

I moved behind the serving counter and busied myself tidying the bags and boxes.

'Has the shop been open long?' asked the woman as she browsed the Christmas figures on the table display.

'Just over a year.'

'Is it your shop?'

'Yes. I'm the Charlee in the shop name.'

'Is that your real name?' The woman moved over to one of the dressers. 'Like *Charlie and the Chocolate Factory*?'

'My Grandpa used to have a chocolate shop and St...' I hesitated. I didn't want to call her Stacey but it was too complicated for a stranger. 'My mum used to call it his chocolate factory so she named me Charlee when I was born, but spelt differently with me being a girl.'

'I like it.'

'Thank you.'

She turned her back again and continued browsing. I watched her profile as she studied a display of chocolate drops. There was something familiar about her, but I was sure we hadn't met.

'What's the best flavour?' she asked.

'All of them!' I took it as an invitation to join her at the stand. 'Obviously, I'm slightly biased because I make them.'

She raised her eyebrows. 'You make them all?'

'Oh yes. Everything is made right here on the premises by me and my team. Nothing's bought in except the ingredients.'

'Even that giant Santa in the window?'

I smiled. 'All me.'

'Very impressive.'

'Thank you.'

She turned back to the chocolate drops so I took my opportunity to focus on them again. 'I like milk chocolate best and my personal favourite is salted caramel. I can't get enough of the stuff, but my colleague Jodie prefers dark chocolate and if it's orange-flavoured, she's in heaven, so the orange fizz are her favourites. One of our apprentices loves white chocolate and the other loves the mint ones. They're on three for two at the moment, so there's a perfect opportunity for customers to try a few and find their own favourite.'

She tapped her finger against her cheek. 'I don't think I could decide. It would probably be six for four or even nine for six.'

'Don't let me stop you,' I joked.

'Actually, there is something I wanted to ask you. Those chocolates with the letters on, would you do a discount if someone wanted quite a few?'

'It depends what they want. If we're talking three of the smallest arrangements, then no, but if we're talking several of the larger ones, there's always a deal to be done. Did you have something in mind?'

She nodded. 'I'm leaving work soon and I want to get a thank you gift for everyone on my team. There are twelve of them. I thought about a bottle of wine but one's pregnant and two of them don't drink so chocolates are probably safer. I was wondering about spelling out thank you and their names.'

'That's a lovely idea,' I said. 'I'd need to work out the price based on their names as some may be a larger box than others, but I'd imagine I could do you a 20 per cent discount on that volume, if that would be of interest.'

'Really?' Her eyes lit up. 'Thank you. That would be great. I'll have a think about it and let you know but, in the meantime, I think you might have convinced me to give the salted caramel drops a go.'

'You will *not* be disappointed,' I said as she reached for a bag off the display.

'Oh, goodness, I'm a sucker for a bargain. I'll have three.'

I laughed. 'Please don't feel you have to. You are allowed to purchase a single bag.'

'Not possible,' she said. 'Like you, I love milk chocolate. Cinder toffee and the milk chocolate orange fizz are also calling to me.'

'Good choices.'

We made our way over to the till and I rang up her purchases. 'I'll put our card in the bag and if you to decide to go for the leaving gifts, you're welcome to ring, email, or send us a Facebook message.'

'You said your granddad had a chocolate shop...?' she asked while we waited for the card payment machine to connect. 'Was that in Whitsborough Bay?'

'No. It was in Brockington, near Hull. That's where I was brought up.'

'What brought you to Whitsborough Bay, then?'

I ripped off the two receipts and handed the customer her copy. 'My grandparents brought me up but they've both passed away now. When my Nanna died from cancer last year, my boyfriend at the time suggested this might be a good place to set up shop so I moved. He wasn't right about many things, but he was right about that.'

'I'm sorry about your grandparents. And about the boyfriend.'

I smiled. 'My grandparents were amazing. My boyfriend was far from it. But thank you.'

She took the bag and glanced out of the window. 'I'm kidding myself that the rain has slowed down, aren't I?'

'Sorry. I think it might have just got heavier again. You're welcome to stay a bit longer.'

She walked towards the door and picked up her brolly. 'My boots are already squelching so it probably doesn't make much difference either way. I'll go for it.' She loosened the fastener from the brolly. 'It was lovely speaking to you, Charlee. I'm really impressed with your chocolate factory. I wish you every success for the future.'

'Thank you. And good luck paddling out there.'

She laughed as she opened the door and made a dash for it.

'Do you think she'll order those leaving gifts?' Jodie asked, appearing from the workshop with my mug of hot chocolate.

I shook my head.

'Really? I thought she sounded pretty keen.'

'No. I'm fairly certain I'll never see her again.'

Jodie stared at me, frowning. 'What am I missing? Why are you smiling?'

I took my mug from her and gulped down the cool liquid. 'I'm smiling because I think that was Stacey. I think that was my birth mother.'

28

'Mummy! Look! Ooh, Mummy, look!'

I swear my uterus contracted with each cute little squeal as the excited toddler gazed in awe at the chocolate angels, elves, snowmen, penguins and Santas.

'You can pick one of the little ones,' his mum said.

'That one,' cried the little boy, pointing at a snowman.

As she reached for it, he pointed at a penguin instead. 'That one! No! Santa!'

'We might be some time,' she said, turning to me, rolling her eyes.

I smiled. 'I made some really small ones this morning but I haven't packaged them yet. I could do you a bag of mixed figures. They're about a third of the size and you get six in a bag, which is a mini one of each of those, plus Rudolph.'

'Rudolph!' the toddler shrieked. 'Want Rudolph!'

'About a third of the size?' his mum asked.

I nodded. 'And they're hollow so it's not like he'll be having too much chocolate.'

'That sounds wonderful, thank you.'

I left Jodie in the shop while I went into the workshop to fill a bag from the cooling trays. I heard the bell tinkle a couple of times but when I walked back into the shop, there was only the one customer with her son.

'I've popped an extra Santa in there, just for you,' I said. 'No extra charge.'

'Thank you. That's so kind. I'll be back in later in the week to get some stocking fillers for the kids, when a certain somebody's at nursery.'

When she'd paid and gone, Jodie handed me an envelope. 'Some bloke in a suit popped in and asked if I'd give you this.'

'Did he leave his name?'

'Nope. He looked like he was on official business.'

Ripping open the envelope, I pulled out a single sheet of paper on town council headed paper. 'Oh! I know what this is. Remember a couple of months ago when a woman from the council dropped by? They'd got a grant to do some mystery shopping for some of the independent businesses as part of a tourism project, so I said to count us in. Well, it's happened. We've been mystery shopped.'

'Ooh, how exciting. I wonder who it was.'

'It was on Thursday last week,' I said, reading down the report. 'Oh. Pants.'

'We got a bad report?'

'No, nothing like that. It's actually a glowing report. Top scores. I'm saying pants because our mystery shopper was the woman who asked about the chocolate letters for leaving gifts.'

'Oh. So that means she doesn't really want them. Pants indeed.'

I shook my head. 'It's pants because that means she wasn't Stacey.'

'Charlee! I thought you'd decided she wasn't worth another minute of your time!'

I slipped the report back into the envelope. 'I had and, after I'd convinced myself that the mystery shopper was Stacey, I felt like I'd got closure. I'd met her, she'd said sorry that Nanna had died, she knew it was cancer that took her, and she'd congratulated me on an impressive business as though she was saying she was proud of me. I realised that's all I wanted from her. I didn't want or need to hear why she'd given me away because I've read the letters so I already know.'

I'd finally had a chance to tell Jodie what I'd discovered in the letters over a Chinese takeaway on Sunday night. From the early letters, I'd gleaned that Stacey had unexpectedly fallen pregnant when she was twenty. She'd been backpacking round Europe, meeting lots of new friends and partying hard, which was obviously code for sleeping around because she didn't know who the father was. She loved her uncommitted lifestyle and wasn't ready to give it up for a baby.

Stacey and Nanna had been really close back then and she'd phoned home in tears after she took a pregnancy test. Nanna had convinced her to fly home and talk about it. Stacey was determined to have a termination but Nanna convinced her to go through with the pregnancy and see how she felt at the end of it, promising that they'd bring me up if Stacey didn't want to.

Nanna had obviously hoped that Stacey would fall in love with the life growing inside of her but a difficult pregnancy and a traumatic birth did the opposite. Stacey supposedly went for some fresh air eight hours after my birth, and never returned. A day later, she was in Spain and my grandparents now had the opportunity to bring up a second child; something they'd always longed for but obviously hadn't expected to get in this way.

* * *

The rest of the day passed with a steady flow of customers and I pushed all thoughts of Stacey out of my mind again. It was pointless thinking about her. Nearly three weeks had passed since I'd written to her and she hadn't been in touch. She'd either moved again so the letter hadn't made it to her, or she'd read it and wasn't bothered. No, that was unfair. She probably *was* bothered about her mum dying, but she wasn't bothered about me. She'd never wanted me and I needed to accept that it was nothing personal; it was about her. I'd never missed out. I'd had an incredibly happy childhood, full of love and laughter. As far as I could see, the only downside to being brought up by grandparents was the generation gap which resulted in them leaving my life earlier than parents might have done in the normal scheme of things. Which left a huge gap and an ache that would probably never go away.

We had a post-school rush in the shop but things calmed down from about 4.45 p.m., which they often did. Jodie fiddled with the music and the familiar opening drum beats of Band Aid filled the shop. 'I thought we'd have *Now Christmas* on for a change,' she said, giggling.

As we dusted and straightened the stock, Jodie taking the side wall and me the back, we took it in turns to sing along, doing exaggerated impressions of each artist. We were so into the song that we didn't hear the doorbell or see the customer come in. It was only when I turned round to play an air guitar riff – something that I've never, ever done in my whole life – that I spotted the woman.

'Oh my goodness, I'm so sorry,' I said.

Jodie called, 'Sorry,' too as she turned down the music.

I tucked the duster into the pocket on the front of my apron.

'Apologies for the appalling karaoke. Can I help you with anything?'

She looked me up and down, one hand on her hip, her other palm pressed against her cheek. 'I can't believe it. After all these years, it's really you.'

'Sorry?'

'It's Charlee, isn't it?' she said, a slight European burr to her voice. She ran a slender hand through her long dark hair. 'I'd have recognised you anywhere. You have so much of your father in you.'

29

'Oh my God, Charlee. This is huge,' Jodie whispered as I pulled on my coat. 'Are you okay? Do you want me to come with you? Are you okay? I've already asked that. But are you?' I'd never seen her quite so agitated.

'I'm fine. My birth mother who I have never met before is in my shop and wants to take me out for a drink and, strangely, I feel very calm about that. Unlike you. Are *you* okay?'

'I'm in shock. I genuinely didn't expect you to ever hear from her. How can you be so calm about this?'

I shrugged. 'Shock too, perhaps? It'll probably hit me later.' I fastened my coat buttons. 'Are you sure you don't mind finishing up on your own?'

'It's no problem. You go with her, but either come and tell me all about it straight after or ring me, no matter how late. I'll be pacing the flat, desperate to know. Promise?'

'I promise.' I hugged Jodie tightly then pulled my bag onto my shoulder. 'Wish me luck.'

'Luck. Loads of it.'

* * *

Stacey and I walked to the pub in relative silence, agreeing that there was much to be said but that it was pointless starting a conversation then having to stop to order drinks. I'd thought it might be awkward, but it felt more like a companionable silence. She admired the enormous tree outside the shopping centre and I pointed out some of my favourite Christmassy shop window displays and a party dress I adored in the window of one of the clothes shops.

We secured a table in a quiet corner of The Old Theatre. She removed her charcoal wool coat and a cream scarf, draped them over the back of a spare chair and headed to the bar.

I removed my coat and watched her placing our drinks order. She looked younger than her fifty years, with straightened dark hair reaching her shoulder blades and big brown eyes. She was about the same build as me and, even though she was wearing jeans, boots and a plain top, just like me, she looked so much more stylish in them than I did.

Moments later, she placed a bottle of wine and two glasses on the table. 'I know you asked for a small one but I thought we might need more,' she said, pouring us both a glass. 'Or I might.'

'Thank you,' I said, reaching for my glass and taking a grateful gulp.

'Thank you for letting me know about my mother,' she said as she sat down. 'I wish I'd known she was ill.'

I didn't want to be on the defensive, but I couldn't help it. 'Nanna said she wasn't in touch with you and I had no reason to doubt her. I had no idea where you lived or even if you were still alive.'

'Oh, Charlee, I wasn't having a go at you,' she said gently. 'I was just thinking out loud. I know it's not your fault and it's not

Mum's either. I know I've moved around a lot over the years, but I've always let her know where I am so she could have contacted me if she'd wanted to. She obviously didn't want me to know.'

She didn't sound angry or bitter; more resigned. For a moment, I actually felt sorry for her. She had, after all, just found out that she'd lost her mum. Even though they hadn't seen each other since I was born, they'd remained in contact. It had to have hurt. 'I'm sorry you had to find out by letter.'

'It's okay. You had no other way of doing it. Was it cancer?'

I nodded. 'She'd fought it once already. You probably already knew that?' I paused as she nodded. 'When it came back, I think she was too tired to fight it again. She was ready to join Grandpa. She died the day after I turned thirty.' My voice cracked and I blinked back the tears. I didn't want her to see me cry. 'I scattered her ashes on Spurn Point where we'd scattered Grandpa's.'

Stacey smiled. 'They both loved it there. I'm sorry for your loss. I know you were all really close.'

The loss hit me like a train. I tried to blink back the tears but there were too many. 'I miss them so much,' I admitted. 'They were my parents.' I didn't say it to hurt her, but it was how I felt.

'I know. And if your childhood was half as happy as mine, you were a very lucky girl.'

I rummaged in my bag for a tissue and dabbed at my eyes. 'Did you just come here to thank me for letting you know about Nanna?'

She sipped on her wine then sighed. 'I came here to explain why I didn't bring you up myself.'

'There's no need. I already know.'

Her eyebrows shot up in surprise. 'How?'

'Nanna kept your letters and postcards. The man who bought their house from me found them under the floorboards and I read them so I know all about you and your crazy life travelling round Europe, finding yourself unexpectedly pregnant by God knows who, and not...' I gasped. 'Hang on. When you first came into the shop, you said I had so much of my father in me.'

'You do.'

'But you said in your letters that you had no idea who my father was.'

She shrugged. 'It was easier that way.'

'So there weren't loads of men?'

'Oh no. Far from it. There's only ever been one man for me and, for four delicious months, he was my whole life and I thought we'd be together forever. Unfortunately, we don't always get what our heart desires.' Her eyes glistened with tears as she gazed past me, clearly lost in the past for a moment. She gave herself a little shake and looked me in the eyes again. 'I know exactly who your father was... is, Charlee. You do too.'

'What? I do not!'

She shook her head. 'All those years and he never even gave the slightest hint that you were his daughter?'

'Who?'

'None of them said *anything*?'

She looked genuinely surprised, but I hadn't a clue what she was talking about. 'Who's my father?'

Stacey bit her lip; a gesture I recognised from myself. 'Your father... and this is going to be a bit of a shock to you given that they've obviously managed to keep it secret... but your father is Pierre DuPont.'

Pierre? My former boss and great friend? 'Bullshit! He is not!'

'Think about it, Charlee. You *know* he is.'

Oh. My. God! A million little things suddenly made sense. He'd always treated me like a surrogate daughter, but I'd assumed that was just because I was reliable, great with customers and good at my job so I'd earned his respect and made him proud; not because I actually *was* his daughter. The dark hair, dark eyes and olive complexion weren't just coincidence; they were shared genes. No wonder customers often assumed I was his daughter and that Gabby and I were sisters. They'd recognised an actual biological connection.

I registered something else Stacey had said. 'You said *they* knew? Are you saying Lillian and Gabby knew?'

Stacey nodded.

I picked up the bottle and topped up my glass. 'You'd better start talking.'

'Okay. Here goes from the start. Despite what you might think, given my absence from their lives, I genuinely loved my parents. They were an amazing couple and I had a wonderfully happy childhood. From a young age, I would spend Saturdays in Dad's chocolate factory, as I called it, eagerly lapping up everything that he showed me. I knew that I wanted to be a master chocolatier from the very start. Give me a bowl of chocolate and a piping bag, and I'm in heaven. I'm sure you feel the same.'

'I do.' But I was stunned to hear that she did. I'd never heard of her love of chocolate from my grandparents but that was hardly surprising when I'd been told so little about her. I wasn't sure how I felt about us having a shared passion. It had been easier to imagine we had nothing in common.

Stacey smiled. 'I suppose it's in our blood. Anyway, the plan was for me to take over the chocolate factory one day. Working with chocolate every day and running my own business was exactly what I wanted, but I started to feel really anxious about it. It wasn't the thought of actually running the chocolate factory, but more the thought that I'd be doing that forever and would never experience anything different. I'd only ever lived in Brockington and I'd only ever worked in Dad's shop. It scared me. I felt trapped. Does that make any sort of sense?'

I smiled wryly. 'Perfect sense. I felt the same and retrained as a pastry chef because of it.' Another thing in common. This was unnerving.

'Oh yes, I remember Mum saying something about that when she...' Stacey shook her head. 'I'll come to that part later. So, there I was, having this panic about the future when my best friend, Miriam, asked me if I wanted to take a year out and backpack round Europe with her. Definitely! Mum and Dad were a little surprised at my decision but they understood and reassured me that, if I changed my mind about my career while I was away, they'd support me in whatever I decided to do. I was certain about being a chocolatier, but I was also certain that I needed some time out first.

'Miriam and I set off on our travels in late August after we'd finished college. We found temporary jobs like cleaning and waitressing and would tend to work for a bit, travel for a bit, then work again. After about six months of travelling, we reached a small town in the south of France called Roussillon. It was really pretty and, to be honest, the novelty of constantly being on the move had worn off so we made an agreement to stay in Roussillon for longer than usual, as long as we were both able to find work. Miriam found a job as an English language assistant in a local school. I didn't fancy waitressing again so I thought I might see if any of the shops needed staff. That's when I came across a chocolaterie with a sign in the window seeking staff.'

'Pierre's chocolaterie?' I'd known that he'd owned one in France before moving to the UK and taking over Grandpa's although I hadn't known the name of the town.

Stacey took a sip of her wine and nodded. 'Yes. Pierre's. I'd studied French at school and had been reasonably competent but I'd become fluent during my travels. There's nothing like living and working in the country for honing your language skills.

When I told him that I was a trained master chocolatier, he seemed doubtful because of my age, so I pointed at the various chocolates he had on display and told him exactly how he'd have made each of them.' She smiled at the memory. 'I still remember the stunned expression on his face, bless him. He offered me the job there and then.'

My mind was racing ahead. Pierre was married to Lillian now but Gabby was older than me so the maths didn't work. 'Where was Lillian?'

'She'd walked out on him taking Gabby with her. Gabby was only four months old and Pierre hadn't seen it coming. She left leaving a note that read something like, "I don't love you anymore. Don't look for us. Gabby isn't yours."'

'No! Pierre's not Gabby's dad?

Stacey shook her head. 'He *is* her dad, but Lillian said she wasn't because—'

'Sorry, I'm interrupting your flow. Continue the story and I'll keep quiet.'

'I don't mind. You probably have a million questions.'

'Yes, but I'll ask them later. Please continue.'

Stacey took another sip of wine. 'So Lillian had walked out saying that Pierre wasn't to look for them. Naturally he did, but even her parents had no idea where she was and were as stunned as him at the suggestion that he wasn't Gabby's father. None of her friends knew where she was or, if they did, they weren't telling him.

'Several weeks passed and I settled into the chocolaterie. Pierre taught me some different techniques and I learned about catering to the French palette instead of the English one. It was a fantastic experience and I was so glad we'd chosen to stay in the town. Then I got home from work one day to find Miriam packing her bags. She'd fallen in love with one of the teachers and he'd asked her to move in with him. We had a huge argument about it. I accused her of being selfish because there was no way I could afford the rent and bills on my own, and she accused me of being selfish for only thinking of me and not being happy for her for finding love. I laughed at her and said that it was lust, not love, and that it probably wouldn't last until the summer.'

'Did it?' I bit my lip. 'Sorry. I'm interrupting again.'

Stacey smiled. 'Miriam and Laurent are happily married with five children and two grandchildren. I was happy to be proved wrong and I'm grateful that she forgave me and has remained my best friend for all these years. As for me, I told Pierre that I'd have to leave work because I had nowhere to live. He didn't want to lose a talented chocolatier and insisted I stay in the spare room in his apartment above the chocolaterie. Working together and living together, we became really close. It was only friendship at first, but it quickly became more.'

She smiled again. I could tell from the warmth in her voice and the sparkle in her eyes every time she mentioned Pierre that she had loved– and still did – love him.

'I was nineteen and he was thirty-four but they were just numbers. The fifteen years between us made no difference. But then...' She sighed and looked down.

'What happened next?' I prompted, desperate to know more.

'We'd had ten glorious weeks together when Lillian returned. It was early August and I remember that day so well. Pierre was chasing me round the shop with a piping bag, threatening to squirt me, when the door opened. This stunning brunette was standing there holding a baby and I knew. I knew it was her.' She paused and took a gulp of her wine. 'I told Pierre that I was taking my lunch break and that he could find me by the fountain when he was ready. Two hours I sat there. When Pierre finally appeared, he looked like that same broken man I'd met on the day I enquired about the job.'

'Where had Lillian been?' I asked.

'In some sort of clinic. Before Gabby, they'd tried for a baby for six years, during which time Lillian had two miscarriages and a stillbirth at seven months. Their relationship had understandably been strained to breaking point and they'd been ready to separate when Lillian discovered she was pregnant with Gabby. Pierre's not the sort to walk out on his responsibilities so he stayed with Lillian, even though he didn't love her anymore. Lillian couldn't relax. She spent the whole pregnancy waiting for something to go wrong. When a healthy baby arrived, she became convinced that they'd still lose her, perhaps to cot death. She barely slept at night, constantly checking to make sure Gabby was still breathing. She'd managed to keep her worries from Pierre because she'd insisted on separate rooms so that he wasn't disturbed by the baby crying when he had a business to run. One day, Lillian was playing with Gabby on the bed and, exhausted, she fell asleep. When Lillian awoke, she'd rolled over and realised that one inch further and she'd have smothered Gabby. At that point, she knew she needed some help so she checked in to a clinic where she was diagnosed with chronic pre- and post-natal depression and anxiety, or something like that.'

'I understand checking into a clinic, but I don't understand why she didn't tell Pierre.'

'Apparently she was worried that Pierre would see her as an unfit mother and, because they'd been on the verge of divorcing before she fell pregnant, she thought that he might still leave her and take Gabby from her. So she ran away and told him that Gabby wasn't his to stop him from doing that. You and I both know that Pierre would never have done anything like that, but Lillian's head was a mess and this seemed to make sense to her.'

'Poor Pierre and Lillian,' I said, my heart breaking for them. 'That's so tragic. I had no idea they'd been through anything like that.'

'Nobody should go through anything like that,' Stacey said, her eyes full of sadness. 'Lillian had received a lot of help at the clinic, but I could tell she still had issues.'

'What did you do? It must have been so awkward.'

Stacey shrugged. 'It was horrendous so I did the only thing I could do. I left. Pierre didn't love her anymore, but they were still married and they had a baby together. Lillian needed him. Gabby needed him. I knew he loved me but I couldn't make him choose between his family and me, so it was my turn to leave him a note.'

'What did it say?'

'Something like, "I love you too much to ask you to choose between your family and me. Be happy." Then I packed my bags and caught the train to Spain. And kept moving. And kept moving. And kept moving. I thought that if I didn't settle anywhere and didn't form any relationships, I couldn't get hurt again. And then I discovered that I was pregnant with you. I was nineteen, miles away from home, and I was alone.'

Although she didn't say the word, it was obvious to me that she'd also been terrified. I would have been in her position. For the first time ever, I felt empathy towards her. This wasn't a woman who'd slept around and had no idea who my father was. This was a woman who'd loved very deeply and had sacrificed her own happiness so the man she loved could keep his family.

She sipped on her wine then resumed her story. 'I agonised over what to do but the only thing I was sure of was that Pierre had a right to know. I travelled back to Roussillon to tell him. I wasn't sure what I wanted from him. I wasn't even sure whether I wanted to go through with the pregnancy, but I couldn't lie to him like Lillian had. My timing was horrendous. There was a festival on in the town and everyone was out in the streets celebrating. Pierre was there with Lillian and Gabby. I watched them for a while and they looked like the perfect happy family, laughing and fussing over the baby. I couldn't do it. I couldn't be the one who broke that up and perhaps tip Lillian over the edge again, so I left town without telling Pierre.'

'That must have been hard.'

'One of the two hardest things I've ever done in my life.' She looked down into her glass and lightly ran her finger round the rim. 'You've read all my letters or just a few?'

'All of them. I know you didn't want to keep me.'

She looked up at me, her eyes filled with tears. 'I'm so sorry, Charlee. I would never have told you that as I can't begin to imagine how awful it must be to hear that. I loved Pierre so much and the constant reminder of him and a love that couldn't be would have been too much for me. I rang my mum in tears, telling her that I was going to come home for a termination and I wanted her to be with me.'

'She talked you out of it, though. Obviously, or I wouldn't be here.'

'I'd already pretty much talked myself out of it by the time I got home, so Mum didn't need to do much convincing. I knew I couldn't keep you myself, though. I mentioned adoption and that's when Mum and Dad came up with the suggestion that I see how I felt after the birth and, if I didn't change my mind, they'd bring you up instead. If that happened, I could be as involved or detached as I wanted.'

'And you chose detached.'

'You were so beautiful,' she said, playing with her wine glass. 'But you were your father. You were born with a shock of dark hair and olive skin and all I could see was him. So I did the only thing I knew how to do. I left. I kept on running, convinced that if

I kept moving, I wouldn't form any relationships and I wouldn't need to think about you. I couldn't break the home ties, though. I kept sending Mum postcards and letters. I made out that I had this amazing life that I'd never have experienced if I'd been burdened with an unwanted baby. I never asked about you, which you'll know from reading my letters, but she wrote back and told me all about you. She sent photos, pictures you'd drawn at school, your first tooth, a lock of hair after your first haircut.' Stacey paused and wiped her eyes. 'I pretended I wasn't interested. I never thanked her or acknowledged what she'd sent, but I didn't ask her to stop. Instead, I moved on even more frequently so I had an excuse to write home again meaning news would follow about my little girl who was growing up without me.' Tears trailed down Stacey's face and she wiped at them, sniffing. 'Sorry. I was determined not to do this.'

I hadn't realised I was crying too until she passed me a tissue. I'd hated her when I'd read those letters. I'd pegged her as selfish, self-centred, and heartless, never stopping to think that there was a corresponding set of letters that could tell a very different story.

Stacey emptied the remnants of the bottle into our glasses. 'I think we need another one.'

Without waiting for a response, she strode up to the bar, giving me a chance to pull myself together before she returned.

Silently, she topped up our glasses again.

'When did you tell Pierre?' I asked.

'A person can't keep running forever. I found myself back in France, in Paris. I liked it there. It felt like home so I decided to stay for a while. On the way to work each day, I passed a choco-laterie. Some days, I'd rush past it. Other days, I'd gaze into the window and allow myself a moment to think about Pierre and you. On this particular day, I looked in the window and they'd arranged chocolates into a large number six to celebrate their sixth anniversary. It was your sixth birthday that day. For six whole years, I'd been running and hiding and lying as easily as I'd been breathing. I realised that it wasn't fair to keep the truth from Pierre so I wrote to him. He came to Paris to find out more and, after that, we stayed in touch. I'd send him duplicates of the letters and photos Mum sent me. It probably seems pretty strange to hear that you were in both our lives for all those years, yet you had no idea. Or at least I'm assuming you had no idea.'

'As far as I was aware, you weren't in touch with Nanna at all.'

'I was. Regularly. For the next decade, I continued to move, although not quite as often, and I kept writing to Mum and passing on duplicates of her responses to the post box that Pierre had set up. Pierre and I met up when we could and he kept saying he wanted to leave Lillian to be with me. I wouldn't let him. I knew how painful it was to walk away from a child and I wasn't prepared to let him do that to himself or to Gabby. I said earlier that walking away from Pierre without telling him about you was one of the two hardest things I'd ever done. Walking out on you was the other.'

My head was reeling, not only about my parentage but how Stacey had felt about me for all of these years. I'd imagined she'd not given me a second thought and the letters had backed that up.

'If you felt this way about me, why didn't you come back to Brockington and become part of my life?'

She sighed. 'It's a great question and I've asked myself the same thing over and over. At first, it was a self-preservation thing. Then it became more about Mum and Dad. I could tell from Mum's letters how devoted they were to you and how much it meant having a second chance at being parents. They'd always wanted a big family and it never happened for them. How could I let them have one, two, three, six, ten years with you then waltz back in and stake my claim? It would have broken their hearts.'

We sat in silence for a moment while I mulled it over. I could see her logic, but I didn't think that Nanna and Grandpa would have reacted like that. I think they'd have welcomed her back and it's not like they'd not have had a role to play in my life. They were still my grandparents.

'I know what you're probably thinking,' Stacey said. 'You're probably thinking that I should have done it anyway. I thought about it constantly, but I never took that step and, as the years passed, it felt too late. If I had a time machine, perhaps I'd have done things differently. Actually, there's no perhaps about it. I *would* have done things differently. I'm genuinely sorry for any pain or confusion I caused you.'

I wasn't sure what to say. I couldn't say it was fine, and I couldn't say she hadn't really caused me any pain or confusion because, despite my main feeling being indifference, those two emotions certainly had featured over the years. I decided to change the subject instead. 'How did Lillian find out?'

'You were sixteen and had passed your GCSEs with flying colours. Mum and Dad took you out to celebrate and there was this photo of you jumping in the air. You know the one?'

I nodded. 'They got me to pretend I was at a graduation ceremony, as though I was throwing a mortar board into the air.'

'You looked so happy. Pierre and I both loved that photo and he kept a copy in his wallet but Lillian found it. She only needed to glance at the photo to know you were Pierre's so the truth came out.' Stacey bit her lip and shook her head. 'She went mad. She told him she never wanted to see him again and she'd make sure that Gabby knew what a liar and cheat he was. She told the whole town. They were a close-knit community and they looked after their own. Lillian was a fifth-generation Roussillon resident and

Pierre was an incomer through marriage. The villagers boycotted the chocolaterie and his landlord tripled the rent. He had no choice but to close the business.'

'That's awful.'

'He was distraught. Completely ostracised with no business left, Pierre packed up his belongings and moved to Hull. He wasn't going to make himself known to you, at my request, but he thought that he could at least see you occasionally. When Dad put up the shop for sale, it seemed like fate had decided to give him a break at last. He'd hoped you would continue working at the shop after he took over but you'd decided to change direction so it wasn't to be. Living in the same village, he regularly saw you around and you were still a frequent visitor to *La Chocolaterie*. The day you asked him if there was any chance of your old job back, he rang me in tears.'

I remembered him being tearful when I'd asked and he'd apologised for being over-emotional saying he knew how much it would mean to Grandpa having me working back at the business he'd started. It seemed perfectly plausible.

'Where were you at this time?' I asked Stacey, trying to think about the destinations on the more recent postcards and letters.

'Germany, Denmark, Switzerland, Norway. Pretty much everywhere. Pierre kept begging me to move back to Hull to be with him. I wanted to but it wasn't that simple. I couldn't be in your life anonymously like he could. I'd be recognised. Mum and Dad would see me. You might even recognise me if you'd seen photos of me. With hindsight, I should have just gone for it. So what if I was recognised? You were an adult. You could choose whether you wanted me in your life or not. You weren't even living at home at this point so I wouldn't have been jeopardising anything. But I faffed about and hesitated by which time Lillian had seen the light. She'd accepted that she'd walked out on Pierre without warning, declaring that Gabby wasn't his, so she could hardly blame him for turning to another woman while she was away.'

'So he took her back?'

Stacey nodded. 'Only because I was adamant that I'd never be with him. He was lonely in a strange country and he did still care deeply for Lillian, even if it was me who held his heart. And, of course, he loved Gabby. She'd decided she wanted to train as a chocolatier, despite showing no interest before, so they set up a new family home in Brockington and I missed my opportunity.'

I sipped on my wine, so much unexpected information swimming round my mind. 'So I worked next to my biological father and my half-sister for all those years, with no idea who they really were?'

'Yes.'

'How did Gabby find out?'

'Gabby's quite a jealous person, as you'll have noticed. She struggled to master the skills that seemed to come so naturally to you. Pierre would often stay behind after hours trying to teach her, and it frustrated her that she found it so hard. After a few years of struggling, she threw a strop one night and said something like, "How is it that I'm your daughter and I'm crap at this, but she seems to pick up new skills in minutes? Are you sure she's not your daughter instead of me?"'

'Ooh.'

'Exactly. She'd hit the nail on the head, or at least in relation to the part about you. You know Pierre. His face is an open book.'

I leaned back in my seat and ran my fingers through my hair. 'I can probably pinpoint the exact time that happened. We'd never gelled but she seemed to go from being a bit snide to being a complete bitch overnight and I never knew why. I wonder why she didn't say anything.'

'Because she'd have lost the power. As long as you were just the employee instead of part of the family, she had one up on you. She's not a very nice person.'

Of course! Wow!

'Is there anything else you want to know?' Stacey asked when I fell silent.

'Probably a million things, but I can't think straight at the moment. That was a lot of unexpected information.'

She nodded. 'I understand. I hope I did the right thing coming to see you in person. I felt I at least owed you that.'

'I'm glad you did.' I sipped on my wine, trying to find the best way to broach the future. 'So where do we go from here?'

Stacey's cheeks flushed, and her eyes sparkled with tears. 'Oh, Charlee, it's not my decision to make. I would absolutely love to be part of your life, but I'm the one who walked out on you and, as far as you were concerned, severed all contact. I have no right to turn up out of the blue and expect anything from you. I came here today with no expectations. The worst-case scenario, and one which I fully anticipated and deserved, was that you'd throw me out without letting me explain. And, believe me, I know you'd have been justified in doing so. The best-case scenario was that you'd allow me to buy you a drink and hear me out. I honestly hadn't dared to think beyond that.'

There was something vulnerable and endearing about her. Despite the anger I'd directed towards her from reading her letters, I was surprised to discover that I really liked her and I wanted to take the time to get to know her. And I knew that it wasn't because I was desperate to cling to her simply because I wanted a family.

'If I did let you be part of my life, what might that look like? I asked.

She put her hand over her mouth, and a tear escaped down

her cheek. 'Oh, Charlee, I really don't know,' she said. 'It has to be what you want.'

'But what do *you* want?'

Stacey wiped the tear and took a deep breath. 'It's probably easier to say what I don't want... or rather, what I don't expect. I don't expect you to call me "mum" because I haven't earned that right. I don't expect you to treat me like a mother figure because I know that your Nanna was that person and I could never and would never try to replace her. Perhaps we could spend a little bit of time together – or a lot if you want – and simply get to know each other. Who knows where that may go in the future. What do you think?'

I sipped on my wine while I mulled it over. 'I think that it's been good to spend time with you tonight and find out about where I came from. I think my head is about to explode with so many revelations. I think I need some time to digest it. But...'

Stacey's face fell when I tailed off. 'It's fine. You can say it. I've done what I came to do and you now know about your past. We can leave it there.'

I laughed. 'It was actually going to be a positive "but". I was going to say, but once I've got my head round everything and spoken to Pierre, I'd like to spend some more time with you and see where that takes us.'

The relief on her face was palpable. 'You really mean that?' Tears spilled down both her cheeks this time.

'I really mean that.' And I did. I liked her and, more than that, I got her. I understood what had happened and why. I found myself wondering if I'd have done things differently if I'd been in her shoes and I wasn't sure that I would have done. 'I'm drained now, though. Do you mind if we call it a night?'

Stacey smiled. 'Of course not.'

Drinks finished, we exchanged contact details and Stacey told me where she was staying. Her B&B was in the opposite direction to where I needed to be so we stood slightly awkwardly outside the pub, cheeks red from the alcohol, breath hanging in the cold night air. What was the correct thing to do in circumstances like these? Hug? Air kiss? Shake hands?

Stacey saved us. 'I don't know what the protocol is. A handshake?'

I smiled. 'Me neither.' I shook her hand. 'Don't be a stranger.'

Her eyes brimmed with tears again. She nodded and smiled, then turned and headed in the opposite direction.

Releasing a long breath, I shook my head, then set off down the pedestrianised precinct. That was some evening. I didn't know what to think or feel. The man who I adored as a friend and employer and, yes, had looked up to as a father figure, especially after Grandpa died, was actually my biological father. The woman I hated who'd made my working life hell was my biological half-sister. And the other woman who I'd spent a lifetime being indifferent towards for giving me up at birth had never actually given me up. Physically, she had, but emotionally she'd been tied to me and had actually selflessly given my grandparents that second chance of a family by letting them raise me.

Everything had turned on its head. That family that I'd craved, I now had. Pierre had four brothers and three sisters, which meant I had aunties, uncles, cousins and second cousins. But after thirty-one years without any of them, did that really make them family? What was family? Was it shared genes or was it the people who were there for you no matter what? An image of Jodie popped into my head, fussing round me earlier as I pulled on my coat, nervous and worried about me meeting my birth mother for the first time. Oh my goodness! Why hadn't I realised it before? We may not have had blood ties but Jodie was as close to me – if not closer – than a sister could be. *She* was my family, and I needed to tell her that. I could imagine her all alone in the flat above the shop, pacing up and down, chewing her fingernails down to the quick, desperate for news.

I took a right down Castle Street and headed towards the shop. I needed to tell Jodie what had happened and I needed to assure her that, despite an unexpected family sprouting up this evening, she would always be the 'family' that I valued the most.

30

'Wow! I did *not* see that coming.' Jodie slumped back in the armchair in her flat, shaking her head. 'How are you feeling?'

I shrugged. 'Like I'm in a really surreal dream. I keep expecting to wake up at any minute.'

'I think I might have joined you in that dream. I can't believe Pierre never said anything to you.'

'I know! Imagine working alongside your daughter for ten years, knowing that she hasn't a clue that you're related. Pierre's such a good man. If Stacey didn't want him to say anything, he'd have respected that. I'm actually more surprised that Gabby didn't let it slip when she was in one of her sulks.'

'Oh my God! This means Satan's Mistress is your half-sister.'

I laughed at the name that Jodie had awarded Gabby after meeting her for the first time. 'Yep. Every rose has its thorn.'

'So how does it feel knowing that Pierre is your dad... assuming she's telling the truth, that is?'

'I thought about that, but what reason would she have to lie? She knew all about him and his family and, let's face it, I do look like him.'

Jodie studied my face. 'You really do. I can't believe I never spotted it before.'

'Why would you? There would be no possible reason for you or me or anyone who knew us to think that we were related. New customers often thought I was his daughter but we'd laugh and say that it was only because we had dark hair and a similar skin tone. That must have been so weird for him, knowing they were spot on.' I shook my head. 'As for how I feel knowing he's my dad, I don't know. In some ways it doesn't change anything because I always looked upon him like a father figure anyway, especially after Grandpa died. We've stayed in regular contact since he moved back to France so what's going to change? I probably do need to accept his invite to visit, but I'd have done that next year anyway.' I'd spoken to Pierre every couple of weeks, and emailed regularly in between. When I was setting up the shop, he'd been eager for photos and we'd discussed the merits of different tempering machines, moulds, and packaging materials. It had been helpful to chat to him about the business side of things and he'd given some great advice. We'd talked about me visiting and he said that, although he missed me and would love to see me, I needed to give the business my full focus in the first year of trading. He suggested that, if I took a holiday, I'd spend it worrying about the shop and wouldn't relax at all. He knew me so well.

'I'm not going to suddenly start calling him "dad",' I said. 'That wouldn't seem right. Or would it? I don't know. I think I'm going to ring him tomorrow and let him know that I know. We'll take it from there. Stacey promised not to let him know we've met so that I can be the one who surprises him.'

'And what about Stacey?'

'I had her completely pegged wrong, didn't I?'

'You weren't to know. Does she want to be part of your life now? Properly, I mean.'

'Yes, but she doesn't expect to be. It's completely up to me but I don't know what I want right now. I need more time to process things.' I told her about the conversation I'd had with Stacey and we speculated about what the future would look like with my birth mother in my life and how my relationship with Pierre might change.

* * *

'Do you want to crash here?' Jodie asked, rubbing her eyes and yawning sometime later. 'There's fresh bedding in your room.'

I looked at my watch and did a double-take. 'It's after two! How did that happen?'

'We had a lot to talk about.'

'We're going to be useless at work tomorrow.' I stood up and stretched. 'Yes, I will stay, if you don't mind.' At the start of the year, we'd talked about whether I should give notice on Coral Court and move in with Jodie but I'd decided to stay put. I was concerned I'd never take a break from work otherwise, especially with Ricky gone from my life, and I suspected Jodie would feel obligated to support me. Even though it didn't make sense financially, that physical distance between home and work provided a valuable work/life balance for us both. I'd stayed over with Jodie on several occasions when we'd been up chatting till the early hours or we'd rolled in after a night out and I couldn't be bothered to walk home. I even had a selection of emergency clothes, some PJs and a full set of toiletries in the second bedroom now to make things easier.

'You know you're welcome to stay any time.' Jodie stood up too and took our empty mugs into the kitchen area. 'Now that you've got into a routine with your work/life balance, I'd suggest that you give notice on your flat and move in properly, except that would be pointless as you'd only move straight out again.'

I frowned. 'What makes you say that? I've lived with you before. I know all your bad habits already.'

'It's nothing to do with me or my bad habits, not that I have any of those, you cheeky mare. It's because you'll be moving into a lovely new barn conversion with a rather lush plumber friend of ours who has finally opened his eyes and seen beyond the friend-zone.'

An image of that brief kiss popped into my head, making my heart race and my stomach do somersaults. 'Do you think so?'

'I know so. When we were out after the lights switch-on, I could see it, Sarah could see it, Nick could see it. In fact, *everyone* could see it. Nick even joked that we should open a book on what time you'd finally kiss. Everyone was convinced it would be that night. And then his phone rang.' Jodie walked towards her bedroom door. 'It'll happen, Charlee. Just maybe not as quickly as we'd have hoped thanks to Libby's little Ecstasy incident. He's a decent bloke so he's not going to abandon her while she's still got issues, but I guarantee that it's you he wants to be with. You've found the man of your dreams and you've found the family you longed for. It's shaping up to be a pretty good Christmas, don't you think?'

Although she was smiling, there was a slight edge to her voice when she said the bit about family and I could have kicked myself. I'd dropped by to say something specific to Jodie and I'd managed to get side-tracked.

'I realised something when I was with Stacey this evening,' I said, making my way round the sofa. 'I'd be lying if I said it wasn't nice discovering that I've got a load of blood relatives who I might have a relationship with, but I've already got a family. It only consists of me and one other person but that person means the world to me. She's my real family. Apologies if this sounds cheesy. I know that we're not bound by blood, but you're like a sister to me, Jodie, and I don't know what I'd do without you.'

I stretched out my arms for a hug. 'I thought you'd never realise,' she said, holding me tightly. 'You'll never have to be without me. I'll always be here for you.'

'I know, and I'll always be here for you too.'

31

On Friday, a few days later, I planned to go to the shop early to make a large batch of moulded Christmas figures. We were approaching the penultimate shopping weekend before Christmas – likely to be very busy in the shop - so I wanted to ensure we had plenty of stock.

When my alarm sounded at 5 a.m., I glanced out of my bedroom window into darkness but, stepping out of the shower fifteen minutes later, the sky had turned pink and heavy flakes were drifting down.

By the time I left Coral Court, the streets had turned into a winter wonderland. I paused under the entrance canopy, a bubble of excitement welling inside me just like it used to when I was a child and snow meant being pulled to school on a wooden sledge and snowball fights at playtime.

A thick blanket of snow had already covered the ground, coating the parked vehicles and hugging the trees and it didn't look like it was going to stop anytime soon. With my wellington boots and thick socks keeping my feet warm and dry, I jumped in all the deepest snowdrifts and created patterns with my foot-prints in the fresh snow all the way into town.

I paused at the end of Castle Street drinking it all in. Each of the Victorian lampposts wore several inches of snow like a top hat. The warm golden glow lit up the snow flurries as they waltzed their way to the ground and the snow covering the cobbles was completely untouched. I stretched out my arms to either side and weaved my way between the lampposts with my head tilted back so the snow could kiss my face.

Halfway down the street, I changed direction and headed back towards Charlee's Chocolates where I stood in the middle of the street, stuck my tongue out and caught a snowflake on it. I breathed in the cool morning air and smiled contentedly. Everything felt so magical and I had this feeling in my gut that something amazing was about to happen. I'd already found my family, so did that mean that something was finally going to happen between Matt and me?

I unlocked the shop door and took one last look heavenwards. 'If you're up there, Nanna and Grandpa, you know what my Christmas wish is.'

* * *

We'd barely been open for five minutes when the doorbell tinkled.

'Matt!' I put down the box of chocolate drops I was restocking and rushed to him with my arms outstretched. 'How's Libby?'

He hugged me and gave me a quick kiss on the cheek, sending the butterflies in my stomach into a frenzy. 'She's doing really well.'

'And how are you?'

He wrinkled his nose. 'It's been an interesting couple of weeks. I'm sorry I haven't been in touch much.'

'That's okay. You've had a lot on your plate.'

'Hi Matt,' Jodie said, emerging from the workshop with a box of paper carrier bags. 'Still snowing, eh?'

Matt brushed the flakes out of his hair, laughing. 'Just a bit.'

'Has Charlee told you her exciting news?' Jodie asked.

'No.' He smiled at me. 'What's happened?'

'Something unexpected. My birth mum came to the shop on Tuesday and I found out who my dad is.' It still didn't feel real saying it, as though I was reciting the lines from a play instead of real life.

'Charlee, that's huge. How—?'

But he was interrupted by the door going and a couple of customers coming in and walking straight to the till, which usually meant they needed help. Jodie was on hand to deal with one of them, but the other was going to need me.

'I'd better let you get on. I know this is a bit short notice, but do you have any plans for tonight?'

'Nothing exciting. I was going to catch up on the accounts.' I made a snoring sound to indicate how much that job thrilled me.

'Would you be willing to ditch the paperwork and let me take you out for a drink?'

'Consider it ditched.'

Matt smiled. 'There's something I want to talk to you about and I need to hear all about your big news. That's amazing. Pick you up from your flat at 7.30?'

'See you then.'

'Wear warm clothes, a coat, and some boots. We're going somewhere a bit different.'

'Sounds intriguing.'

Matt leaned in and kissed me on the cheek again, making me hold my breath.

* * *

'Wow! It's beautiful!'

The 'somewhere a bit different' turned out to be the haybarn at Matt's parents' farm. Coloured lanterns were strung round the entrance, and strings of star-shaped fairy lights hung like curtains on the wooden walls.

'We had a party here for our Erin and she insisted on lights everywhere. We've never taken them down.' He led me over to a wooden bench next to a lit chiminea. 'Don't panic about the flames. I promise there's no hay anywhere near.' He lifted a couple of bottles of lager out of a cool box, opened them, and passed me one. 'I hope this is okay. I thought that we were bound to bump into someone we knew if we went to a pub, so this is the safest way to ensure no interruptions after last time.'

'It's lovely and a good idea.' Gazing round the barn, I had that same feeling I'd had in Castle Street this morning that something special was about to happen. With the lanterns and fairy lights, the barn certainly felt like the sort of place where a little Christmas magic could happen and wishes could come true.

We sat down on the padded seat cushion and Matt peeled a strip off the label on his bottle. He was clearly building up to something and I sensed he might need a little coaxing to start speaking.

'So what did you want to tell me?' I asked.

'You've got to tell me your news first.'

I shook my head. 'Oh no you don't. You asked me out tonight because you wanted to talk about something so you're first. I insist.'

Matt took a sip from his bottle. 'You're sure?'

'I'm sure.'

'Okay.' He took a big gulp from his bottle this time. 'I want to tell you something about Libby, but nobody knows this. Not even my parents.'

'Go on...'

He fiddled with the label again, clearly nervous about what he was about to reveal. I'd never seen him nervous before. Was he going to tell me that Libby was pregnant? I bit my lip and hoped that I could be a good enough friend to act like I was genuinely delighted for him.

'I need to go back to the beginning so please bear with me if it doesn't seem relevant at first.'

'Okay...' My stomach lurched. *Be a good friend. Whatever he says, he obviously needs someone to talk to.*

'When we were at school, Libby was one of the cool kids. You know the sort? Pretty, sporty, popular. Completely out of my league.'

I wanted to object but me telling him he was gorgeous wasn't exactly timely.

'I was one of the geeks at school. In fact, I was a walking stereotype of a geek. I wore glasses, had braces, had this crazy wild curly hair, and was into science and maths; not the sort of kid she'd lower herself to speak to, which was fine by me because I actually couldn't stand her. We'd probably have gone through school having nothing to do with each other but our parents had met at some event when we were fourteen and became great friends. Her parents would often come to the farm to visit mine and they'd bring Libby with them. Being the same age and at the same school, I was expected to entertain her.'

He paused and I nodded at him to continue.

'The first couple of times, she was exactly the pain in the arse

I'd expected her to be. She moaned about the mud, the midges, and the smell. The cows scared her and she reckoned the sheep were staring her out. Yeah. I know! She seemed drawn to the horses so, stuck for anything better to do, I asked her if she wanted to ride one day. It turned out that she'd had riding lessons when she was little but had a fall and hadn't ridden since. I decided to make her my pet project. If I could get her confident enough to ride again, even if only round the paddock, she might start being nice and the family visits might be bearable. It took some doing but over the next few months she got her confidence back and, during that time, I got to see a different side to her. Obviously I saw her vulnerability as she faced her fears, but I also saw this relaxed person who was fun to be around. I thought maybe the farm Libby was the real her and the school Libby was an act. She still didn't speak to me at school but she'd give me this secret smile when she saw me.' He smiled wistfully. 'That's when I fell for her.'

'I didn't realise you'd been together that long,' I said when he paused.

He shook his head as he sipped his drink. 'We weren't. Nothing happened back then. Not even a hint of anything but friendship and I never told her how I felt. She started coming outside her parents' visits so she could ride more often and sometimes we'd walk across the fields afterwards and talk about anything and nothing.

'When we were seventeen, she turned up one evening in a right state, demanding to go for a ride. She wouldn't tell me what was wrong, but we saddled up and went for a canter. When we stopped, she slumped forward on her horse, crying. As I helped her down, the long-sleeved T-shirt she was wearing rode up her arm and I saw she was covered in cuts.'

'What sort of cuts?'

'Self-inflicted ones. Both arms.'

'Oh, my God! Why?'

'She was a daddy's girl. She idolised that man, but she'd come home from school earlier that week to find several suitcases in the hall. She thought they were going on a surprise holiday, but the surprise was that he'd met someone else and was moving out. She hadn't seen it coming and took it personally. In her eyes, it wasn't her mum he was rejecting; it was her. She locked herself in her room, grabbed a pair of scissors and started slashing things like books, clothes, her curtains. And then she slashed her arms.'

I put my hand over my mouth. 'No! That's awful.'

'The day I found out, she'd just discovered that the affair had been going on for two years and that her Dad's new woman was pregnant with twins. Libby saw it as the ultimate rejection of her. She thought she wasn't important to him now that she was almost an adult and was convinced that she was being replaced by brand new babies who'd get all his love.'

'Did she get any help?'

'She wouldn't do anything. She blamed her mum for driving her dad away so they fell out. She wouldn't go to a doctor or a teacher. The only person she'd speak to was me but I was way out of my depth. I spent ages online researching how to support her. One day, I told Libby that I couldn't deal with it on my own and would have to tell someone, but she was adamant she'd stopped. She showed me her arms and there were no fresh wounds so I had to trust her.'

'Had she stopped?'

'Yes, but it was only because she'd found a new release: alcohol. We'd finished college by this time and were both working. She spent all her wages on going out and she started sleeping around. She stopped riding but would still turn up at the farm occasionally, usually hammered. I was so worried about her.

After pulling too many sickies, she lost her job. She was depressed and self-harming again, and then she started doing drugs and was pretty much on a downward spiral. She stopped coming to the farm and wouldn't return my calls. Said me worrying about her killed her buzz. We lost touch then, when she was twenty-one, she hit rock bottom. She turned up at the farm, begging me to go with her while...'

He paused again and I had a feeling I knew what was coming next. 'She was pregnant?'

He nodded. 'She didn't know who the father was. She'd been at a party. There'd been drugs, drink and lots of partners. It could have been anyone. After the termination, she knew she had to sort herself out, but she wasn't strong enough to do it on her own.'

'So you helped?'

'Every step of the way. If I wasn't working, I was with Libby. It took a long time, but I started seeing glimpses of the person I thought of as the real Libby and those moments became more and more regular. She started riding again, she found a job she loved, she made new friends through work like Gina, and she had counselling to deal with her issues.

'For my twenty-fifth birthday, she booked a riding weekend for us both in the Peak District. She told me she didn't think she'd still be alive if it hadn't been for me and how grateful she was that I'd been there for her despite all the crap she'd thrown at me which would have made most men run for the hills. She said I was her rock and she couldn't imagine coping without me but she was scared that, one day soon, I'd meet someone and I wouldn't be there for her and she'd be on a downward spiral again.'

Matt paused and sighed. I could hear the strain in every word and tried to push away an image in my head of a log cabin, an open fire and the pair of them snuggled together under a blanket so I could focus completely on him and how hard it clearly was to relive all of this.

'I told her that I cared about her and we could explore always being together if that was what she really wanted but I thought it was best for her if we took things slowly.' He ran his hands through his hair and shrugged. 'I don't really know how it happened but we went away that weekend as friends and came back engaged.'

'What do you mean, you don't know how it happened?'

He shrugged. 'We talked about the future and marriage was even mentioned way, way down the line but I definitely never proposed. I think Libby joined a few too many dots.'

I winced. 'Why didn't you correct her?'

He took another swig on his drink. 'Do you know how many times I've asked myself that over the years? I suppose it's because I loved her, or thought I still did at the time, and there was this stupid gallant streak in me that wanted to protect her exactly like I'd been doing for the past decade. She'd said I was her rock and she was worried what might happen without me in her life. I didn't want her to self-harm again, or take drugs, or drink herself into a stupor, or sleep around, so I just accepted it all and hoped for the best.'

'Oh my God, Matt! Are you saying that you've stayed with Libby for, what, seven or eight years to keep her safe and not because you loved her?'

He peeled at the label once more. 'I sound like a right shit when you put it like that, don't I?'

I quickly shook my head. 'No. You sound like a knight in shining armour. You rescued her but got captured yourself.'

He smiled and my heart raced at those dimples. 'That's such a great way of describing it.'

'So where does this leave the two of you now?'

'There is no the two of us.'

My heart raced even faster. 'You've split up? When?'

'When Libby was discharged from hospital, she wanted to stay with Gina rather than in the caravan which made sense because she'd be more comfortable there. I took some clothes over on the first day, but she was sleepy so Gina said there was no point me staying. I probably should have been a good fiancé, sitting there and holding her hand while she slept, but I was angry with her. After everything I'd done for her, she'd gone down that path of self-destruction again, presumably because she was mad at me for going out with my friends instead of going to her works do. She'd taken drugs and she'd been with someone else.'

'You had every right to be angry,' I said. 'I would have been in your situation.'

'Thank you. Anyway, I got a call from Gina the next day. Libby wanted me to visit because she wanted to apologise. I assumed she wanted to say sorry for the drugs and the men, but she actually wanted to apologise for everything she'd put me through since she'd first visited the farm when she was fourteen. Like you just now, she described me as her knight in shining armour. She said she'd needed me and I'd always been there for her, rescuing her from her many mistakes, but it was her turn to rescue me from mine. She said that she might owe me her life, but I didn't owe her mine so she was going to do the right thing for once and let me go. I protested and said it was just the trauma from what had happened but she took my hand and said, "Look me in the eye and tell me that you love me with all your heart, that you want to marry me, and that you believe we can live happily ever after together".'

He shook his head. 'I couldn't do it, Charlee. I'd kidded myself for years that I could make it work and, believe me, I've thrown everything at it, but it was never enough. I expected Libby to start crying or to yell at me, but she just smiled and said, "We gave it our best shot but we both know it was never going to last." Turns out she'd never truly loved me. She'd needed me and she'd been scared of what might happen to her if she didn't have me to lean on so she convinced herself our friendship would be enough. It wasn't.

'We've moved her stuff out of the caravan and she's living with Gina for a while. She's told Gina everything and Gina's conscious that she's gone a bit crazy herself since her divorce came through so they're going to have a chilled Christmas together and look forward to a fresh start next year.'

'I'm so sorry, Matt,' I said.

He fixed his gaze on me. 'Are you?'

Only two words but they seemed to be loaded with meaning. I felt my cheeks burning as I looked into his eyes. I wasn't sorry that he'd split up with her because it was absolutely the right thing for him, but I was sorry for everything he'd been through.

'I know that Libby wasn't my favourite person but I feel like I understand her a bit better now, and I'm sorry for you because, even if you didn't love her, break-ups are tough. What will happen about the house now?'

'I'll still finish it and I'll move into it but without Libby. I don't know if you remember it but we'd had a stupid argument over cushions the day I met you.'

'I do remember.'

'Libby admitted she couldn't see herself ever moving into the house and, for her, getting hung up on stupid things like cushions and candlesticks helped her stop thinking about the big picture and the huge mistake we were making. She deliberately kept pushing and pushing me, hoping that I'd snap and call it off because she didn't think she was strong enough to be the one to walk away. Meanwhile, I was worried that arguing too much might send her back on the self-harm path so I took all the shit she shovelled at me.'

I sipped on my lager, taking it all in. Matt was free and he'd never loved Libby. That didn't mean he was going to want to jump straight into another relationship with me, though. If he'd been seeing her for eight years and his life had been embroiled with hers for at least a decade before that, he likely needed a heck of a lot of space.

'You're probably wondering why I'm telling you all this,' Matt said.

'Because we're friends and it's the sort of thing that friends tell each other?' I suggested. 'You were there for me after my break-up with Ricky so it's my turn to be here for you after yours. Hopefully we can see each other a bit more often now that Libby isn't around to get jealous about it.'

'I'd like that,' Matt said. 'But I've got a bit of a problem.'

'What's that?'

'I've spent the last eight years in a relationship that should only ever have been a friendship and I can't and won't put myself through that again.'

Oh crap! He'd realised that I saw him as more than a friend and, despite what Jodie, Sarah, Nick and all the others thought they'd seen on the night of the Christmas lights switch-on, he clearly saw me as nothing more and he wanted to set me straight. I stared into the chiminea flames, bracing myself for the blow and hoping my emotions wouldn't betray me.

'Libby never minded me spending time with Jodie, you know. It was only ever you she had the problem with. You know why, don't you?'

I shrugged. 'Can't have been my chocolate-making skills

because she made it very clear that she wasn't impressed with those.'

Matt laughed. 'She had her claws out that day. In fact, she did on most days she saw you. She knew, you see. From that very first day when I came to sort out your flood, she knew.'

I looked up. He was smiling and his eyes were twinkling. I thought nothing could beat the sight of Matt in a tux but the casually dressed version beside me now, bathed in the soft glow from the fire, had just edged ahead. It felt like there was a spark but I'd been wrong before. I'd thought Ricky had looked at me with love but I'd been mistaken.

'What did she know?' I whispered, my heart thumping.

'She knew what it's taken me nearly a year to admit to myself. I've been in a relationship with Libby when I should have just been her friend, and I've been in a friendship with you when...' He stopped and looked towards the fire; his shoulders slumped as he ran his hand through his curls.

'Sorry, Charlee. I'm not very good at this. I've never done this before. With Libby it just sort of happened by mistake and... it's just that... erm... I thought that if I brought you here, I'd be more relaxed and... erm... it might just sort of happen again, but not by mistake this time and...' He released a shuddery breath and clapped his hand against his forehead. 'Shit! I'm making such a mess of this.'

And at that moment I knew exactly what I'd seen in his eyes. The fumbling and the wanting to get it right were adorable and made me love him even more. He'd rescued Libby and me so many times and now it was my turn to rescue him.

I shuffled a little closer along the bench. 'I sometimes find that actions speak louder than words.'

He looked up and gulped. 'Do you think so?'

I shuffled closer still, letting my bottle of lager slip from my fingers and drop to the ground. 'It's worth a try. What did you want to tell me?'

Matt cupped my face in his hands and gently tilted it towards his. I closed my eyes, fireworks exploding in my stomach as he lowered his lips to mine and I melted into his kiss. That brief kiss at the end of Castle Street at the Christmas lights switch-on had promised something good, but this was spectacular. I'd been waiting a year to do this and, from the sounds of it, so had Matt even though he hadn't admitted it. And it was certainly worth the wait.

32

'Do you think I'm doing the right thing?' I asked Matt as I checked on the shepherd's pie in the oven. It was Saturday night a week later, two days before Christmas. 'Or have I read too many of my Nanna's romance novels?'

Matt pulled me to him and gently kissed me. 'You're definitely doing the right thing. If Pierre and Lillian were happy together, you wouldn't have dreamed of getting involved, but they're not. He told you himself they've reached the end of the line.'

I smiled and kissed him again, grateful for the reassurance. After Stacey's revelations, I'd needed to get my head round it all so I left it a couple of days before contacting Pierre. The headspace helped me realise that this was huge news to be given face to face. I usually FaceTimed Pierre but I opted for a phone call instead, not sure I'd be able to stop myself blurting out the news if I saw his face.

He told me he had plans to return to the UK to spend Christmas and New Year with Gabby and was hoping to see me while he was here. I asked if Lillian would be joining him.

'All is not well with Lillian,' he said.

'Oh no! She's poorly again?'

'*Non, ma petite chocolatière,* Lillian is very well. It is our marriage that is not well. It has never been well but you cannot say we did not try.' He sounded so sad, I wished I could crawl down the phoneline and hug him. 'We both know this for a long time, but neither of us wanted to be the one who ends it.'

'And now?'

'We will start the divorce in the New Year.'

'I'm so sorry, Pierre.' I genuinely was sorry as they had to both be hurting. But a seed of an idea had sprouted as I confirmed tonight to see him.

The entry buzzer sounded and nervous butterflies flitted round my stomach as I greeted Pierre and told him to come up to the second floor.

'I can't believe how nervous I am,' I said to Matt. 'It's only Pierre.'

'But it isn't anymore, is it? It's a special moment.'

I wiped my clammy hands down my apron then hung it up and stepped into the hall. We'd agreed that Matt would stay in the lounge for now as I was going to tell Pierre what I'd discovered as soon as I saw him.

Tears clouded my eyes and a lump welled in my throat as I peered through the peephole, watching for him on the stairwell. I'd have felt emotional seeing Pierre after sixteen months apart anyway, but now that I knew he was my dad, my emotions were all over the place.

I drew in a deep shuddery breath as he emerged round the corner. My dad. I still felt as though I was in a dream. I didn't want to open the door crying so I forced back the tears, smiled, and flung open the door.

'*Bonsoir, ma petite chocolatière,*' Pierre said enthusiastically. 'I have missed you so much.' He passed me a bottle of wine and a bunch of flowers.

'Thank you. I've missed you too.'

I placed the gifts on the floor as he stepped into the hall, pushing the door shut behind him. He held his arms wide and we hugged and exchanged kisses on each cheek.

'*Bonsoir,* Pierre.' I stepped back and looked into his eyes. 'Or should I say, *Bonsoir, Papa?*'

Pierre stared at me, wide-eyed and wide-mouthed and clapped his hand across his heart. '*Je n'arrive pas y croire.* You know? How can this be?'

He couldn't believe it. I still couldn't either. 'I met Stacey and she told me.'

'She did? When was this?'

'At the start of last week but I didn't want to tell you over the phone.'

Pierre shook his head. 'Oh, Charlee, can you forgive me for not saying? I wanted to so many times, but I promised Stacey and I could not let her down.'

'I know. That's because you love her.'

His eyes widened even further. 'You know this too?'

'I know everything. Have you got another hug for your daughter?'

'*Ma chérie,* I have a lifetime of them.'

We held each other tightly. Tears ran down my cheeks and I could feel him shaking so I knew he was finding it just as emotional as me. Wait until he saw what else I had in store for him later! It was such a relief for me to have it out in the open and I'd only known for eleven days. How must it feel for Pierre after keeping the secret close to his heart since I was six? Eleven days was nothing compared to twenty-five years.

When we finally broke apart, I picked up the wine and flowers and opened the lounge door. 'Come through. I want to introduce you to someone. Matt?' Matt stepped out of the kitchen. 'This is my boyfriend Matt, who I was telling you about the other day. Matt, this is my dad Pierre.' *My dad.* Two words I never imagined I'd say and yet they felt so comfortable on my tongue.

Matt went to shake hands but Pierre surprised him by grabbing him by both arms and kissing him on each cheek. I probably should have warned him to expect a traditional French greeting.

'Can I offer you a glass of wine?' Matt asked, taking the wine and flowers from me. 'We have a bottle open. I can't remember what it's called but Charlee says it's your favourite.'

'I would like that very much. *Merci.*'

Matt disappeared into the kitchen to get the wine while I settled onto the sofa with Pierre.

'You must tell me everything,' he said, stroking his hand over his beard like he always did when he was anxious. 'Are you happy with this news? Are you mad at me?'

'I've just found out that one of my most favourite people in the world who I've always looked to like a father really is my dad. Right now, I couldn't be happier.'

He hugged me once more then we settled back with glasses of wine Matt had brought in as I explained about Stacey's visit and how suddenly lots of things from the past made sense now that I knew about my heritage.

'I am sorry again that Gabby did not treat you like her sister,' he said.

I shrugged. 'I suspect it's because I'm her sister that she treated me like that. It's fine. Who knows. Maybe one day we'll laugh about it, but I won't hold my breath on that one. I wanted to ask you about Lillian. She was always nice to me but that must have been difficult, knowing who I was.'

'Ah, yes. Lillian wanted to hate you, but how could she when you are so wonderful? She knew it was not your fault and she fell under your spell. You became like another daughter to her, *n'est pas*? She would not say this out loud, but I know she feels this in here.' He tapped his heart. 'She sends her love and wishes you a happy Christmas.'

'Thank you. Please tell her I wish her the same. I've missed her too.'

The door buzzer sounded again.

'Excuse me,' I said, jumping up and buzzing our guest straight in without confirming who it was. I didn't want to ruin the surprise.

Matt was under strict instructions to keep Pierre distracted so that he couldn't hear her voice when I opened the door. I was desperate to see their reactions when they were reunited.

I hadn't seen Stacey since that evening in The Old Theatre because she'd needed to head home early the next morning, but we'd spoken on the phone and exchanged a few messages.

'Thank you for inviting me. It's really good to see you again.' Stacey shuffled awkwardly from one foot to the other, probably thinking that another handshake didn't seem appropriate. 'These are for you.' She handed me some wine and flowers; the same wine as Pierre had chosen and the same colours in the bouquet.

'You didn't have to, but thank you.' I smiled and gave her a quick hug. 'It's good to see you again too. Come in. Let me take your coat. Is it still snowing?' It had started snowing lightly shortly after lunch, but hadn't settled at first. As it fell more heavily across the afternoon, it started to lay. I'd worried that the snow might mean that Stacey and Pierre wouldn't make it or that only one of them would manage.

'It's started again, but the trains were running fine. For now. I'm not hopeful for tomorrow, though.'

I hung Stacey's coat up, indicated where she could leave her overnight bag, and took a deep breath as I pushed the lounge door open.

'This is my boyfriend, Matt,' I said. Matt stood up, smiling, blocking the view so Stacey couldn't see Pierre and vice versa. He gave Stacey a kiss on her cheek.

I bit my lip. 'And this is...' Matt stepped aside, as planned '... Well, I think you already know each other.'

She gasped. 'Pierre!'

He rose from the sofa, his eyes wide. '*Mon Dieu!* Stacey!'

They may have been shocked to see each other, but there was no mistaking the fireworks exploding as they kissed each other on either cheek then embraced. I glanced at Matt and he gave me a reassuring smile. Definitely the right decision.

'I suspect you two have a lot to talk about so Matt and I are going for a drink round the corner. There's a shepherd's pie in the oven and some carrots and peas ready in pans to heat up. There's plenty of wine. We'll be back in a couple of hours and, if you two haven't admitted by then that you're meant to be together, we'll knock your heads together.'

They both looked at me, mouths agape, evidently rendered speechless.

'This is my Christmas gift to both of you and, so that you don't spend the next two hours pussy-footing around things, there are two things you need to know. Pierre, Stacey still loves you, and always has done. Stacey, Pierre's marriage is over and he still loves you too. Happy Christmas. See you later.'

'Charlee, what...?' Stacey began. 'I... What...?'

I grinned at her. 'You see that Christmas present under the tree with the red wrapping paper? That's for you, Stacey, and you need to open it tonight before we return. And the one with the gold paper is for you both, also to be opened tonight. We'll see you later.'

I grabbed Matt's hand and we darted out of the flat, before they could say anything else. We pulled on our coats as we ran down the stairwell and out onto the snowy street.

The gift for Stacey was Nanna's cream photo album full of her childhood Christmases. I suspected that looking through it would be extremely emotional and it felt like Pierre should be there to support Stacey; not me. How funny that I'd made the decision to keep it when I cleared the attic. I'd never imagined that, a year later, I'd have met my birth mother and discovered the identity of my father.

The gift for them both was my Christmas album. Pierre and Stacey had already seen some photos of me growing up, courtesy of Nanna, but I thought that giving them the album would be a lovely way of fully letting them in. Jodie, Matt and I had spent several evenings choosing other photos of me throughout the years which we'd had printed and added so the album had become more of a story of my life instead of just my Christmases. The album held precious memories for me, but we'd scanned in the photos so I still had copies but in digital format,

Matt stopped me when we rounded the corner, pulled me close and tenderly kissed me. 'I think that went brilliantly. How do you feel?'

'Pretty amazing right now. Hopefully they'll finally take their chance to be together.'

'I reckon they will. What you did tonight was really special. You're such a romantic.'

'It's all those books of Nanna's I've read. That and watching her and Grandpa together over the years. I always hoped I'd find what they had.'

Matt brushed my hair back from my face. 'Do you think you might have found it now?'

My heart raced as I gazed into his eyes. We'd been inseparable all week and I had no doubt that it was the real thing, but I didn't want to be the first to say 'I love you' in case I scared him off.

'That depends on you,' I said, trying and failing to sound casual.

He smiled and cuddled me to him. 'That wasn't a very fair question, was it? I'm not great at the romantic stuff, but I'd like to learn. And, as you could tell from the way I bumbled through it in the haybarn last Friday night, I'm not very good at talking about feelings either, but I'll keep trying.' He stepped out of the hug and looked at me so tenderly, I could have melted. 'I love you, Charlee. I should have said that last week or all the times we've been together since. I don't know why I haven't but it's how I feel.'

'Will you say it one more time, please? I just want to check I heard you right.'

Matt laughed. 'You heard me right. I love you, Charlee. I've loved you for the past year, even if I didn't admit it to myself until recently. And, if you'll let me, I'll love you until the end of time. Maybe a bit longer.'

'And you said you're not romantic,' I said, tears rushing to my eyes. 'That was lovely. And I love you too. I've also loved you for the past year and I *did* admit it to myself. Serious case of unrequited love.'

'Unrequited love?' He raised his eyebrows and I could see it had just clicked. 'At the Awards do when we danced to Daniel Bedingfield, you said unrequited love was the story of your life and I thought you were talking about Ricky.'

I shook my head. 'I know. I was talking about you but you were with Libby so I couldn't say anything even though I really wanted to. Jodie had just given me a lecture about either telling you how I felt or getting over you. She set me a deadline. I had until the stroke of midnight on New Year's Eve to kiss you or kiss goodbye to my feelings for you.'

'Then it looks like I was just in time,' Matt said, leaning forward to kiss me. Flakes of snow settled on my head and shoulders, but I didn't feel their chill because my heart was on fire.

33

'It's Christmas Day tomorrow!' Jodie squealed, as she joined me in the shop on Sunday morning, wearing an elf hat with pointy ears and a tingling bell. 'And it's still snowing.'

'I know! I'm so excited!'

Jodie grinned. 'I'm not surprised. You've bagged yourself the best Christmas gift ever.'

'I can't stop smiling. It's going to be such a different Christmas to the disaster from last year.'

'Nobody deserves it more than you. Are you sure Matt's parents don't mind me joining you tomorrow?'

'They said the more the merrier. You'll really like them. You know Matt's nieces already. Matt's brother, Tim, is lovely and so's his wife, Kendal.' I didn't mention that Kendal's brother Dean was also joining us – her older single brother who'd been staying at the farm for the past couple of weeks while he house-hunted, ready to move back into the area after leaving the army. Her single brother who couldn't be more perfect for Jodie if I'd picked him out of a catalogue; something with which Matt wholeheart-edly agreed.

Despite loving to meddle herself, Jodie couldn't bear it if she thought anyone was trying to matchmake for her. If I'd mentioned Dean at any point, she'd have refused to come up to the farm so Matt and I had agreed that the best plan was to conveniently forget to mention the additional dinner guest and let Cupid do his thing.

'How did it go with Pierre and Stacey last night?' she asked while she boiled the kettle.

'Better than I could ever have imagined.' When Matt and I returned from the pub, we'd felt like parents returning home, wondering if we'd catch our teenage daughter and boyfriend up to no good. We made sure we were unnecessarily loud when we opened the door and we loitered in the hall hanging up our coats for far longer than we needed to.

'The food was untouched, but plenty of wine had been drunk. We chatted for a while but I was shattered. When I started yawning, they said they'd better leave and Stacey invited him back to her hotel for a nightcap. Pierre sent me a text later that simply said "*merci*" followed by a stack of smiley faces and kisses. I'll FaceTime him later and find out how it went.'

Jodie made the drinks. 'Aw, it's so sweet. I hope they make a go of it after all these years. But if they tie the knot and you get to be bridesmaid at their wedding, don't forget that your "sister" here is available for bridesmaid services too.'

I laughed. 'I'm not sure they'll be rushing down the aisle any time soon but, if it does come to that, I'll definitely suggest it.'

She sighed wistfully. 'It's like something out of *Love Actually*. "Love is all around". There's you and Matt, Stacey and Pierre, Sarah and Nick, me and... oh wait! Me and Teddy Brown Bear to cuddle again.'

'It'll happen. You've still got time to ask Santa for the man of your dreams.'

'Already have. Tall, athletic, blonde, older, mature, and completely and utterly faithful. The opposite of Karl, as it happens.'

I had to bite my lip to stop myself from smiling. That was Dean to a tee. 'Sounds like you'll need an extra big stocking this year. I just hope that Santa doesn't get your dream man stuck in the chimney.'

* * *

We had an amazing Christmas Eve in the shop. I was lucky that Ashleigh and Kieran had both been available to work because we never seemed to stop. I lost count of the number of times customers said they were buying, 'a few last-minute stocking fillers' or I heard, 'I don't know what to get the wife. Women like chocolates, don't they?' I'd smile politely at that one, and subtly add, 'and perfume, and jewellery.' I'm sure my words fell on deaf ears most times, but that was their problem; not mine.

The atmosphere was electric. I couldn't decide whether that was because it was Christmas Eve, or whether the snow had escalated the excitement. Castle Street was the perfect setting for that magical Christmas feeling. Full of Victorian character buildings and old-fashioned lamps there was almost a Dickensian feel to the place.

At around 3 p.m., we hit a lull and I took a moment to step outside the shop. I looked up beyond the strings of fairy lights into the snow-laden sky, thinking of Nanna and Grandpa. *Thank you for making my Christmas wish come true and also for giving me a family again. If it's not too greedy, could I make another wish? I'd love Pierre and Stacey to finally get their happy ever after.* I kissed my fingertips then blew the kiss into the sky. *Happy Christmas to you both.*

'Right, Ashleigh and Kieran,' I announced, stepping back inside. 'I think it's calmed down enough to let you both go an hour early and start celebrating Christmas with your families.' I handed them each a gift bag full of chocolatey loveliness and a Christmas bonus.

'I love seeing you like this,' Jodie said after we waved them off. 'I was a bit worried about you for a while there.'

'I was worried about me too! I've never felt so stressed. Thank you for being the best friend and non-biological sister ever.'

She hugged me. 'Same to you.'

* * *

Matt called in shortly before our 4 p.m. closing time. He ran the vacuum cleaner round the shop while Jodie and I nipped up to the flat for a quick freshen up and change before joining some of the other traders in The Old Theatre for Christmas Eve drinks.

The pub was packed and buzzing with excitement. I thought about my conversation earlier with Jodie about the two very different Christmases. This time last year, I'd been in the flat on my own, heartbroken and lonely. What a difference a year could make.

As we headed up town for a last drink in Minty's, I dug my phone out intending to check the forecast for Christmas Day and was surprised to see three missed calls from Stacey. She must have called while I was in The Old Theatre and it had been so loud in there, there'd been no chance of hearing a ringing phone.

There was also a text:

⊠ From Stacey
Called you but got voicemail so hope you don't
mind a thank you by text instead. What you did

for Pierre and me yesterday was the best
Christmas present ever. We've agreed that too
many years have been wasted so we're moving in
together. We don't know where but it will definitely be England, not France. I hope you have
a wonderful day tomorrow with Matt and his
parents. If you have time, Pierre and I would
love to see you again before you're back to
work but there's no pressure. We know there's a
lot to take in. I can't thank you enough for my
photo album. I had no idea Mum had created
that. Sobbed like a baby! What a precious gift.
As for that album of your life so far, there
aren't enough words to describe how wonderful
that was. Pierre and I will treasure it forever
and look forward to adding more photos to it.
But the best gift of all has been finally
meeting you. Happy Christmas xx

'Are you okay?' Matt asked, as I wiped my eyes, feeling quite
overcome with emotion.

Silently, I passed him my phone so he could read the text for
himself. 'It worked,' I whispered. 'Our matchmaking worked.' I
glanced towards Jodie, who was having a snowball fight with
Sarah. 'I've found love with you, and now Pierre and Stacey are
back together so that's two of my Christmas wishes come true. Do
you think there's any chance of a hat-trick?'

34

'They're laughing,' I whispered to Matt as we hid behind the haystacks in the barn, spying on Jodie and Dean. 'That's a good sign.'

'We need kissing, not laughing,' Matt whispered back.

'Aw, you old romantic. And you thought you were rubbish at this stuff.'

I'm pretty certain they knew they were being set up because it wasn't exactly subtle. Kendal had started it, introducing Dean as 'my *single* brother' and Jodie as 'Charlee's *single* friend'. Matt insisted on them sharing a two-seater sofa while we had champagne and exchanged gifts, and his mum had placed name cards on the dining table, sitting Jodie and Dean across a corner for ease of conversation.

Jodie had rolled her eyes at me a few times, but it was good-natured because I could tell she liked Dean and they seemed to have plenty in common as they chatted together.

After dinner, he'd declared loudly, 'Jodie, why don't you and I go for a walk all on our own before someone pushes us both out the door, nudging and winking.' As soon as they'd gone, Matt and

I pulled on our wellies and ran out to spy on them, feeling like naughty schoolchildren.

The haybarn was at the highest point on the land, like the farmhouse, so we had a great view. Suddenly Jodie and Dean turned in our direction. We ducked back down behind the haystacks but they waved at us. We reluctantly emerged from our hiding place and waved back. They laughed and disappeared down a farm track.

'Seeing as we've been busted, this gives me the perfect opportunity to give you your main Christmas present,' Matt said.

'My *main* present? You've already given me loads of gifts.' And they'd all been really thoughtful ones which was no mean feat considering how close to Christmas we'd got together.

'I couldn't wrap this one. Come on.' He took my hand and led me back towards the farmhouse, then took a right down a track before we reached it.

'It must have been amazing growing up here,' I said, taking in the rolling fields either side, housing a mixture of crops and animals.

'As kids, Tim and I probably took it for granted because it was all we'd known, but I started appreciating it more when Lucy and Erin came along and I saw it through their eyes. Wide open spaces. Stunning views. Animals. What's not to love?'

'How come they haven't done a barn conversion?'

'They thought a newbuild on a housing estate close to school was more practical but the girls love it here so much, I think they're regretting it. Now that they've seen what my conversion looks like, I wouldn't be surprised if they don't start their own next year.'

'Am I going to finally get to see yours?' I asked. So far, I hadn't had an opportunity. While he'd been with Libby, it hadn't seemed appropriate to visit and, since we'd started seeing each other, it had been too dark to explore by the time the shop closed.

'I think it's time.' He slid his arm round me and snuggled me to his side as we walked.

We passed some more barns and storage buildings, some obviously in use and others in a state of disrepair. 'That's been my home for the past year,' he said, pointing at a static caravan on the left with his van parked beside it.

'Cosy. I bet you can't wait to move out of there.'

'Seriously, Charlee, if I never see the inside of another caravan for the rest of my life, it won't be a moment too soon.'

We rounded a corner to head up another incline and I gasped. Nestling in front of some trees stood the most spectacular L-shaped barn conversion. Constructed from pale grey stonework with timber-framed windows. The larger part of the 'L' was two-storey and the other part appeared to be single-storey with a pitched roof suggesting a vaulted ceiling inside.

A gravel drive had been laid leading up to a double garage but the rest of the grounds were churned up mud and rubble. I could imagine how they'd look with grass, flowerbeds, and possibly a pond.

'Oh, Matt, it's even more beautiful than I imagined.'

'You really like it?'

'I absolutely love it.'

'The outside still needs a lot of work, which will be the project for spring, but the inside is close to finished. It's all plastered and ready to paint, the kitchen and bathrooms are fitted, but there's no furniture yet so it's very echoey. Would you like to see inside?'

I nodded eagerly as we tramped across the gravel to a timber-framed entrance porch.

'There's a side door into a utility room and boot room which will be the usual way in, but I want you to see it for the first time through the front door.'

Matt unlocked the sturdy oak door and pushed it open. He flicked a couple of light switches as we stepped into a large stone flagged entrance hall. There was a grand wooden staircase in front of us and a beautifully decorated tree beneath it.

'No furniture, but you've put up a tree?' I asked.

'Kendal helped me. She came decoration shopping with me. There's meant to be a theme because I've learned all about the importance of themes from a certain master chocolatier I know, but Lucy and Erin kept putting random decorations in the trolley when we weren't looking. Kendal and I spotted some of them but there were still some infiltrators that made it through the till.'

'Theme or no theme, it's gorgeous,' I said. 'I love big entrance halls with trees in them. They make a home feel so welcoming.'

He smiled. 'I know. You told me.'

'And you remembered?'

'I remember everything you say.' He leaned forward and kissed me softly at first then with longing.

'I've been dying to get you alone all day so I could do that,' he said as we pulled away breathless.

'It was worth the wait.'

He kissed me again and I imagined racing upstairs to the master bedroom and tumbling onto the bed. Except he'd said there was no furniture yet so we'd have to wait a bit longer. He hadn't stayed over at Coral Court because we'd wanted our first night together to be somewhere special in a place that held no memories of Ricky or Libby.

I reluctantly pulled away from his kiss. 'I could do this all afternoon but I think you'd better finish the tour or it'll be dark and I'll only have seen the entrance hall.'

He smiled at me. 'Good plan. The one-storey part to the left is the kitchen-diner. There's a toilet and an office down here too but I'll show you the lounge before the light fades and we miss the view.'

Matt opened the door to the lounge and flicked on another light.

'Wow!' The lounge had high beamed ceilings. An inglenook fireplace with a real fire filled the wall opposite the door and, overlooking the back, were floor to ceiling windows.

'Some of the windows are actually bi-folding doors,' Matt said. 'The plan is to build a deck out there on the same level as the house so that the outside and inside seem like one seamless space.'

I wandered towards the doors. 'Is that the sea in the distance?'

'Yes. On a sunny day, you can see it much better. Not bad, eh?'

'It's stunning!' Acres of grass, flanked by trees, perfectly framed the sea view. I imagined sitting on the deck with Matt, enjoying a glass of wine, and drinking in that view as the sun went down.

I turned back round. 'I love that you've got another tree in here.'

'It looked like it needed one.'

'Nice chairs too.' I pointed to the pair of battered candy-striped deckchairs either side of the fireplace.

'What are you talking about? They're vintage! A couple more of those and the lounge will be complete. It's a style statement.' Matt grinned. 'Come on. I'll show you the kitchen.'

As I'd hoped, the kitchen-diner had the most incredible vaulted ceiling.

'They're all the original beams,' Matt said. 'We've kept as much of the original barn as we could.'

'So much history and character,' I said, marvelling at how sympathetically the restoration had been done.

The kitchen had been fitted with a large island in the centre of the room and tall cupboards on the side walls. At either end of the room were open spaces.

'There'll be a dining table at that end, overlooking the garden,' Matt said, pointing to the back of the barn. 'The other end will have sofas and be a relaxing space.'

Turning in a small circle, I took in the pale blue Aga, the mix of pale blue and cream units, and a log burner at either end of the room.

'What do you think?' Matt asked.

'Do you know what you've created here? You've created my dream kitchen. In fact, you've created my dream house. These are the units I fell in love with in that catalogue you showed Jodie and me.'

He nodded. 'When we broke up, Libby said she'd suspected I wanted to be with you from the start but the moment she was certain was the day the kitchen arrived and it was the one I'd told her you loved rather than the one she'd picked out. She said it was also the moment she knew she had to let me go because she realised she wasn't bothered that I'd done that.'

I ran my fingers along the granite worktops. 'It's all so beautiful, Matt. I can't wait to stop over, assuming I'm invited. When will you be able to properly move in?'

'Everything was connected earlier this week so I've got heat, light, water, and all the appliances work. I could have moved in on Tuesday, but I haven't got any furniture yet so I decided to wait.'

'I think I'd have still been tempted if I'd been you, unless you're unable to tear yourself away from luxurious caravan living, that is.'

He laughed. 'You saw how knackered that caravan looks from outside. Believe me, it's ten times worse inside.'

'So why didn't you grab a sleeping bag and move in?'

'I had my reasons.' He looked at me with such tenderness in his eyes. 'I need to give you your Christmas gift. It's hanging from the tree in the hall.'

He took my hand and led me out of the kitchen.

'Look for the teddy bear.'

I looked the tree up and down then spotted him nestled among the branches next to what looked like a fox wearing a skiing jacket; clearly one of Erin or Lucy's random choices. 'There he is!'

'Lift him down but, be warned, he's heavier than he looks.'

'He's the colour of chocolate,' I observed, removing the small dark brown jointed bear.

'I'm glad you said that, because a chocolate bear was the brief I gave.'

'Ooh! Is this one of Jemma's from next-door? I've wanted one of these for ages.' Jemma was the manager of Bear With Me, the specialist teddy bear shop next door to Charlee's Chocolates. She made gorgeous miniature teddy bears called Ju-Sea Jem Bears which she sold alongside her mum's larger Ju-Sea Bears. I'd popped into the shop a few times over the Christmas period, loving the magical, festive feel inside. I'd treated Jodie to one for Christmas but hadn't been able to justify the price-tag for a treat to myself but now I had a chocolate-coloured one of my very own.

Matt nodded. 'The bear might have something round his neck.'

I turned him round and spotted a shiny brass key dangling down his back. Oh my God! Did this mean what I thought it meant? I looked up at Matt, questioningly.

'A key?' Matt frowned. 'Hmm. I wonder what that opens.' He nodded towards the front door and winked at me. 'Do you want to give it a try?'

My hands were shaking so much that I missed the lock on my first couple of attempts but made it into the hole on my third. I turned the key and listened to the click. Facing Matt, I said, 'It would seem that it unlocks your front door.'

'So it does. The reason I didn't move in is that I don't want to do it alone. I want to do it with you. I love you, Charlee, and I want us to start our life together here. I know that I was originally meant to be moving in with Libby, but she's had nothing to do with the design of this place. She ordered some cushions and some candlesticks and she's kept those. I chose everything else from room sizes to light fittings and, as it turns out, those choices were mainly influenced by you. When we go upstairs, I think you'll recognise the décor in the bathroom too. I know it isn't painted and I know there's no furniture yet, other than a couple of stylish deckchairs, but will you move in with me?'

I rushed towards him, flung my arms round him and kissed him. 'I'd love to. Can we stay here tonight?'

'If you like.'

I nodded. 'There's something we haven't been able to do yet and I can't think of a better way to spend our first Christmas evening together.' I put my hands up to my cheeks. 'Oh, my God! I'm blushing. I'm rubbish at this stuff.'

Matt laughed and pulled me into a kiss.

'What a pair we make. I get embarrassed saying I love you and you get embarrassed about... you know. Argh! It seems I'm just as bad.'

I laughed too. 'Thank you, Matt. You've just taken Christmas gift giving to a whole new level. I'm not sure I'll ever be able to give you anything so amazing.'

'You could and I'm hoping that you will do in a minute. You liked your first gift from the tree which means that I can give you your second one and, if you accept it, you'll be giving me the best Christmas present ever. This time you're looking for an angel.'

I immediately looked up to the top of the tree, but there was a silver star up there.

'She's a bit lower,' he said. 'And to your right.'

I stepped closer to the tree and peered into the branches at eye-level. 'Found her!'

'Lift her off.'

I unhooked the sparkly silver angel and, as I did, something metal dropped to the floor. 'Oh no! I've broken her halo,' I said, kneeling down on one knee to retrieve it. 'Sorry.' I looked at the halo between my fingers. But it wasn't a halo. I twisted round to face Matt who was on one knee too.

'The house is for us to start our lives together, and the ring is for us to stay together for always. Will you marry me, Charlee?'

I squealed with excitement as I flung my arms round him. 'Yes!'

He slipped the platinum diamond engagement ring on my finger and, under the tree in my dream home, I kissed the man of my dreams. This Christmas had already eclipsed all others and it just kept getting better and better.

35

I was on a blissful loved-up high over the week that followed. Matt and I packed up my belongings at Coral Court and moved into the barn. Between us we owned an assortment of chipped mugs, mismatched pans, a pair of old deckchairs, an inflatable mattress and a couple of sleeping bags, but it was all we needed to start our new life together because we had each other.

His family were delighted about our engagement although he'd already told them his plans as he'd been too excited to keep it to himself. Jodie was so thrilled, she clung to me sobbing. We'd asked them to keep it quiet from everyone else as we had a big moment planned for announcing it and that moment had just arrived.

'Thank you for joining us at the farm tonight to see the New Year in,' Matt announced, looking round the sea of happy faces in the haybarn. 'Many of you join us every year, but you'll have noticed a few unfamiliar faces tonight. Mum and Dad have very kindly let me hijack the party this year because, as well as seeing in the New Year, there's something extra special to celebrate tonight.'

Matt looked towards me and gave me a dazzling smile, making me feel quite weak at the knees. The annual New Year's Eve party had a black tie tradition so he was back in that tux again, looking delectable, and this time I could openly appreciate it without feeling guilty.

'In the run-up to last Christmas, I was called out to an emergency leak at Charlee's Chocolates on Castle Street. I met and became friends with the owner, Charlee Chambers. This Christmas, I asked Charlee to marry me and she said yes, so tonight is actually our engagement party.'

Taking their cue, Tim and Kendal pulled down some sheeting covering several 'happy engagement' banners, and Dean pulled a cord, releasing a net full of silver and purple balloons from the ceiling. There were gasps and applause and I blushed as everyone turned to look in my direction.

'So please join me in a toast to my beautiful fiancée, Charlee, to the best Christmas ever, and to an amazing start to the New Year.'

I sipped on my champagne as cries of 'Congratulations!', 'To Charlee!', 'To Charlee and Matt!' and 'Happy New Year!' rippled round the haybarn as Matt joined me and kissed me.

Sarah, Nick and many of our friends from Bay Trade and Castle Street were the first to offer hugs and congratulations, delighted with the news. Friends of Matt's parents, neighbours and relatives swamped us for the next thirty minutes or so, congratulating us and admiring the ring, with his relatives welcoming me to the family. Matt stood by my side throughout, giving me a running commentary on who everyone was.

I imagined there'd be curiosity surrounding Libby's swift exit from Matt's life and my appearance. They were all tactful enough not to say anything in front of us although I giggled as several guests made a beeline for Matt's parents afterwards, no doubt desperate to find out what had happened.

When everyone had expressed their congratulations, Matt slipped his arm round my waist and gently kissed me. 'You look absolutely stunning this evening. Not that you don't usually but tonight... that dress.'

I smiled as I gave him a little twirl. Ginny who ran The Wedding Emporium at the other end of Castle Street had a stunning range of prom dresses for hire and I'd chosen a deep purple one with off the shoulder tulle sleeves and silver crystals round the waist and down the top of the tulle skirt. We'd chosen the silver and purple balloons to match my dress.

'I could say the same about you in that suit,' I said running my hand down his lapel. 'Last time I saw you in this, I thought I was going to have to lose you from my life because I wasn't sure I could cope with seeing you all the time, thinking it was never going to be more than friends.'

He brushed his thumb lightly across my cheek. 'I have a confession to make. Last time I wore this, I came so unbelievably close to telling you how I felt about you, especially when we were on the dance floor.'

'I thought you were going to say something and then I thought I'd imagined it.'

'You didn't imagine it.'

I glanced round the busy haybarn. It had been beautifully decorated for the party with an eight-foot Christmas tree and swathes of holly, ivy and fairy lights wrapped round the pillars. Sarah had made several floral displays with red and white flowers and trailing ivy.

'It's so beautiful in here tonight and it feels extra special to have our engagement party in the place we had our first proper kiss. I love it in here.'

'Enough to have our wedding here too?' Matt asked.

We'd been so focused on planning for the party and settling into the house that we hadn't spoken about wedding venues but it was a brilliant suggestion. Gazing round the room once more at the tree and the flowers, I could see how fantastic it would look for a wedding.

I drew Matt into another kiss. 'I'd love to get married here. I couldn't think of anywhere more beautiful or more meaningful.'

* * *

'I wish Pierre and Stacey could have come,' I said to Matt, as we topped up our drinks a little later after we'd both mingled. 'It feels like all the important people in our lives are in this one barn, and there's only them missing.' Pierre had promised Gabby he'd see New Year in with her and he couldn't let her down.

'It's a shame but we'll see them tomorrow for lunch so we can give them our news then.' He put his arms round me and kissed me.

'Get a room you two,' hissed Jodie, filling up her glass.

'How's it going with Dean?' I asked, unable to resist.

'Stop it! We're just friends.' But I could tell from the smile in her voice and the twinkle in her eyes that it wouldn't stay that way for long. I'd be stunned if the pair of them didn't kiss at midnight but it was down to Jodie and Dean from now on. I wouldn't meddle any further.

'I'd like to propose a toast,' I said to Matt, holding up my glass. 'To Ricky and Gabby.'

He frowned. 'Because they're your two most favourite people in the whole world? Are you sure?'

'I'm sure. It may seem strange but if it hadn't been for Gabby being so horrible, I'd never have left my job. If it hadn't been for

Ricky's suggestion, I'd never have come to Whitsborough Bay and opened Charlee's Chocolates. If it hadn't been for him refusing to help me and enlisting his useless mate Toadie instead, I'd never have had a leak in my flat and if it hadn't been for Ricky shagging BJ behind my back, he'd have come round and sorted out the leak, and I'd never have met you.'

'I see your logic. In that case, I'll add Libby to the toast because, if she hadn't let me go, I might have continued to make the biggest mistake of my life out of some stupid, misguided sense of loyalty, duty and long-gone feelings for her.'

'To Ricky, Gabby and Libby,' we said, toasting each other.

'What are we toasting?' a voice said behind me.

I turned round and squealed. Pierre and Stacey had made it after all. I hugged them both. 'I thought you couldn't get here until tomorrow.'

'We told Gabby you know our family secret,' Pierre said. 'And we told her that we are together at last and very happy. She had a strop and told us to spend New Year with you, so we called her bluff and said yes we would so here we are!'

I put my hand to my cheek and shook my head. 'I'm sorry she didn't take it well. Maybe with time...?'

'Oh my goodness!' Stacey gasped. 'What's that on your finger?'

'Ah yes,' I said, moving my hand from my cheek and gazing at my ring. 'We've got some news for you...'

* * *

As midnight approached, I sipped on my champagne, taking in the laughter and the genuine warmth from friends and family, new and old. I thought about Christmas Day and New Year's Day last year when I'd been a mess, crying for the loss of my family and my boyfriend and rueing the day I'd moved to Whitsborough

Bay. I could never have imagined that, just a year later, I'd have a family, a fiancé, a dream home and an award-winning business. Talk about a tale of two Christmases. They couldn't have been more extreme!

I could imagine Nanna and Grandpa smiling down on me right now, joyous that my wishes had all come true, including finding a love just like theirs. Matt was made from the same mould as Grandpa: an absolute gent, passionate about his work, devoted to his friends and family, and liked by all who met him. What a shame they'd never get to meet him but, if they'd still been around, I'd never have come to Whitsborough Bay so we'd never have met. Things were obviously exactly how they were meant to be.

'Five... four... three... two... one... Happy New Year!'

As streamer cannons and party poppers exploded round us, Matt and I stood in the middle of the haybarn, arms round each other, and kissed. Six weeks ago, Jodie had challenged me to spend New Year's Eve kissing Matt or kissing our friendship goodbye. I'd expected the latter and had to pinch myself that it was actually the former, and that it wouldn't only be a New Year's Eve kiss. I could kiss him any time I liked.

There was a chorus of 'Auld Lang Syne' as the guests exchanged kisses, hugs and clinked glasses. I nudged Matt and pointed towards Dean approaching Jodie at the other side of the barn. I sighed as he kissed her on the cheek and gave her a hug.

'Give them time,' Matt whispered. 'It'll happen when it's right for them both, just like it did for us. And just like it has for your parents.' He nodded towards where Pierre and Stacey were locked in a kiss. My heart melted for them, reunited after all these years, and I felt nothing but excitement at the thought of spending more time with my dad and getting to know my mum this New Year.

The lights dimmed a little further.

'It's time to grab your nearest and dearest for a little smooch to a song that means a lot to the future Mr and Mrs Richards,' announced the DJ.

I glanced at Matt, tears in my eyes, as Daniel Bedingfield's soft voice sang the opening line to 'If You're Not the One.'

He kissed me gently then wrapped his arms round me and held me close as we swayed to the music. 'We might have to find a new song,' he whispered. 'Because you are the one. Forever. Happy New Year, Charlee!'

'Happy New Year, Matt!' And I had no doubt whatsoever that it would be. An extremely happy one.

ACKNOWLEDGMENTS

Thank you so much for reading *Christmas Wishes at the Chocolate Shop*. I hope you enjoyed Charlee's heartwarming story about two very different Christmases as much as I loved creating Charlee, Jodie, Matt (and even Ricky – villains are so much fun to create!) as well as the delectable Charlee's Chocolates.

This book was originally released under the title of *Charlee and the Chocolate Shop* for Christmas 2017 and it was the first Christmas book I ever wrote. It was an independent release but I struggled to make an impact as an indie author and was thrilled to receive a traditional publishing deal from the amazing Boldwood Books in 2019. Boldwood acquired the rights to my entire backlist and *Christmas Wishes at the Chocolate Shop* is the very last book from that list to get the Boldwood polish and a re-issue.

It's been a challenging edit because my writing style has developed over my years as an author and I noticed the change in this particular book more than any of my others. Even though readers of the original version loved it, it didn't pack the emotional punch my stories usually have so, instead of the quick edit my editor and I original anticipated, it became a mammoth exercise where I added in several new scenes and restructured most of the sentences while still keeping the overall story the same. I love it all the more and hope you do too.

Because Charlee's grandparents were such an important part of her life, if felt appropriate to dedicate this to mine, none of whom are with us today. Louisa Jane and Ted were my dad's parents who died in 2000 and 2006, respectively. My grandma was a wonderful woman. Every time I think of her, I picture a Yorkshire Terrier tucked under her arm, and her laughing as she tried to tell a joke and messed up the punchline. She came from the generation who always wore a housecoat, had tea at 4 p.m. and kept a room at home 'for best' which basically meant it never got used! My older brother and I would sometimes stay with her during the school holidays and she'd take us on a walk which she called a 'magical mystery tour'. We were allowed to help ourselves to some goodies from her sweetie drawer (only a grandparent would have a sweetie drawer) and we'd have to run past 'the witch's house' a few doors up. It was years later when she actually admitted she had no idea who lived in that particular house, never mind whether they were a witch! If you've read any of my other books, you may have spotted these traits in other grandmothers as they were too delightful not to use!

My granda, Ted, wasn't the easiest of men but I relished the occasional moments where his cheeky sense of humour shone through and I'll always remember his delight when I bought him a hot water bottle one Christmas with a soft cover in the shape of a chimp. He absolutely loved it and I'll always cherish a photo I have of him cuddling it and my grandma cuddling her teddy bear version.

Polly and Jack were my mum's parents. Sadly I never met Polly as she died when Mum was eighteen. My granda Jack died when I was only eight so I didn't know him well but I do have fond memories of him being a lovely man and I also remember him always having jars of sweets in his kitchen. Hmm, sweets seem to be a common theme in my memories of my grandparents which is perhaps what subconsciously led me to writing a story set in a chocolate shop where grandparents were a strong influence.

I loved writing a story set in a chocolaterie and particularly enjoyed my research. I couldn't possibly write about a chocolate shop without spending time in one and sampling lots of chocolates, could I? I already had a fairly good knowledge of chocolate-making as I'd worked for Nestlé for several years and spent time in their UK-based chocolate factories. However, that was chocolate production on a large scale and I needed to understand what might happen in a small independent business instead.

I'm extremely grateful to Amelia Forrest, former owner of Amelia's Chocolate in Scarborough who agreed to me being her apprentice for the day. She demonstrated every part of the process, showed me her product ranges, and talked about running the business side. Running a small business is something I have knowledge of as I ran my own teddy bear shop for two years, but this was very different to running a chocolate shop where the products are made fresh on site rather than bought in from suppliers. I was honoured when Amelia let me help her make and package the favours for her own impending wedding and, of course, sample a few. It was hard, but somebody had to do it ;-) Yummy! Sadly, Amelia's Chocolate ceased trading in summer 2019 so I wish Amelia well and hope she's still making her amazing chocolates.

I owe an enormous gratitude to my original team of beta readers. Jo Bartlett and Sharon Booth are extremely talented authors whose work I can't recommend enough and Jo is now part of #TeamBoldwood. They both gave me insightful feedback on where the story could be tweaked. My mum, Joyce, plus my close friends, Susan and Liz, were also invaluable in helping smooth out the edges. They were good at spotting typos, questioning gaps, and identifying any repetition or unexplained parts including those moments when I'd gone far too Northern and they didn't know what I was wittering on about!

For this edited version, my biggest thanks go to my fabulous editor, Nia Beynon, who has worked on every one of my books to date and is completely embroiled in the worlds of Whitsborough Bay and Hedgehog Hollow. Nia gives such insightful feedback to improve the story and the way it's written. Also from Boldwood, thank you to Claire Fenby for the amazing digital marketing support.

Thank you to Sue Lamprell for the sterling work as copy editor and proofreader, Debbie Clement for the simply divine cover (my new favourite), Rachel Gilbey for organising another fabulous blog tour, Emma Swan for her vocal talents as the narrator on the audio version, and ISIS Audio and Ulverscroft for the recording and distribution of the audiobook.

My final thanks go to you, my wonderfully supportive readers. Not only is *Christmas Wishes at the Chocolate Shop* the final book in my backlist for a Boldwood re-release, it's also the final book in my original twelve-book contract with them. All twelve of those books have been published in a two-year period and it has been a phenomenal two years during which I have gone from being an invisible, struggling indie writer trying to squeeze in writing round a demanding full-time day job to being a bestselling full-time author; my dream come true. Thanks to the fabulous work from Boldwood Books and all your love and support for my stories, I have secured another twelve-book deal through which to bring you many more brand new uplifting stories of love, friendship and community.

I read every review and I appreciate every single message of support and encouragement. The kindness and the book love from the reading and blogging community has been outstanding and I am so incredibly grateful for everything you've all done. Please do follow me on social media, check out my Pinterest boards for visual inspiration behind each of my books, and keep reviewing and recommending my stories to your friends and family. Thank you again from the bottom of my heart.

Big hugs

Jessica xx

MORE FROM JESSICA REDLAND

We hope you enjoyed reading *Christmas Wishes at the Chocolate Shop*. If you did, please leave a review.

If you'd like to gift a copy, this book is also available as an ebook, digital audio download and audiobook CD.

Sign up to Jessica Redland's mailing list for news, competitions and updates on future books.

http://bit.ly/JessicaRedlandNewsletter

ABOUT THE AUTHOR

Jessica Redland is the top 10 bestselling author of over thirteen novels, including *The Secret to Happiness*. Inspired by her hometown of Scarborough she writes uplifting women's fiction which has garnered many devoted fans.

Visit Jessica's website: https://www.jessicaredland.com/

Follow Jessica on social media:

[f] facebook.com/JessicaRedlandWriter

[twitter] twitter.com/JessicaRedland

[instagram] instagram.com/JessicaRedlandWriter

[BB] bookbub.com/authors/jessica-redland

ALSO BY JESSICA REDLAND

Welcome to Whitsborough Bay Series
Making Wishes at Bay View
New Beginnings at Seaside Blooms
Finding Hope at Lighthouse Cove
Coming Home to Seashell Cottage

Other Whitsborough Bay Books
All You Need is Love
The Secret to Happiness

Christmas on Castle Street
Christmas Wishes at the Chocolate Shop
Christmas at Carly's Cupcakes
Starry Skies Over The Chocolate Pot Café

The Starfish Café Series
Snowflakes Over The Starfish Café

Hedgehog Hollow Series
Finding Love at Hedgehog Hollow
New Arrivals at Hedgehog Hollow
Family Secrets at Hedgehog Hollow
A Wedding at Hedgehog Hollow

ABOUT BOLDWOOD BOOKS

Boldwood Books is a fiction publishing company seeking out the best stories from around the world.

Find out more at www.boldwoodbooks.com

Sign up to the Book and Tonic newsletter for news, offers and competitions from Boldwood Books!

http://www.bit.ly/bookandtonic

We'd love to hear from you, follow us on social media:

facebook.com/BookandTonic

twitter.com/BoldwoodBooks

instagram.com/BookandTonic

Printed in Great Britain
by Amazon